Life Is
Elsewhere

BOOKS BY MILAN KUNDERA

The Joke

Laughable Loves

Life Is Elsewhere

Farewell Waltz
(EARLIER TRANSLATION: *The Farewell Party*)

The Book of Laughter and Forgetting

The Unbearable Lightness of Being

Immortality

Slowness

Identity

Jacques and His Master (PLAY)

The Art of the Novel (ESSAY)

Testaments Betrayed (ESSAY)

Milan Kundera

Life Is Elsewhere

Translated from the French by
Aaron Asher

Perennial
An Imprint of HarperCollinsPublishers

FIRST EDITION

Library of Congress Cataloging-in-Publication Data
Kundera, Milan.
    [Život je jinde. English]
    Life is elsewhere/[Milan Kundera]; translated from the French by Aaron Asher.
      p. cm.
    Written first in Czech; published in French as *La vie est ailleurs.*
    ISBN 0-06-099702-8
    I. Asher, Aaron.   II. Title.
PG5039.21.U6 Z3513 2000
891.8'6354—dc21   99-086224

08 ❖/RRD 10 9 8

CONTENTS

PART ONE

The Poet Is Born

1

When the poet's mother wondered where the poet had been conceived, there were only three possibilities to consider: a park bench one night, the apartment of a friend of the poet's father one afternoon, a romantic spot outside Prague late one morning.

When the poet's father asked himself the same question, he concluded that the poet had been conceived in his friend's apartment, for on that day everything had gone wrong. The poet's mother had refused to go to the friend's place, they had quarreled about it twice and reconciled twice, and while they were making love the door lock of the adjoining apartment rasped, the poet's mother took fright, they broke off, and then they resumed lovemaking and finished in a state of mutual tension to which his father attributed the poet's conception.

The poet's mother, on the other hand, never admitted that the poet had been conceived in a borrowed apartment (she was repelled by the bachelor's untidiness, by rumpled sheets and pajamas on a stranger's bed), and she also rejected the possibility that he had been conceived on a park bench, where she had let herself be persuaded to make love, reluctantly and without pleasure, thinking with disgust of the prostitutes who made love this way on such benches. So she became absolutely convinced that the poet had been conceived on a sunny summer morning in the shelter of a huge boulder that stood with sublime pathos among the other boulders in a small valley where the people of Prague liked to stroll on Sundays.

For several reasons this setting is an appropriate place for the poet's conception: in the late morning sun it is a setting of light rather than darkness, day rather than night; it is in the middle of open nature, thus a place from which to take wing; and finally, though not very far from the apartment buildings on the city's outskirts, it is a romantic landscape strewn with boulders looming out of wildly rough terrain. For the poet's mother all this seemed to express what she was experiencing at the time. Wasn't her great love for the poet's father a romantic rebellion against the dullness and regularity of her parents' life? Wasn't there a hidden likeness between the untamed landscape and the boldness she, the daughter of a rich merchant, showed in choosing a penniless engineer who had just finished his studies?

And so the poet's mother was living a great love, despite the disappointment that followed a few weeks after the beautiful morning at the foot of the boulder. When she disclosed to her lover, with joyous excitement, that the intimate indisposition that monthly disturbed her life was several days overdue, the engineer asserted with appalling indifference (but, it seems to me, a feigned and ill-at-ease indifference) that it was an insignificant disruption of her cycle, which would soon resume its benign rhythm. The poet's mother, perceiving that her lover refused to share her joyous hopes, was hurt, and she stopped talking to him until the day the doctor confirmed her pregnancy. The poet's father said that he knew a gynecologist who would discreetly relieve her of her worries, and she burst into tears.

The poignant end of rebellions! First she rebelled against her parents for the sake of the young engineer, and then she ran to her parents for help against him. Her parents didn't let her down: they spoke plainly to the engineer, who clearly understood that there was no way out, agreed to an ostentatious wedding, and readily accepted a sizable dowry that would enable him to establish his own construction business; then he packed his belongings into a couple of suitcases and moved into the villa his new wife had lived in with her parents from the day she was born.

The engineer's prompt capitulation, however, couldn't hide from the poet's mother that the adventure she had precipitated herself into with a heedlessness she found sublime was not the great shared love she believed she had a full right to. Her father was the owner of two flourishing shops in Prague, and the daughter's morality was that of balanced accounts; since she had invested everything in love (she had been ready to betray her own parents and their peaceful home), she wanted her partner to invest an equal amount of feeling in their joint account. Striving to redress the injustice, she wanted to withdraw from the joint account the affection she had deposited there, and after the wedding she presented a haughty and severe face to her husband.

The poet's mother's sister had recently left the family villa (she had married and rented an apartment in the center of Prague) and so the old retail merchant and his wife lived on the ground floor and the engineer and their daughter above them in the three rooms—two large and one smaller—furnished exactly the way they were twenty years before when the villa was built. Acquiring an entirely furnished home was a rather good deal for the engineer, because he really owned nothing but the contents of the aforementioned two suitcases; nonetheless, he suggested some small changes in the appearance of the rooms. But the poet's mother didn't allow the man who had wanted to put her under the knife of a gynecologist to dare disrupt the time-honored arrangement of rooms that harbored the spirit of her parents, twenty years of sweet routine, and mutual intimacy and safety.

This time, too, the young engineer capitulated without a struggle, permitting himself only a moderate protest, which I note: in the couple's bedroom there was a small tabletop of heavy gray marble on which stood a statuette of a naked man; in his left hand the man was holding a lyre against his plump hip; his right arm was bent in a pathetic gesture as if the fingers had just struck the strings; the right leg was extended forward, the head slightly inclined, and the eyes turned toward the sky. Let me add that the man had an extremely beautiful face, that he had curly hair, and that the whiteness of the alabaster from which the statuette had been sculpted gave the figure something tenderly feminine or divinely virginal; it's not, moreover, by chance that I use the word "divinely": according to the inscription carved on the pedestal, the man with the lyre was the Greek god Apollo.

But the poet's mother could rarely look at the man with the lyre without being angered. Most of the time it was his rear end that faced the onlooker, and sometimes he served as a peg for the engineer's hat or a shoe was hung from his fine head or a smelly sock of the engineer's stretched over him, the latter a particularly odious defilement of the master of the Muses.

That the poet's mother was impatient with all this was not solely due to her meager sense of humor: she had in fact correctly guessed that with the buffoonery of putting a sock over Apollo's body her husband was letting her know what he politely hid from her with his silence: that he rejected her world and had only temporarily submitted to it.

Thus the alabaster object truly became an ancient god, that is, a supernatural being who intervenes in the human world, schemes, scrambles destinies, reveals mysteries. The newlywed wife regarded him as her ally, her dreamy femininity transforming him into a living creature whose eyes at times took on the colors of illusory irises and whose mouth seemed to draw breath. She fell in love with the naked little man, who was being humiliated for and because of her. Gazing at his lovely face she began to hope that the child growing in her belly would resemble this handsome foe of her husband's. She wanted the resemblance to be so strong that she would be able to imagine the child as this young man's rather than her husband's; she implored him to use his magical powers to rectify the fetus's features, to transform and transfigure them as the great Titian once did when he painted a masterpiece over a bungler's spoiled canvas.

Instinctively modeling herself on the Virgin Mary, who became a mother without the intervention of a human begetter and thus the ideal of maternal love without a father's troublemaking interference, she felt a provocative desire to name her child Apollo, a name that to her meant "he who has no human father." But she knew that her son would have a hard time with such a pretentious name and that it would make both him and her a laughingstock. So she looked for a Czech name that would be worthy of a young Greek god and came up with Jaromil (which means "he who loves spring" or "he who is beloved by spring"), and this choice was approved by everyone.

Moreover, it was spring and the lilacs were blooming when they drove her to the hospital; there, after some hours of suffering, the young poet slipped out of her onto the soiled sheet of the world.

2

Then they put the poet into a crib next to her bed and she heard the delightful cries; her aching body was filled with pride. Let's not begrudge her body that pride; until then it had not experienced it, even though it was well built: it did have a rather inexpressive rump and the legs were a bit too short, but the bosom, on the other hand, was unusually youthful, and beneath the fine hair (so fine it was difficult to set) a face that may not have been dazzling but had an unobtrusive charm.

Mama had always been more conscious of her unobtrusiveness than of her charm, all the more since she had lived since infancy with an older sister who was an outstanding dancer, was clothed by Prague's best couturier, and tennis racket in hand, moved easily in the world of elegant men, turning her back on the parental home. The flashy impetuosity of her sister confirmed Mama's sullen modesty, and in protest she learned to love the emotional gravity of books and music.

Admittedly, before she met the engineer she had gone out with a young medical student, the son of friends of her parents, but this relationship had been incapable of giving her body much self-confidence. The morning after being initiated by him into physical love in a summer house, she broke up with him with the melancholy certainty that neither her feelings nor her senses would ever experience a great love. And since she had just finished high school, she announced that she wanted to find the meaning of her life in work and had decided to register (despite her father's practical man's disapproval) in the faculty of arts and letters.

Her disappointed body had already spent four or five months on the wide bench of a university lecture hall when it encountered an arrogant young engineer in the street who called out to it and three dates later possessed it. And because this time the body was greatly (and to its great surprise) satisfied, the soul very quickly forgot its ambition of a university career and (as a reasonable soul always must) rushed to the body's aid: it gladly agreed with the engineer's ideas and went along with his cheerful heedlessness and charming irresponsibility. Even as she knew that they were foreign to her family, she wanted to identify herself with the engineer's qualities, because in contact with them her sadly modest body ceased to doubt and, to its own astonishment, began to enjoy itself.

Was she then happy at last? Not quite: she was torn between doubt and confidence; when she undressed before the mirror she looked at herself with his eyes and sometimes found herself arousing, sometimes vapid. She handed her body over to the mercy of another's eyes—and that caused her great uncertainty.

But even though she fluctuated between hope and doubt, she had been completely torn away from her premature resignation; her sister's tennis racket no longer demoralized her; her body finally lived as a body, and she understood that it was beautiful to live like that. She wanted this new life to be more than a deceptive promise, to be a lasting reality; she wanted the engineer to tear her away from the lecture-hall bench and from her parental home and turn a love adventure into a life adventure. That is why she welcomed her pregnancy with enthusiasm: she saw herself, the engineer, and her child as a trio rising to the stars and filling the universe.

I've already explained this in the previous chapter: Mama quickly realized that the man who sought a love adventure dreaded a life adventure and wanted no change at all like the image of a duo rising to the stars. But we also know that this time her self-confidence did not crumble under the pressure of the lover's coldness. Something very important had in fact changed. Mama's body, recently still at the mercy of the lover's eyes, entered a new phase of its history: ceasing to be a body for the eyes of others, it became a body for someone who could not yet see. Its outer surface was no longer so important; the body was touching another body by means of an internal membrane no one had ever seen. Thus the eyes of the external world could only perceive its inessential aspect, and even the engineer's opinions no longer meant anything to the body, for they could have no influence over its great destiny; the body had finally attained total independence and autonomy; the belly, which kept growing bigger and uglier, was for that body a steadily increasing supply of pride.

After the delivery, Mama's body entered a new phase. When she first felt the groping mouth of her son sucking at her breast, a sweet shiver radiated from her chest through her entire body; it was similar to her lover's caress, but it had something more: a great peaceful bliss, a great happy tranquillity. She had never felt this before; when her lover had kissed her breast, it had been a moment that should have made up for hours of doubt and mistrust; but now she knew that the mouth pressed against her breast brought proof of a continuous attachment of which she could be certain.

And then there was something else: when her lover touched her naked body, she always felt ashamed; their coming close to each other was always a surmounting of otherness, and the instant of embrace was intoxicating just because it was only an instant. Shame never dozed off, it exhilarated lovemaking, but at the same time it kept a close eye on the body, fearing that it might let itself go entirely. But now shame had disappeared; it had been done away with. These two bodies opened to each other entirely and had nothing to hide.

Never had she let herself go in this way with another body, and never had another body let itself go with her in this way. Her lover could play with her belly, but he had never lived there; he could touch her breast, but he had never drunk from it. Ah, breast-feeding! She lovingly watched the fishlike movements of the toothless mouth and imagined that, along with her milk, her son was drinking her thoughts, her fantasies, and her dreams.

It was an *Edenic* state: the body could be fully body and had no need to hide itself with a fig leaf; they were plunged into the limitless space of a calm time; they lived together like Adam and Eve before they bit into the apple of the tree of knowledge; they lived in their bodies beyond good and evil; and not only that: in paradise there is no distinction between beauty and ugliness, so that all the things the body is made of were neither ugly nor beautiful but only delightful; even though toothless, the gums were delightful, the breast was delightful, the navel was delightful, the little bottom was delightful, the intestines—whose performance was closely overseen— were delightful, the standing hairs on the grotesque skull were delightful. She watched over her son's burps, pees, and poops not only with concern for the child's health; no, she watched over all the small body's activities with *passion*.

This was an entirely new thing because since childhood Mama had felt an extreme repugnance for physicality, including her own; she thought it degrading to sit on the toilet (she always made sure that no one saw her going into the bathroom), and there were even times when she had been ashamed to eat in front of people because chewing and swallowing seemed repugnant to her. Now her son's physicality, amazingly elevated above all ugliness, purified and justified her own body. The droplet of milk that sometimes remained on the wrinkled skin of her nipple seemed to her as poetic as a dewdrop; she would often press one of her breasts lightly to see the magical drop appear; she caught it with her index finger and tasted it; she told herself that she wanted to know the flavor of the beverage with which she nourished her son, but it was rather that she wanted to know the taste of her own body; and since her milk seemed delectable to her, its flavor reconciled her to all her other juices and secretions; she began to find herself delectable, her body seemed as pleasant, natural, and good to her as all natural things, as a tree, a bush, as water.

Unfortunately, she was so happy with her body that she neglected it; one day she realized that it was already too late, that she had a wrinkled belly with whitish streaks, a skin that didn't adhere firmly to the flesh beneath but looked like a loosely sewn wrap. The strange thing is that she wasn't in despair about this. Even with the wrinkled belly, Mama's body was happy because it was a body for eyes that still only perceived the world in vague outline and knew nothing (weren't they *Edenic* eyes?) of the cruel world where bodies were divided into the beautiful and the ugly.

Though the distinction was unseen by the eyes of the infant, the eyes of the husband, who had tried to make peace with his wife after Jaromil's birth, saw them all too well. After a very long interval, they began again to make love; but it was not what it had been: for their embraces they chose covert and ordinary moments, making love in darkness and with moderation. This surely suited Mama: she knew that her body had become ugly, and she feared that caresses too intense and passionate would quickly lose her the delectable inner peace her son gave her.

No, no, she would never forget that her husband had given her pleasure filled with uncertainties and her son serenity filled with bliss; and so she continued to search nearby (he was already crawling, walking, talking) for comfort. He fell seriously ill, and for two weeks she barely closed her eyes while she tended the burning little body convulsed with pain; this period, too, passed for her in a kind of delirium; when the illness began to subside, she thought that she had crossed through the realm of the dead with her son's body in her arms and had brought him back; she also thought that after this ordeal together nothing could ever separate them.

The husband's body, swathed in a suit or in pajamas, reserved and self-enclosed, was withdrawing from her and day by day losing its intimacy, but the son's body at every moment depended on her; she no longer suckled him, but she taught him to use the toilet, she dressed and undressed him, arranged his hair and his clothes, was in daily contact with his gut through the dishes she lovingly prepared. When he began, at the age of four, to suffer from a lack of appetite, she became strict; she forced him to eat and for the first time felt that she was not only the friend but also the *sovereign* of that body; that body rebelled, defended itself, refused to swallow, but it had to give in; with an odd satisfaction she watched this vain resistance, this capitulation, this slender neck through which one could follow the course of the reluctantly swallowed mouthful.

Ah, her son's body, her home and her paradise, her realm . . .

3

And her son's soul? Was that not her realm? Oh, yes, yes! When Jaromil uttered his first word and the word was "Mama," she was wildly happy; she thought that her son's intellect, still consisting of only a single concept, was taken up with her alone, and that although his intellect would grow, branch out, and bloom, she would always remain its root. Pleasantly inspired, she meticulously followed all of her son's attempts to use words, and knowing that life is long and memory fragile, she bought a date book bound in dark red and recorded everything that came from her son's mouth.

So if we were to look at Mama's diary we would notice that the word "Mama" was soon followed by other words, and that "Papa" was seventh, after "Grandma," "Grandpa," "Doggie," "You-you," "Wah-wah," and "Pee-pee." After these simple words (in Mama's diary the date and word were always accompanied by a brief commentary) we find the first tries at sentences. We learn that well before his second birthday he proclaimed: "Mama nice." A few weeks later he said: "Mama naughty." For this remark, made after Mama had refused to give him a raspberry drink before lunch, he was smacked on the behind, upon which he shouted, in tears: "I want other Mama!" A week later, however, he gave his mother great joy by proclaiming: "I have pretty Mama." Another time he said: "Mama, I give lollipop kiss," by which he meant that he would stick out his tongue and lick her entire face.

Skipping a few pages, we come upon a remark that catches our attention with its rhythm. His grandmother had promised Jaromil a pear, but she forgot and ate it herself; Jaromil felt cheated, became angry, and kept repeating: "Grandmama not fair, ate my pear." In a certain sense, this phrase is like the previously cited "Mama naughty," but this time no one smacked his behind because everyone laughed, including Grandmama, and these words were often repeated in the family with amusement, a fact that of course didn't escape Jaromil's perspicacity. He probably didn't understand the reason for his success, but we can be certain that it was rhyme that saved him from a spanking, and that this was how the magical power of poetry was first revealed to him.

More such rhymed reflections appear in the following pages of Mama's diary, and her comments on them clearly show that they were a source of joy and satisfaction to the whole family. This, it seems, is a terse portrait: "Maid Hana bends like a banana." A bit farther we read: "Walk in wood, very good." Mama thought that this poetic activity arose not only from Jaromil's utterly original talent but also from the influence of the children's poetry she read to him in such great quantities that he could easily have come to believe that the Czech language was composed exclusively of trochees. But we need to correct Mama's opinion on this point: more important here than talent or literary models was the role of Grandpapa, a sober, practical man and fervent foe of poetry, who intentionally invented the most stupid couplets and secretly taught them to his grandson.

It didn't take long for Jaromil to notice that his words commanded great attention, and he began to behave accordingly; at first he had used speech to make himself understood, but now he spoke in order to elicit approval, admiration, or laughter. He looked forward to the effect his words would produce, and since it often happened that he didn't obtain the expected response, he tried to call attention to himself with outrageous remarks. This didn't always pay off; when he said to his father and mother: "You're pricks" (he had heard the word from the kid next door, and he remembered that all the other kids laughed loudly), his father smacked him in the face.

After that he carefully observed what the grown-ups appreciated in his words, what they approved of, what they disapproved of, what astonished them; thus he was equipped, when he was in the garden with Mama one day, to utter a sentence imbued with the melancholy of his grandmother's lamentations: "Life is like weeds."

It's hard to say what he meant by this; what is certain is that he wasn't thinking of the hardy worthlessness and worthless hardiness that is the distinctive feature of self-propagating plants but that he probably wanted to express the rather vague notion that, when all is said and done, life is sad and futile. Even though he had said something other than what he wanted to, the effect of his words was splendid; Mama silently stroked his hair and looked into his face with moist eyes. Jaromil was so carried away by this look, which he perceived as emotional praise, that he had a craving to see it again. During a walk he kicked a stone and said to his mother: "Mama, I just kicked a stone, and now I feel so sorry for it I want to stroke it," and he really bent down and did so.

Mama was convinced that her son was not only gifted (he had learned to read when he was five) but also that he was exceptionally sensitive in a way different from other children. She often expressed this opinion to Grandpapa and Grandmama while Jaromil, unobtrusively playing with his tin soldiers or on his rocking horse, listened with great interest. He would look deeply into the eyes of guests, imagining rapturously that their eyes were looking at him as a singular, exceptional child, one who might not be a child at all.

When his sixth birthday was approaching and he was a few months from entering school, the family insisted that he have his own room and sleep by himself. Mama looked upon the passage of time with regret, but she agreed. She and her husband agreed to give their son the third and smallest room on their floor as a birthday present, and to buy him a bed and other furniture for a child's room: a small bookcase, a mirror to encourage cleanliness, and a small desk.

Papa suggested decorating the room with Jaromil's own drawings, and he soon set about framing the childish scrawls of apples and gardens. Then Mama went over to Papa and said: "I want to ask you for something." He looked at her, and Mama's voice, at once shy and forceful, went on: "I'd like some sheets of paper and paints." Then she sat down at a table in her room, laid a sheet of paper in front of her, and on it started to draw letters in pencil; finally she dipped a brush in red paint and redid the penciled letters in that color, the first a capital *L*. It was followed by a small *i* and an *f*, and went on to form this line: "Life is like weeds." She examined her work with satisfaction: the letters were straight and well shaped; and yet she picked up a new sheet of paper, again wrote the line in pencil, and colored it in dark blue this time, for that seemed to her much better suited to the ineffable sadness of her son's maxim.

Then she remembered that Jaromil had said, "Grandmama not fair, ate my pear," and with a happy smile she started to write (in bright red), "Grandmama fair, loves her pear." And after that, with a hidden smile, she again remembered "You're pricks," but she refrained from copying this thought and instead penciled and colored (in green), "We'll dance in the wood, our hearts feeling good," and then (in purple), "Dear Hana bends like a banana" (Jaromil had actually said "Maid Hana," but Mama found the word offensive), then she remembered Jaromil bending down to stroke a stone, and after a moment's thought she wrote and painted (in sky blue), "I can't harm or even alarm a rock," and with a bit of embarrassment but with all the more pleasure (in orange), "Mama, I give you a lollipop kiss," and finally (in gold), "My mama is the most beautiful in the world."

The day before his birthday his parents sent the overexcited Jaromil down to sleep with his grandmother while they moved the furniture amd decorated the walls. The next morning, when they brought the child into the renovated room, Mama was tense, and Jaromil did nothing to dispel her agitation; he was dumbfounded and silent; the main object of his interest (which he showed only feebly and shyly) was the desk; it was an odd-looking piece of furniture resembling a school desk, with the slanted desktop (its hinged lid covering a space for books and notebooks) attached to the seat.

"Well, what do you say? Do you like it?" asked Mama impatiently.

"Yes, I like it," the child responded.

"And what do you like best?" inquired Grandpapa, who with Grandmama was watching the long-awaited scene from the room's doorway.

"The desk," said the child. He sat down and began raising and lowering the lid.

"And what do you say about the pictures?" Papa asked, pointing to the framed drawings.

The child raised his head and smiled. "I know them."

"And how do you like them hanging on the wall?"

The child, still sitting at his little desk, nodded to indicate he liked the drawings on the wall.

Mama was heartbroken and wanted to vanish from the room. But there she was, and she couldn't allow the framed, colored inscriptions on the wall to be passed over in silence, for she would have taken such silence for condemnation. That is why she said: "And look at this writing."

The child lowered his head and looked inside the little desk.

"You know, I wanted . . . ," she went on in great confusion, "I wanted you to be able to remember how you grew up, from cradle to school, because you were a bright little boy and a joy to us all. . . ." She said this as if in apology, and since she was nervous, she repeated the same thing several times. At last, not knowing what to say, she was silent.

But she was wrong to think that Jaromil was not pleased by his gift. He didn't know what to say, but he wasn't disappointed; he had always been proud of his words, and he didn't want to utter them into the void; now that he saw them carefully copied in color and transformed into pictures, he experienced a feeling of success, a success so great and unexpected that he didn't know how to respond, and it gave him stage fright; he understood that he was *a child who uttered striking words*, and he knew that this child should at this moment say something striking, yet nothing striking came to mind, and so he lowered his head. But when he saw out of the corner of his eye his own words on the walls, set, fixed, more durable and bigger than himself, he was carried away; he had the impression of being surrounded by his own self, of being vast, of filling the entire room, of filling the entire house.

4

Jaromil already knew how to read and write before he started school, and Mama decided that he could go directly into second grade; she obtained special authorization from the ministry, and after passing an examination before a committee, Jaromil was permitted to take a place among pupils a year older than he. Because everyone in school admired him, the classroom seemed to him merely a reflection of the family house. On Mother's Day the pupils performed at the school celebration. Jaromil was the last to step up on the podium, and he recited a touching little poem that was much applauded by the audience of parents.

But he soon realized that behind the audience that applauded him there was another that was slyly and antagonistically on the lookout for him. In the dentist's crowded waiting room one day, he ran into one of his schoolmates. As the boys stood side by side with their backs to the window, Jaromil saw an old gentleman listening with a kindly smile to what they were saying. Encouraged by this sign of interest, Jaromil asked his fellow pupil (raising his voice a bit so that the question would be heard by all) what he would do if he were the country's minister of education. Since the boy didn't know what to say, Jaromil began to elaborate his own thoughts, which was not very difficult because all he needed was to repeat the speech with which his grandfather regularly entertained him. And so if Jaromil were

minister of education, there would be two months of
school and ten months of vacation, the teacher would
have to obey the children and bring them their snacks
from the bakery, and there would be all kinds of other
remarkable reforms, all of which Jaromil loudly and
clearly put forward.

Then the door to the treatment room opened, and a
patient came out, accompanied by the nurse. A woman
holding a book with her finger in it to mark the place
turned to the nurse and asked, almost pleading: "Please
say something to that child! It's dreadful the way he's
showing off!"

After Christmas the teacher had the pupils come to
the front of the room one by one to tell what they had
found under the tree. Jaromil began to enumerate a
construction set, skis, ice skates, books, but he quickly
noticed that the children didn't share his fervor, that, on
the contrary, some of them were looking indifferent,
indeed hostile. He stopped without breathing a word
about the rest of his presents.

No, no, don't worry, I don't intend to retell the tired
old story of the rich kid his poor schoolmates hate; in
Jaromil's class there were in fact children from families
better off than his, and yet they got along well with the
others, and no one resented their affluence. What was it
about Jaromil that annoyed his schoolmates; what was
it that got on their nerves, that made him different?

I almost hesitate to say it: it was not wealth, it was his
mama's love. That love left its traces on everything; it
was recorded on his shirt, on his hair, on the words he

used, on the schoolbag in which he carried his notebooks, and on the books he read at home for pleasure. Everything was specially chosen and arranged for him. The shirts made for him by his frugal grandmother resembled, God knows why, girls' blouses more than boys' shirts. He had to keep his long hair off his brow and out of his eyes with one of his mother's barrettes. When it rained Mama waited for him in front of the school with a large umbrella, while his friends took off their shoes and waded through the puddles.

Mother love imprints a mark on boys' brows that rebuffs the friendliness of schoolmates. Eventually Jaromil gained the skill to hide that stigma, but after his glorious arrival at school he experienced a difficult time (lasting a year or two) during which his schoolmates, who taunted him with a passion, also beat him up several times just for the fun of it. But even during that worst time he had some friends to whom he would remain grateful throughout his life; a few words need to be said about them:

His number one friend was his father: sometimes he would go out into the yard with a soccer ball (he had played soccer as a student), and Jaromil would plant himself between two trees; his father kicked the ball toward Jaromil, who pretended that he was the goalkeeper of the Czech national team.

His number two friend was his grandfather. He would take Jaromil to his two businesses—a large housewares store that Jaromil's father was now running, and a cosmetics shop, where the salesgirl was a young woman who greeted the boy with a friendly smile and let him sniff all the perfumes, soon enabling him to recognize the various brands; he would close his eyes and make his grandfather test him by holding the little bottles under his nose. "You're a genius of smell," his grandfather would congratulate him, and Jaromil dreamed of becoming the inventor of new perfumes.

His number three friend was Alik. Alik was a wild little dog that had been living in the villa for some time; even though it was untrained and unruly, the dog provided Jaromil with fine daydreams of a faithful friend who waited for him in the corridor outside the classroom and, to the envy of his schoolmates, accompanied him home after school.

Daydreaming about dogs became the passion of his solitude, even leading him into a peculiar Manicheism: for him dogs represented the *goodness* of the animal world, the sum total of all natural virtues; he imagined great wars of dogs against cats (wars with generals, officers, and all the tactics he had learned while playing with his tin soldiers) and was always on the side of the dogs, in the same way as a man should always be on the side of justice.

And since he spent much time with pencil and paper in his father's study, dogs also became the chief subject of his drawings: an endless number of epic scenes in which dogs were generals, soldiers, soccer players, and knights. And since as quadrupeds they could hardly perform their human roles, Jaromil gave them human bodies. That was a great invention! Whenever he had tried to draw a human being, he encountered a serious difficulty: he couldn't draw the human face; on the other hand, he succeeded marvelously with the elongated canine head and the spot of a nose at its tip, and so his daydreams and clumsiness gave rise to a strange world of dog-headed people, a world of characters that could quickly and easily be drawn and situated in soccer matches, wars, and stories of brigands. The adventure serials Jaromil thus drew filled many a sheet of paper.

The only boy among his friends was number four: a classmate whose father was the school janitor, a sallow little man who often informed on pupils to the principal; these boys would take revenge on the janitor's son, who was the class pariah. When the pupils one after another started to turn away from Jaromil, the janitor's son remained his sole faithful admirer and thus was invited one day to the villa; he was given lunch and dinner, he and Jaromil played with the construction set, and they did their homework together. The following Sunday Jaromil's father took them both to a soccer match; the game was wonderful and, just as wonderful, Jaromil's father knew all the players' names and talked about the game so like an expert that the janitor's son never took his eyes off him, and Jaromil was proud.

It seemed like a comical friendship: Jaromil always carefully dressed, the janitor's son threadbare; Jaromil with his homework carefully prepared, the janitor's son a poor student. All the same Jaromil was contented with this faithful companion at his side, for the janitor's son was extraordinarily strong; one winter day some class-mates attacked them, but the attackers got more than they bargained for; though Jaromil was exhilarated by this triumph over superior numbers, the prestige of successful defense cannot compare with the prestige of attack:

One day, as they were taking a walk through the sub-urb's vacant lots, they encountered a boy so clean and well-dressed that he could have been coming from some children's tea dance. "Mama's darling!" said the janitor's son, barring the way. They asked him mocking questions and were delighted by his fright. Finally the boy grew bold and tried to push them aside. "How dare you! You'll pay for this!" Jaromil shouted, cut to the quick by this insolent contact; the janitor's son took these words as a signal and hit the boy in the face.

Intellect and physical force can sometimes complement each other remarkably. Didn't Byron feel great affection for the boxer Jackson, who trained the discriminating aristocrat in all kinds of sports? "Don't hit him, just hold him!" said Jaromil to his friend as he pulled up some stinging nettles; then they made the boy undress and flogged him with the nettles from head to toe. "Your mama'll be glad to see her darling little red crayfish," said Jaromil, experiencing a great feeling of fervent friendship for his companion and fervent hatred for all the mama's darlings of the world.

5

But exactly why did Jaromil remain an only child? Did Mama simply not want another one?

On the contrary: she very much hoped to regain the blissful time of her first years as a mother, but her husband always found reasons to put her off. To be sure, the yearning she had for another child didn't lessen, but she no longer dared to be insistent, fearing the humiliation of further refusal.

But the more she refrained from talking about her maternal yearning, the more she thought about it; she thought about it as an illicit, clandestine, and thus forbidden thing; the idea that her husband could make a child for her attracted her not only because of the child itself but because it had taken on a lasciviously ambiguous tone; "Come here and make me a little daughter," she would imagine saying to her husband, and the words seemed arousing to her.

Late one evening, when the couple had come home a bit tipsy from the house of friends, Jaromil's father, having stretched out beside his wife and turned off the light (let me note that, ever since their wedding, he had always taken her blindly, letting his desire be guided not by sight but by touch), threw off the blanket, and coupled with her. The rarity of their erotic relations and the influence of wine made her give herself to him with a voluptuous sensuality she had not felt for a long time. The idea that they were making a child together again filled her mind, and when she sensed that her husband was approaching his spasm of pleasure she stopped controlling herself and began to shout ecstatically at him to abandon his usual caution, to stay inside her, to make her a child, to make her a pretty little daughter, and she clutched him so firmly and convulsively that he had to struggle to free himself so as to make sure that his wife's wish would not be granted.

Then, as they lay exhausted side by side, Mama moved closer to him and, now whispering in his ear, again said that she wanted to have another child with him; no, she no longer wanted to insist on it, she only wanted to explain why a few moments ago she had shown her desire so abruptly and emphatically (and maybe improperly, she was willing to admit); she added that this time they would surely have a little daughter in whom he would see himself just as she saw herself in Jaromil.

The engineer then told her (it was the first time since their wedding that he had reminded her of it) that he had never wanted to have a child with her; that he had been forced to give in regarding the one child, and that now it was her turn to give in; that if she wanted him to see himself in a child, he could assure her that he would see the most accurate image of himself in a child that had never been born.

They lay side by side, silent for a moment, and then Mama began to sob and she sobbed all night, her husband not even touching her and saying barely a few soothing words that couldn't even get through the outer wave of her tears; she felt that she understood everything at last: the man she lived with had never loved her.

The sadness into which she had sunk was the deepest of all the sorrows she had ever known. Fortunately the consolation her husband had refused her was provided by another creature: History. Three weeks after the night I've just described, her husband was called up for active duty in the military, and he took his gear and left for the country's border. War was about to break out at any moment, people were buying gas masks and preparing air-raid shelters in their cellars. And Mama clutched the misfortune of her country like a saving hand; she experienced it with emotion and spent long hours with her son colorfully describing the events for him.

Then the Great Powers reached an agreement in Munich, and Jaromil's father came home from one of the fortifications now occupied by the German army. After that the whole family would sit downstairs in Grandpapa's room evening after evening to go over the various moves of History, which until recently they had believed to be dozing (maybe, since it was watchful, pretending to be asleep) but which had now suddenly leaped out of its lair and overshadowed everything with its great bulk. Oh, how good Mama felt to be protected by this shadow! Czechs were fleeing the Sudeten region en masse, Bohemia was left defenseless in the center of Europe like a peeled orange, and six months later, early in the morning, German tanks swept into the streets of

Prague, and during that time Jaromil's mother was always close to the soldier who had been prevented from defending his homeland, completely forgetting that he was a man who had never loved her.

But even during periods when History impetuously rages, everyday life sooner or later emerges from its shadow and the conjugal bed shows all its monumental triviality and astounding permanence. One evening, when Jaromil's father again put his hand on Mama's breast, she realized that the man who was touching her was the same man who had brought her down. She pushed his hand away, subtly reminding him of the harsh words he had said to her some time before.

She didn't want to be spiteful; she only wanted to signify by this refusal that the great matters of nations cannot make us forget the modest matters of the heart; she wanted to give her husband the opportunity to rectify today the words of yesterday and to raise up the person he had brought down. She believed that the nation's tragedy had made him more sensitive, and she was ready to greet with gratitude even a furtive caress as a sign of repentance and the beginning of a new chapter in their love. Alas, the husband whose hand had just been pushed away from his wife's breast turned over and quickly fell asleep.

After the great student demonstration in Prague, the Germans closed the Czech universities, and Mama waited in vain for her husband again to slip his hand under the blanket and put his hand on her breast. Grandpapa, having discovered that the pretty salesgirl in the cosmetics shop had been stealing from him for ten years, went into a rage and died of a stroke. Czech students were taken away in cattle cars to concentration camps, and Mama consulted a doctor, who deplored the bad state of her nerves and recommended a rest. He told her about a boardinghouse on the edge of a small spa, surrounded by a river and lakes, which every summer attracted crowds of people who liked swimming, fishing, and boating. It was early spring, and she was enchanted by the thought of tranquil lakeside walks. But then she was afraid of the delightful dance music that, forgotten, lingers in the air of restaurant terraces like a poignant recollection of summer; she was afraid of her own longing, and she decided that she couldn't go there alone.

Ah, of course! She knew right away with whom she would go. Because of the sorrow her husband had caused her and because of her desire for another child she had for some time nearly forgotten him. How stupid she had been, how badly she had treated herself by forgetting him! Repentant, she bent over him: "Jaromil, you're my first and my second child," she said, pressing his face to her breast, going on senselessly: "You're my first, my second, my third, my fourth, my fifth, my sixth, and my tenth child," and she covered his face with kisses.

6

A tall, gray-haired lady with an erect bearing greeted them at the railroad station; a sturdy countryman grabbed the two suitcases and carried them out to a waiting horse-drawn black carriage; the man got up onto the driver's seat and Jaromil, Mama, and the tall lady sat down on the facing passenger seats to be conveyed through the streets of the small town to a square bordered on one side by a Renaissance colonnade and on the other by a wrought-iron fence before a garden in which stood an old vine-covered château; then they headed down to the river; Jaromil noticed a row of yellow wooden cabanas, a diving board, white pedestal tables and chairs, a line of poplars in the background along the riverbank, and by then the carriage was already on its way to the scattered riverfront villas.

In front of one of them the horse stopped, the man got down from his seat and picked up the two suitcases, and Jaromil and Mama followed him through a garden, a foyer, and upstairs to a room with twin beds placed against each other in the marital arrangement and with two windows, one of them opening onto a balcony facing the garden and the river. Mama went over to the balcony railing and took a deep breath: "Ah, how divinely peaceful!" she said and again inhaled and exhaled deeply, looking at the riverside, where a red boat moored to a wooden landing was rocking.

That evening at dinner downstairs in the small dining room, she met an old couple who occupied another of the guest rooms, and every evening thereafter the murmur of prolonged conversation ruled the room; everyone liked Jaromil, and Mama listened with pleasure to his small talk, ideas, and discreet boasting. Yes, *discreet*: Jaromil would never forget the woman in the dentist's waiting room and would always seek a shield against her nasty look; to be sure he would still thirst for admiration, but he had learned to gain it with terse phrases naively and modestly uttered.

The villa in the peaceful garden; the dark river with the moored boat awakening thoughts of long voyages; the black carriage that stopped in front of the villa from time to time to pick up the tall lady who looked like a princess from a book filled with castles and palaces; the still, deserted swimming pool to which one could descend upon leaving the carriage as if passing from one century to another, one dream to another, one book to another; the Renaissance square with the narrow colonnade among whose columns men with swords once clashed—all this made up a world that Jaromil entered with delight.

The man with the dog was also part of this beautiful world; the first time they saw him he was standing motionless on the riverbank, looking at the water; he was wearing a leather coat, and a black German shepherd sat at his side; their stillness made them look like otherworldly figures. The next time they met him it was in the same place; the man (again in the leather coat) was throwing sticks, and the dog was retrieving them.

The third time (the setting was always the same: poplars and river), the man briefly bowed to Mama and then, as the perceptive Jaromil noticed, he turned to look at them after they passed him. Returning from their walk the next day, they saw the black German shepherd sitting at the entrance to the villa. When they entered the foyer they heard voices in the next room and were in no doubt that the masculine one belonged to the dog's master; their curiosity was great enough to keep them standing in the foyer for a while, looking around and chatting until the tall lady, the boarding-house owner, at last appeared.

Mama pointed at the dog: "Who is that man this dog belongs to? We're always running into him on our walks." "He's the art teacher at the high school here." Mama remarked that she would be very delighted to talk to an art teacher because Jaromil liked to draw, and she was eager to have an expert's opinion. The boardinghouse owner introduced the man to Mama, and Jaromil had to run up to the room to get his sketch-book.

Then the four of them sat down in the small salon—the boardinghouse owner; Jaromil; the dog's master, who was examining the drawings; and Mama, who accompanied his examination with her commentary: she explained that Jaromil always said that what interested him was not drawing landscapes or still lifes but rather action scenes, and, she said, his drawings really did have astonishing vitality and movement, even though she didn't understand why all the people in them had dogs' heads; maybe if Jaromil drew people with real human bodies his modest work might have some value, but the way it was she unfortunately couldn't say whether it made any sense at all.

The dog's owner examined the drawings with satisfaction; then he declared that it was in fact the combination of animal head and human body that captivated him. For that fantastic combination was no chance idea but, as so many of the child's drawings showed, a haunting image, something rooted in the unfathomable depths of his childhood. Jaromil's mother should be careful of judging her son's talent only by his ability to depict the outer world; anyone could acquire that; what interested him as a painter (letting it be understood that teaching for him was a necessary evil to earn a living) was precisely the original inner world the child was laying out on paper.

Mama listened with pleasure to the painter's praise, the tall lady stroked Jaromil's hair and asserted that he had a great future ahead of him, and Jaromil looked down, registering in his memory everything he was hearing. The painter said that next year he would be transferred to a Prague high school, and that he would be pleased if Jaromil's mother were to bring him further examples of the boy's work.

"Inner world!" Those were grand words, and Jaromil heard them with extreme satisfaction. He never forgot that at the age of five he had already been considered an exceptional child, different from others; the behavior of his classmates, who made fun of his schoolbag and shirt, also (at times harshly) confirmed his uniqueness. Until this moment that uniqueness had only been a vague and empty notion; it had been an incomprehensible hope or an incomprehensible rejection; but now it had received a name: "original inner world"; and that designation was immediately given definite content: drawings of people with dogs' heads. Jaromil of course knew very well that he had made this admired discovery of dog-headed humans by chance, purely because he couldn't draw a human face; this gave him the confused idea that the originality of his inner world was not the result of laborious effort but rather the expression of everything that randomly passed through his head; it was given him like a gift.

From then on he paid great attention to his own thoughts and began to admire them. For example, the idea came to him that when he died the world he was living in would cease to exist. At first this thought only flickered in his head, but now that he had been made aware of his inner originality, he didn't allow the thought to escape (as he had allowed so many other thoughts to escape previously) but immediately seized it, observed it, examined it from all sides. He was walking along the river, closing his eyes from time to time and wondering if the river existed when his eyes were closed. Of course, every time he opened his eyes the river was flowing as before, but what was astonishing was that Jaromil was unable to consider this as proof that the river was really there when he was not seeing it. That seemed inordi-

nately interesting to him, and he devoted the better part
of a day to this observation before telling Mama about it.

The nearer they came to their vacation's end, the
greater the pleasure they took in their conversations.
Now they would take their walks after dark, just the
two of them, sit down on a worm-eaten bench at the
edge of the water, hold hands, and look at the wavelets
on which an enormous moon gently rocked. "How
beautiful," Mama said with a sigh, and the child
watched the moonlit circle of water and dreamed of the
river's long course; Mama thought of the empty days
that would soon resume, and she said: "Darling, there's
a sadness in me you'll never understand." Then she
looked into her son's eyes, and it seemed to her that she
saw great love there and a yearning to understand. This
frightened her; she couldn't really confide a woman's
troubles to a child! But at the same time those understanding eyes attracted her like a vice. When mother
and son lay stretched out side by side on the twin beds
Mama remembered that she had reclined this way
beside Jaromil until he was five years old and that she
was happy then; she said to herself: He's the only man
I've ever been happy with in bed; at first this thought
made her smile, but when she looked again at her son's
tender gaze she told herself that this child was not only
capable of distracting her from the things that grieved
her (thus giving her the *consolation of forgetting*) but
also of listening to her attentively (thus bringing her the
consolation of understanding). "I want you to know

that my life is far from being full of love," she said to him; and another time she went so far as to confide to him: "As a mama, I'm happy, but a mama is not only a mama, she's also a woman."

Yes, these incomplete confidences attracted her like a sin, and she was aware of it. When Jaromil once suddenly said to her: "Mama, I'm not so little, I understand you," she was almost frightened. Naturally the boy hadn't surmised anything precise, he only wanted to suggest to Mama that he was able to share her sorrows, whatever they might be, but what he had said was fraught with meaning, and Mama saw his words as an abyss that had suddenly opened: an abyss of illicit intimacy and forbidden understanding.

7

And how did Jaromil's inner world continue to expand?

Not much; the schoolwork that had come so easily to him in the elementary grades became much more difficult in high school, and in that dullness the glory of the inner world disappeared. The teacher spoke of pessimistic books that saw the here and now merely as misery and ruin, which made his maxim that life is like weeds seem shamefully trite. Jaromil was no longer at all convinced that everything he thought and felt was solely his, as if all ideas had always existed in a definitive form and could only be borrowed as from a public library. But who then was he? What could his own self really consist of? He bent over that self in order to peer into it, but all he could find was the reflection of himself bending over himself to peer into that self. . . .

And so he began to yearn for the man who, two years before, had first talked about his inner originality; and since his art grades were barely average (in his watercolors the paint always strayed beyond the penciled outline sketches), Mama decided to accede to her son's request, find the painter, and arrange for private lessons to remedy Jaromil's inadequacies, which were spoiling his report cards.

So one fine day Jaromil went to the painter's apartment. It was a converted attic consisting of two rooms; the first contained a big collection of books; in the second, windowless but with a large skylight in the slanting roof, there were easels holding unfinished canvases, a long table with sheets of paper and small bottles of colored ink scattered on it, and on the wall strange black faces the painter said were copies of African masks; a dog (the one Jaromil already knew) lay motionless on the corner of the daybed watching the visitor.

The painter seated Jaromil at the long table and began to leaf through his sketchbook. "They're all the same," he finally said. "They don't take you anywhere."

Jaromil wanted to reply that these were exactly the figures with dogs' heads that had captivated the painter and that he had drawn them for him and because of him, but he was so disappointed and upset he couldn't say anything. The painter set a blank sheet of paper in front of him, opened a bottle of India ink, and put a brush in his hand. "Now draw whatever comes to mind, don't think about it much and just draw." Jaromil was so frightened that he had absolutely no idea what to draw, but since the painter insisted, he again, dying a thousand deaths, fell back on the head of a dog on top of an ill-formed body. The painter was dissatisfied, and Jaromil, embarrassed, said that he would like to learn how to paint with watercolors, because in class the colors always overflowed his outlines.

"So your mother said," said the painter. "But forget about it for now, and forget about dogs too." He set a big book in front of Jaromil and showed him pages where awkward black lines wiggled whimsically over a colored background, evoking in Jaromil's mind images of centipedes, starfish, beetles, stars, and moons. The painter wanted the boy to use his imagination and draw something comparable. "But *what* should I draw?" he asked, and the painter replied: "Draw a line; draw a line that pleases you. And remember that it's not the artist's role to copy the outlines of things but to create a world of his own lines on paper." And Jaromil drew lines he didn't like at all, covering sheet after sheet with them and finally, according to Mama's instructions, giving the painter a banknote and going home.

The visit had thus been different from what he had expected, not having led to the rediscovery of his lost inner world but rather the contrary: it had deprived Jaromil of the only thing that belonged to him alone, the soccer players and soldiers with dogs' heads. And yet, when Mama asked if the lesson had been interesting, he talked about it enthusiastically; he was being sincere: the visit had not validated his inner world, but he had found an unusual outer world that was not accessible to just anyone and had instantly granted him some small privileges: he had seen strange paintings that had bewildered him but offered the advantage (he understood immediately that it was an advantage!) of having nothing in common with the still lifes and landscapes hanging on the walls of his parents' villa; he had also heard some strange remarks that he appropriated without delay: for example, he understood that the word "bourgeois" was an insult; bourgeois are people who want paintings to be lifelike, to imitate nature; but we can laugh at the bourgeois because (and Jaromil was delighted by this idea!) they were long since dead and did not know it.

And so he gladly went to the painter's, passionately hoping to repeat the success he had gained in the past with his dog-headed people; but in vain: the doodles that were meant to be variations on Miró's paintings were forced and entirely lacking the charm of childlike playfulness; the drawings of African masks remained clumsy imitations of their models and failed to stimulate the boy's own imagination, as the painter had hoped. And since Jaromil found it unbearable to have been at the painter's so many times without hearing a word of praise, he made a decision: he would bring him his secret sketchbook of female nudes.

His models for most of these drawings were photographs of statues he had seen in illustrated books from Grandpapa's library; in the initial pages of the sketchbook they were therefore of sturdy mature women in the lofty poses of the previous century's allegories. Then there was a page with something more interesting: a drawing of a headless woman; better still: the paper had been slit at the level of her neck, so that it looked as if the woman's head had been chopped off and that the paper still bore the mark of an imaginary ax. The slit in the paper had been made by Jaromil's pocketknife; there was a girl in his class he liked very much, and he often gazed at her, wishing to see her naked. To fulfill this wish he obtained a photograph of her and cut the head out; he inserted it into the slit.

That is why all the women in the following drawings were also decapitated and bore the same mark of an imaginary ax; some of them were in very strange positions—for example, in a squatting posture depicting urination; at a flaming stake, like Joan of Arc; that execution scene, which I could explain (and perhaps excuse) as a historical reference, inaugurated a long series: sketches of a headless woman impaled on a sharpened pole, a headless woman with a leg cut off, a woman with an amputated arm, and other situations it is better to be silent about.

Of course Jaromil couldn't be certain whether these drawings would please the painter; in no way did they resemble the pictures he saw in his big books or on the canvases on the easels in his studio; even so it seemed to Jaromil that there was something about the drawings in his secret sketchbook that was close to his teacher's work: their aura of something forbidden; their originality, as compared to the paintings at home; the disapproval his drawings of nude women would provoke, much as the painter's incomprehensible canvases would if they were submitted to a jury consisting of Jaromil's family and their friends.

The painter leafed through the sketchbook and then, without a word, handed Jaromil a big book. He sat down some distance away and began drawing on sheets of paper while Jaromil went through the book, seeing a naked man with buttocks so extended they had to be supported by a wooden crutch; an egg hatching a flower; a face covered with ants; a man whose hand was turning into a rock.

Coming over to Jaromil, the painter said: "Notice what a wonderful draftsman Salvador Dalí is," and then he placed a plaster statuette of a naked woman in front of him: "We've been neglecting draftsmanship, and that's a mistake. We need to start by getting to know the world as it is before we can go about radically transforming it," he said, and Jaromil's sketchbook was soon filled with female bodies whose proportions the painter had corrected and modified with strokes of his pencil.

8

When a woman doesn't live sufficiently through her body, she comes to see the body as an enemy. Mama didn't much like the strange scrawls her son brought back from his drawing lessons, but when she examined the drawings of naked women the painter had corrected, she felt intense disgust. Looking out of the window a few days later, she saw Jaromil down in the garden holding the ladder for the maid, Magda, who was picking cherries while he gazed attentively under her skirt. Feeling herself assailed on all sides by battalions of bare bottoms, she decided to wait no longer. That day Jaromil was supposed to have his drawing lesson as usual; Mama dressed quickly and got there ahead of him.

"I'm not a prude," she said, having seated herself in one of the studio's armchairs, "but you know that Jaromil is entering the awkward age."

She had carefully prepared everything she wanted to say to the painter, but now she was at a loss. She had gone over her sentences in familiar surroundings where a window looked out onto the garden's peaceful greenery, which silently applauded her every thought. But there was no greenery here, there were only bizarre canvases on easels and on the daybed a dog with its head between its paws examining her with the fixed gaze of a distrustful sphinx.

The painter refuted Mama's objections with a few sentences, then he went on: he frankly admitted that he had no interest at all in the good grades Jaromil might receive in art classes that do nothing but kill children's pictorial sense. What interested him in her son's drawings was his original, nearly mad imagination.

"Notice the strange happenstance. The drawings you showed me some time ago depicted people with dogs' heads. The drawings your son showed me recently depicted naked women, but all of them headless. Don't you find it significant, this stubborn refusal to acknowledge man's human face, to acknowledge man's human nature?"

Mama was bold enough to reply that her son was surely not so pessimistic as to deny man's human nature.

"Of course his drawings don't come from some pessimistic logic," said the painter. "Art arises from sources other than logic. Jaromil spontaneously had the idea of drawing people with dogs' heads and women without heads, not knowing how or why. It was his unconscious that dictated these strange but not absurd images to him. Don't you feel there's some kind of link between your son's vision and the war that shakes us every hour of our lives? Hasn't the war deprived man of his face and head? Aren't we living in a world where headless men only desire decapitated women? Isn't a realistic vision of the world the emptiest of illusions? Aren't your son's childish drawings much more truthful?"

She had come here to rebuke the painter, and now she was as shy as a little girl afraid of being scolded; she didn't know what to say.

The painter got up from his armchair and headed for

a corner of the studio where unframed canvases were leaning against the wall. He picked one up, turned it face out, took a few steps back, squatted down, and looked at it. "Come here," he said, and when she (obediently) came near him he put his hand on her hip and drew her toward him, so that now they were squatting side by side and Mama was examining a curious assemblage of browns and reds making up a kind of charred and deserted landscape filled with dying flames that could also be taken for steaming blood; and scraped into the landscape with a palette knife was a strange human figure that seemed to be made of white string (the whiteness was the bared canvas) and seemed to be floating rather than walking and more diaphanous than substantial.

Mama still didn't know what to say, but the painter kept on talking, talking about the phantasmagoria of war, which by far surpasses, he said, the fantasies of modern paintings, talking about the ghastly image presented by a tree among whose leaves scraps of human bodies are entangled, a tree with fingers and an eye looking down from the tip of a branch. Then he said that in a time like this he was no longer interested in anything but war and love; a love that appears behind the blood-soaked world like the figure Mama saw on the canvas. (For the first time in the conversation she felt that she understood the painter, for she too had seen a kind of battlefield on the canvas and had perceived a human figure there.) The painter recalled for her the path along the river where they had first seen each other and then met so often, and he told her that she had suddenly appeared before him out of a fog of fire and blood like the shy white body of love.

Then he turned the squatting Mama's face toward him and kissed her. He kissed her before she knew what was happening. It was, moreover, characteristic of everything about this meeting: events were catching her off guard, running ahead of her imagination and her thinking; the kiss was a fait accompli before she had the time to reflect on it, and any further reflection couldn't change what was happening, for she had barely the time to tell herself quickly that something was happening that should not be happening; but she was not even quite certain about that, which is why she left for later the response to that debatable question and concentrated all her attention on what was, on taking things as they were.

She felt the painter's tongue in her mouth and in a fraction of a second realized that her own tongue was timidly sluggish and that it must feel to the painter like a wet rag; she was ashamed and quickly thought, almost angrily, that it was no surprise her tongue was a rag after all that kissless time; she hastened to respond to the painter's tongue with the point of her own tongue, and he lifted her up from the floor, led her to the daybed (the dog, whose eyes had been fixed on them, jumped off and lay down near the door), set her down on it, started to caress her breasts, and she felt satisfaction and pride; the painter's face looked young and eager, and she thought how long it had been since she

had been young and eager, and, afraid of being incapable of it, she urged herself to behave like a young and
eager woman, and suddenly (this time again, the event
occurred before she had time to think) she realized that
inside her body she was feeling the third man ever to
enter it.

And she realized that she didn't know at all whether
she did or didn't want him, and it occurred to her that
she was still a silly, inexperienced little girl, that if only
she had suspected in the recesses of her mind that the
painter was going to kiss and go to bed with her, what
was happening would never have taken place. This
thought provided her a reassuring excuse, for it follows that she was brought into adultery not by her
sensuality but by her innocence; and the thought of
innocence immediately increased her anger toward the
one who perpetually kept her in a state of innocent
half maturity, and this anger fell like an iron curtain in
front of her thoughts so that she only heard her breath
quicken and she gave up pondering what she was
doing.

Then, when their breathing eased, her thoughts
reawakened, and to escape them she put her head on
the painter's chest; she let him caress her hair, breathed
in the soothing odor of oil paints, and wondered which
of them would first break the silence.

It was neither one nor the other, but the doorbell. The
painter got up, quickly buttoned his trousers, and said:
"Jaromil."

She was very frightened.

"Stay here and be calm," he said to her, and he caressed her hair and went out of the studio.

He greeted the boy at the front door in the other room and asked him to sit down.

"I have a visitor in the studio, so we'll stay here today. Show me what you've brought." Jaromil handed his sketchbook to the painter, the painter examined the drawings he had made at home, and then he put paints before him, gave him paper and a brush, suggested a subject, and asked him to draw.

Then he returned to the studio, where he found Mama dressed and ready to leave. "Why did you let him stay? Why didn't you send him away?"

"Are you in such a hurry to leave me?"

"This is crazy," she said, and the painter again took her in his arms; this time she neither defended herself nor yielded; she stood in his arms like a body deprived of its soul; the painter whispered into the ear of this inert body: "Yes, it's crazy. Love is either crazy or it's nothing at all." He sat her down on the daybed and kissed her and caressed her breasts.

Then he returned to the other room to see what Jaromil had drawn. This time the subject he had given him was not intended to exercise the boy's manual dexterity; Jaromil was to draw a scene from one of his recent dreams. The painter now talked for a long while about this work: what is most beautiful about dreams is the unlikely encounter of creatures and objects that couldn't possibly meet in everyday life; in a dream a boat can sail through a bedroom window, a woman

dead twenty years might be lying in bed and yet here
she is getting into the boat, which immediately changes
into a coffin, and the coffin begins floating between the
flowering banks of a river. He quoted Lautréamont's
famous phrase about the beauty of "the encounter of a
sewing machine and an umbrella on a dissecting table,"
and then he said: "That encounter, however, is no more
beautiful than the encounter of a woman and a child in
a painter's studio."

Jaromil could see that his teacher was a bit different
from the way he had been before, noticing the fervor in
his voice when he talked about dreams and poetry. Not
only did he like that, but he was pleased that he,
Jaromil, had been the justification for such an exhilarating speech, and above all he had registered his
teacher's last remark about the encounter of a child and
a woman in a painter's studio. A short while before,
when the painter had told him that they would stay in
this room, Jaromil had surmised that there was probably a woman in the studio, and certainly not just any
woman, because he was not allowed to see her. But he
was still too far away from the adult world to try to
clear up this puzzle; what interested him more was the
fact that, with that last remark, the painter had placed
him, Jaromil, on the same level as this woman who was
certainly important to the painter, and the fact that
Jaromil's arrival obviously made the presence of this
woman still more beautiful and precious, and he concluded that the painter liked him, that he mattered in
his life perhaps because of a deep and mysterious inner

similarity between them that Jaromil, still a child, could not clearly discern but that the painter, a wise adult, was aware of. This thought filled him with calm enthusiasm, and when the painter gave him another subject he bent feverishly over the paper.

The painter returned to the studio and found Mama in tears.

"Please let me go home right now!"

"Go ahead, you can leave together—Jaromil will soon be finished."

"You're a devil," she said, still in tears, and the painter embraced her and covered her with kisses. Then he returned to the adjoining room, praised Jaromil's work (ah, Jaromil was very happy that day!), and sent him home. Then he returned to the studio, stretched tearful Mama out on the old paint-stained daybed, kissed her soft mouth and wet face, and again made love to her.

9

Mama and the painter's love affair never freed itself from the omens that marked its beginning: it was not a love she had long and dreamily contemplated in advance, firmly looking it in the eye; it was an unexpected love that had grabbed her by the neck from behind.

This love constantly reminded her of her *unpreparedness* for love; she was inexperienced, she knew neither what to do nor what to say. Before the painter's unusual and demanding face, she was ashamed in advance of her every word and gesture; even her body was no better prepared; for the first time she bitterly regretted taking care of herself so badly after she gave birth, and she was frightened when she looked in the mirror at her belly, at its sadly hanging wrinkled skin.

Ah! She had always dreamed of a love in which her body and soul, hand in hand, would grow old together (yes, that was the love she had long contemplated in advance, looking it dreamily in the eye); but now, in this difficult liaison she was suddenly immersed in, she found her soul painfully young and her body painfully old, so that she moved forward into her adventure as if she were tremulously walking on a much-too-narrow plank, not knowing whether it was the youth of her soul or the age of her body that would cause her to fall.

The painter treated her with extravagant solicitude and tried hard to introduce her to the world of his paintings and thoughts. She was delighted by that; she saw it as proof that their first rendezvous was something other than a conspiracy of bodies taking advantage of a situation. But when love occupies both body and soul, it takes more time; Mama had to keep inventing new friends to justify (especially to Grandmama and Jaromil) her frequent absences from the house.

She would sit beside the painter as he worked, but that was not enough for him; he explained to her that painting, as he conceived it, was merely one method among others of quarrying the marvelous from life; and even a child could discover the marvelous at play or an ordinary man by recalling a dream. The painter gave Mama a sheet of paper and colored inks; she was told to make blots on the paper with the various colors and blow on them; rays ran over the paper in all directions and covered it with a multicolored web; the painter displayed Mama's output behind the glass panes of his bookcase and praised them to his guests.

On one of her earliest visits, he gave her several books as she was leaving. At home she had to read them secretly because she was afraid that Jaromil would ask her where she got the books, or another member of the family might ask her the same question, and she would find it difficult to find a satisfactory lie because a glance at them was enough to show that they were very different from the ones in the libraries of their friends or parents. She therefore hid the books in the drawer under her brassieres and nightgowns and read them during the moments when she was alone. The feeling of doing something forbidden and the fear of being caught probably prevented her from concentrating on what she was reading, for she seemed not to be absorbing much of what she read, not understanding most of it even when she reread many pages two or three times in a row.

She would then return to the painter's with the anxiety of a student who was afraid of being quizzed, because the painter would begin by asking her whether she had liked a certain book, and she knew that he wanted to hear not merely a positive answer but also that for him the book was the point of departure for a conversation, and that there were observations in the book on a subject he wanted to be in alliance with her about, as if it were a matter of a truth they defended in common. Mama knew all that, but it didn't make her understand any more of what was in the book, or what in the book was so important. And so, like a cunning pupil, she came up with an excuse: she complained that she had to read the books in secret to avoid being discovered, and she therefore couldn't concentrate on them as well as she wanted to.

The painter accepted this excuse, but he found an ingenious way out: at the next lesson he spoke to Jaromil about the currents of modern art and gave him several books to read, which the boy gladly accepted. When Mama first saw these books on her son's desk and realized that this contraband literature was actually intended for her she was frightened. Until then she alone had taken on the entire burden of her adventure, but now her son (that image of purity) had become an unwitting emissary of adulterous love. But there was nothing to be done, the books were on Jaromil's desk and Mama had no choice but to leaf through them in the guise of understandable maternal concern.

One day she dared to say to the painter that the poems he had lent her seemed needlessly obscure and confused. She regretted uttering these words the moment after she said them, for the painter considered the slightest divergence from his opinions as a betrayal. Mama quickly tried to erase her blunder. As the painter, his brow wrathful, turned away toward his canvas, she rapidly slipped off her blouse and brassiere. She had pretty breasts and knew it; now she proudly displayed them (but not without a remnant of shyness) as she crossed the studio, and then, half hidden by the canvas on the easel, she planted herself in front of the painter. He continued sullenly dabbing at the canvas, several times giving her a baleful look. Then she tore the brush from the painter's hand, put it between her teeth, said a word to him she had never said to anyone, a vulgar, obscene word, repeating it in an undertone several times in a row until she saw that the painter's anger had turned into erotic desire.

No, she had never before behaved this way, and she was nervous and strained; but she had realized from the beginning of their intimacy that the painter demanded from her free and astonishing types of erotic expression, that he wanted her to feel entirely free with him, released from everything, from all convention, from all shame, from all inhibition; he liked to say to her: "I don't want anything except that you give me your freedom, the totality of your freedom!" and he wanted at every moment to be convinced of this freedom. Mama had more or less come to understand that such uninhibited behavior was probably something beautiful, but she was all the more afraid that she would never be capable of it. And the harder she tried *to know her freedom*, the more this freedom became an arduous task, an obligation, something she had to prepare for at home (to consider what word, what desire, what gesture she was going to surprise the painter with to show him her spontaneity), so that she sagged under the imperative of freedom as if under a heavy burden.

"The worst thing isn't that the world isn't free, but that people have unlearned their freedom," the painter told her, and this remark seemed deliberately directed at her belonging so completely to that old world that the painter maintained had to be totally rejected. "If we can't change the world, let's at least change our own lives and live them freely," he said. "If every life is unique, let's draw the conclusion; let's reject everything that isn't new." And then, quoting Rimbaud: "It is necessary to be absolutely modern," and she listened to him religiously, full of trust in his words and full of mistrust toward herself.

It occurred to her that the love the painter felt for her could only be the result of a misunderstanding, and she sometimes asked him why exactly he loved her. He would answer that he loved her as a prizefighter loves a fragile forget-me-not, as a singer loves silence, as an outlaw loves a village schoolteacher; he would tell her that he loved her as a butcher loves the timorous eyes of a heifer or lightning the idyll of rooftops; he would tell her that he loved her as a beloved woman stolen away from a stupid habitat.

She listened to him enraptured and went to see him whenever she could spare a moment. She felt like a tourist who has before her the most beautiful land-scapes but is too worn out to perceive their beauty; she gained no joy from her love, but she knew that it was grand and beautiful and that she must not lose it.

And Jaromil? He was proud that the painter lent him books from his library (the painter had told him more than once that he had never lent anyone books, that Jaromil was the only one with that privilege), and since he had a lot of free time, he dreamily lingered over their pages. At that time, modern art had not yet become the property of the bourgeois multitude, retaining the spell-binding allure of a sect, that allure so easily understood by a child still at an age when one dreams of the romance of clans and brotherhoods. Jaromil felt that allure deeply, and he read the books in a way entirely different from that of Mama, who read them from A to Z like textbooks on which she would be examined. Jaromil, who ran no risk of being examined, never really read the painter's books; he scanned them, strolled through them, leafed through them, lingered over a page, and stopped at one line of verse or another, unconcerned whether or not the poem as a whole had something to say to him. A single line of verse or a sin-gle paragraph of prose was enough to make him happy, not only because of their beauty but above all because they provided entry into the realm of the elect who knew how to perceive what for others remained hidden.

Mama knew that her son was not content to be a mere emissary and that he read with interest the books that were only apparently meant for him; she thus began to discuss with him what they had both read, and she asked him questions she didn't dare ask the painter. She then was terrified to learn that her son defended the borrowed books with more implacable stubbornness than did the painter.

She noticed that in a collection of poems by Éluard he had underlined some lines in pencil: *To be asleep, the moon in one eye and the sun in the other.* "What do you find so beautiful about that? Why should I sleep with the moon in one eye?" *Legs of stone in stockings of sand.* "How can stockings be made of sand?" Jaromil thought that Mama was not only making fun of the poem but that she thought him too young to understand it, and he responded brusquely to her.

My God, she couldn't even stand up to a child of thirteen! When she went to the painter's that day, her state of mind was that of a spy wearing the uniform of a foreign army; she was afraid of being unmasked. Her behavior had lost the last vestige of spontaneity, and everything she said and did resembled the performance of an amateur who, paralyzed by stage fright, recites her lines in fear of being booed.

It was at about that time that the painter discovered the charm of the camera; he showed Mama his first photographs, still lifes made up of an odd assortment of objects, bizarre views of forgotten and abandoned things; then he led her under the luminous skylight and started to photograph her. At first it made her feel a kind of relief, for there was no need to talk; she only had to stand or sit or smile or listen to the painter's instructions and to the compliments he from time to time bestowed on her face.

The painter's eyes suddenly lit up; he grabbed a brush, dipped it in black paint, gently turned Mama's head, and made two oblique lines on her face. "I've crossed you out! I've destroyed God's work!" he said laughing, and he set about photographing her with the two thick lines crossing on her nose. Then he led her to the bathroom, washed her face, and dried it with a towel.

"I crossed you out in order to create you all over again now," he said, again taking up the brush and starting to draw on her. This time it was circles and lines resembling ancient ideographic writings. "A face-message, a face-letter," said the painter, and he took her back under the bright skylight and began again to photograph her.

Then he had her lie down on the floor and beside her head placed a plaster cast of the head of an antique statue on whose face he drew the same lines she had on hers, then photographed these two heads, the living and the lifeless, and then washed the lines off Mama's face, painted other lines on it, photographed her again, had her lie down on the daybed, and began to undress Mama, who, fearing that he would paint on her breasts and legs, even risked a joking remark intended to make him realize that he should not paint her body (it took courage for her to risk a joke, for she was always afraid that her jokes would misfire and make her look foolish), but the painter was tired of painting, and instead of painting he made love to her and, at the same time, he held her head between his two hands, her head covered with his designs, as if he were particularly aroused by the thought of making love to a woman who was his own creation, his own fantasy, his own image, as if he were God lying down with a woman he had just created for himself.

Mama really was at that moment nothing but his invention, one of his paintings. She knew it, and she marshaled all her forces to keep him from seeing that she was not at all the painter's partner, his miraculous counterpart, a creature worthy of love, but merely a lifeless reflection, a mirror proffered with docility, a passive surface on which the painter projected the image of his desire. And in fact she passed the test, the painter had his rapture and blissfully withdrew from her body. But then, once she was home, she felt as if she had undergone a great struggle, and that evening she wept before she fell asleep.

When she returned to the studio some days later, the painting and picture taking resumed. This time the painter bared her breasts and painted on their beautiful contours. But when he tried to undress her completely, for the first time she denied her lover something.

It's hard to conceive of the skill, even the trickery, she

employed, during all her erotic games with the painter, to hide her belly! She would keep on her garter-belt, implying that such seminakedness was more arousing; she would get him to make love in semidarkness instead of in full light; she would gently remove the painter's caressing hands from her belly and set them on her breasts; and when she had exhausted all her tricks, she would invoke her shyness, a trait the painter was familiar with and adored (he often told her that she was the incarnation of the color white, and that he had expressed his first thoughts of her in a painting by scraping white lines with a palette knife).

But now she had to stand in the middle of the studio like a living statue in the grip of the painter's eyes and brush. She resisted, and when she told him, as she had during her first visit, that what he wanted from her was crazy, he answered, as he did then: "Yes, love is crazy," and tore off the rest of her clothes.

And so she stood in the middle of the studio thinking only of her belly; she was afraid to look down at it, but it was before her eyes as she knew it from having despairingly looked at it a thousand times in the mirror; it seemed to her that she was nothing but a belly, nothing but ugly wrinkled skin, it seemed to her that she was a woman on an operating table, a woman who must not think about anything, who must yield herself up and simply believe that all this was temporary, that the operation and the pain would come to an end and that meanwhile there was only one thing to do: hang on.

The painter picked up a brush, dipped it in black

paint, and applied it to her shoulder, her navel, her legs, stepped back and picked up the camera; then he led her to the bathroom, where he had her lie down in the empty bathtub and, placing across her body the metal snake with its perforated head, told her that this metal snake didn't spray water but a deadly gas and that it was now lying on her body like the body of war on the body of love; and then he led her out to another spot and photographed her there too, and she went obediently, no longer trying to hide her belly, but she always had it before her eyes, and she saw the painter's eyes and her belly, her belly and the painter's eyes . . .

And then, when she lay stretched out on the rug, all covered with paint, and he made love to her beside the cool, beautiful antique head, she couldn't hang on any longer and began sobbing in his arms, but he probably failed to grasp the meaning of these sobs, for he was convinced that his ferocious bewitchment, transformed into steady, pounding, beautiful movement, could evoke no response other than tears of rapture and bliss.

Mama realized that the painter had not guessed the cause of her sobs, so she controlled herself and stopped crying. But when she got home she was overcome by vertigo on the stairs; she fell and scraped her knee. Frightened, Grandmama led her to her room, put a hand on her brow, and stuck a thermometer in her armpit.

Mama had a fever. Mama had a nervous breakdown.

10

A few days later, Czech parachutists sent from England killed the German ruler of Bohemia; martial law was declared, and long lists of those who had been shot in reprisal appeared on the street corners. Mama was confined to her bed, and the doctor came every day to stick a needle into her bottom. Her husband would come to sit at her bedside, grip her hand, and gaze into her eyes; she knew that he attributed her nervous collapse to History's horrors, and she thought with shame that she had deceived him while he, in this difficult time, was being good to her and trying to be her friend.

As for Magda—the maid who had been living in the villa for several years and about whom Grandmama, respectful of a sturdy democratic tradition, would say that she considered her more a member of the family than an employee—she came in weeping one day because her fiancé had been arrested by the Gestapo. And a few days later the fiancé's name appeared in black letters on a dark red poster among the names of others who had been shot, and Magda was given a few days off.

When she came back, she said that her fiancé's parents had been unable to obtain his ashes and that they would probably never know the location of their son's remains. She dissolved in tears and continued to weep almost every day. She wept most often in her small room, where her sobs were muffled by the wall, but sometimes she would suddenly begin to weep during lunch; since her misfortune the family had allowed her to eat with them at their table (before that she had eaten alone in the kitchen), and the exceptional nature of this favor reminded her at noon, day after day, that she was in mourning and being pitied, and her eyes would redden and a tear emerge and fall on the dumplings; she did her best to hide her tears and the redness of her eyes, lowering her head, hoping not to be seen, but they were noticed all the more, and someone was always ready to utter a comforting word, to which she would reply with great sobs.

Jaromil watched all this as an exhilarating show; he looked forward to seeing a tear in the girl's eye, to seeing the girl's shyness as she tried to suppress sorrow and how sorrow would triumph over shyness and allow a tear to fall. His eyes drank in that face (surreptitiously, for he had the sense of doing something forbidden), he felt himself invaded by a warm excitement and by the desire to cover that face with affection, to caress it and console it. At night, when he was alone and curled up under the covers, he imagined Magda's face with her big brown eyes, imagined caressing it and saying, "Don't cry, don't cry, don't cry," because he could find no other words to say.

At about that time Mama ended her medical treatments (she had cured herself with a week of sleep therapy) and began again to do the housekeeping and shopping even while constantly complaining of headaches and palpitations. One day she sat down and began to write a letter. The very first sentence made her

realize that the painter would find her silly and sentimental, and she was afraid of his verdict; but she soon
put herself at ease: she told herself that these words, the
last she would ever address to him, required no answer,
and this thought gave her the courage to continue; with
relief (and a strange feeling of rebellion) she created
sentences that were entirely herself, that were entirely
as she had been before she knew him. She wrote that
she loved him and that she would never forget the
miraculous time she had spent with him, but that the
moment had come to tell him the truth: she was different, completely different from what the painter imagined, she was really just an ordinary, old-fashioned
woman afraid that some day she would be unable to
look her innocent son in the eye.

Had she therefore decided to tell him the truth? Ah,
not at all! She didn't tell him that what she called the
bliss of love had been for her a taxing effort, she didn't
tell him how ashamed she had been of her marred belly
or about her scraped knee, her nervous breakdown, or
her having to sleep for a week. She didn't tell him anything of the kind because such sincerity was contrary to
her nature and because she finally wanted again to be
herself and she could be herself only in insincerity;
because if she had confided everything to him sincerely,
it would have been like lying down naked before him
with the stretch marks on her belly showing. No, she no
longer wanted to show him either her inside or her outside; she wanted to regain the protection of her modesty, and therefore to be insincere and write only about

her child and her sacred duties as a mother. By the time she finished the letter she had persuaded herself that it was neither her belly nor her exhausting efforts to follow the painter's ideas that had provoked her nervous breakdown, but her great maternal feelings that had rebelled against her great but guilty love.

At that moment she felt not only boundlessly sad but also noble, tragic, and strong; that she had depicted with grand words the sadness that a few days before had made her suffer now brought her a soothing joy; it was a beautiful sadness and she saw herself, illuminated by its melancholy light, as sadly beautiful.

What a strange coincidence! Jaromil, who at that time spent entire days spying on Magda's weeping eye, was well acquainted with the beauty of sadness and had fully immersed himself in it. He again leafed through the book the painter had lent him, reading and endlessly rereading Éluard's poems and falling under the spell of certain lines: "She has in the tranquillity of her body / A small snowball the color of an eye"; or: "Distant the sea that bathes your eye"; and: "Good morning, sadness / You're inscribed on the eyes I love." Éluard had become the poet of Magda's calm body and of her eyes bathed by a sea of tears; her entire life seemed to him to be contained in a single line: "Sadness-beautiful face." Yes, that was Magda: sadness-beautiful face.

One evening the rest of the family went out to the theater, and he was alone with her in the villa; aware of the habits of the household, he knew that Magda would be taking her Saturday bath. Since his parents and grandmother had arranged their outing to the theater a week in advance, that morning he had pushed aside the keyhole cover on the bathroom door and glued it in place with a wad of moistened bread; to provide a clear view, he took the key out of the door. Then he hid it carefully.

The house was quiet and empty, and Jaromil's heart was pounding. He sat upstairs in his room with a book as if someone might suddenly turn up and ask him what he was doing, but he was not reading, he was only listening. At last he heard the sound of water rushing through the plumbing and the flow hitting the bottom of the bathtub. He turned off the light at the top of the stairs and tiptoed down; he was in luck; the keyhole was still open, and when he pressed his eye against it he saw Magda leaning over the bathtub, her breasts bare, with nothing on but her underpants. His heart was pounding violently, for he was seeing what he had never seen before, would soon see still more, and no one could prevent it. Magda straightened up, went over to the mirror (he saw her in profile), looked at herself for some moments, then turned (he saw her facing him) and headed toward the bathtub; she stopped, took off her underpants, threw them aside (he still saw her facing him), then climbed into the bathtub.

When she was immersed in the bathtub, Jaromil went on watching her through the keyhole, but since the water was up to her shoulders, she once again was nothing but *a face*; the same familiar sad face with eyes bathed by a sea of tears but at the same time a com-

pletely different face: a face to which he had to add
(now, in the future, and forever) bare breasts, a belly,
thighs, a rump; it was *a face illuminated by the body's
nakedness;* it still elicited tenderness from him, but this
tenderness was different because it echoed the rapid
pounding of his heart.

And then he suddenly noticed that Magda was gazing
right at him. He was afraid he had been discovered. Her
eyes were fixed on the keyhole and she was smiling
sweetly (a smile at once embarrassed and friendly). He
quickly moved away from the door. Had she seen him
or not? He had tested the keyhole many times, and he
was sure that a spying eye on his side of the door couldn't
be seen from inside the bathroom. But how to explain
Magda's gaze and smile? Or was Magda merely looking
in that direction by chance, and was smiling only at the
thought that Jaromil could see her? In any event his
encounter with Magda's gaze so disturbed him that he
didn't dare go near the door again.

And yet, when he calmed down, he suddenly had an
idea that went beyond anything he had ever seen or
experienced: the bathroom was unlocked, and Magda
had not told him that she was going to take a bath. He
could therefore pretend ignorance and simply go into the
bathroom. His heart again started pounding; he imagined stopping in the doorway, an expression of surprise
on his face, and saying: *I'm just getting my hairbrush;*
walking past the naked Magda, who is speechless; shame
reflected on her beautiful face, as it is at lunch when she
suddenly begins sobbing; and Jaromil moves along the

bathtub to the washstand, picks up the hairbrush, and then stops at the bathtub to lean over Magda, over the naked body he sees through the greenish filter of water, and again he looks at the face that is ashamed and caresses the shame-filled face. . . . But when his imagination brought him to this point, it clouded over so that he could neither see nor imagine anything more.

To make his entrance look entirely natural, he went quietly back upstairs to his room and then came down again, his every step now heavy and loud; he realized that he was trembling, and he feared that he would lack the strength calmly and naturally to say: *I'm just getting my hairbrush*; he continued nevertheless, and when he had nearly reached the bathroom door and his heart was pounding so hard he could barely breathe, he heard: "Jaromil, I'm taking a bath! Don't come in!" He answered: "Of course not, I'm just going to the kitchen!" And he crossed the corridor in the opposite direction, entering the kitchen and opening and then closing the door as if he were merely there to get something, and went back upstairs.

Once in his room he realized that Magda's words, disconcerting as they were, should not at all have caused him to give in so hastily, that he need only have said: *It's all right, Magda, I'm just getting my hairbrush*, and walked in, because Magda would surely not complain about him; Magda liked him, he was always nice to her. And again he imagined the scene: he is in the bathroom, and Magda is stretched out in the bathtub, completely naked, and she says: *Don't come near me, get out of*

here, but she can't do anything, she can't defend herself, she is as helpless as she is in confronting her
fiancé's death, for she is lying imprisoned in the bathtub
and he is leaning over her face, over her big eyes. . . .

But the opportunity had been irrevocably lost, and
Jaromil heard only the feeble sound of water draining
from the bathtub into distant sewers; the irretrievabil-
ity of this marvelous opportunity broke his heart, for he
knew that the chance to spend an evening alone in the
house with Magda would not come again soon, and that
even if it were to occur, the key would long since have
been replaced and Magda would have double-locked
herself in. He lay on his bed in despair. But what made
him feel worse than the loss of the opportunity was the
despair he felt at the thought of his timidity, his weakness, his stupidly pounding heart, which had deprived
him of his presence of mind and spoiled everything. He
felt a violent *distaste* for himself.

But what to do about such distaste? Distaste is completely different from sadness; it is even its polar opposite; when someone was nasty to Jaromil he often
locked himself in his room and cried; but those were
happy, almost sensually pleasurable tears, almost tears
of love with which Jaromil pitied and consoled Jaromil,
casting his eyes down into his soul; whereas this sudden
distaste that revealed to Jaromil his own ridiculousness
pushed him away from his soul! This distaste was as
direct and terse as an insult; as a slap in the face; the
only escape was to flee.

But when our own pettiness is suddenly revealed to

us, where do we flee to escape it? From debasement the only escape is upward! So he sat down at his desk and opened the little book (that precious book the painter told him he never lent to anyone else) and tried hard to concentrate on the poems he liked best. Once again "the sea that bathes your eye" was there, and once again he saw Magda before him, the snowball in the tranquillity of her body was also there, and the sound of water entered the poem as the murmur of the river entered the room through the closed window. Jaromil was overcome by a languorous desire and closed the book. He picked up a piece of paper and a pencil and began to write—in the manner of Éluard, Nezval, Biebl, and Desnos—short lines, one under the other, without rhythm or rhyme. It was a variation on what he had read, but the variation contained what he had just experienced: there was the "sadness" that "begins to melt and turns into water," there was the "green water" whose surface "rises and rises until it reaches my eyes," there was the body, "the sad body," the body in the water "that I pursue, I pursue through endless water."

He read these lines aloud several times in a melodious, pathetic voice, and he was enthusiastic. At the core of the poem was Magda in the bathtub and he with his face pressed against the door; he thus didn't find himself *outside the limits* of his experience; he was high *above* it. His distaste for himself remained *down below*; down below he had felt his palms become sweaty with fear and his breath speed up; but here, *up high* in the poem, he was above his paltryness; the keyhole episode

74

and his cowardice were merely a trampoline above which he was now soaring; he was no longer subordinate to his experience, his experience was subordinate to what he had written.

The next day he used his grandfather's typewriter to copy the poem on special paper, and the poem seemed even more beautiful to him than when he had recited it aloud, for the poem had ceased to be a simple succession of words and had become a *thing*; its autonomy was even more incontestable; ordinary words exist only to perish as soon as they are uttered, their only purpose is to serve the moment of communication; subordinate to things, they are merely their designations; whereas here words themselves had become things and were in no way subordinate; they were no longer destined for immediate communication and prompt disappearance, but for durability.

What Jaromil had experienced the day before was expressed in the poem, but at the same time the experience slowly died there, as a seed dies in the fruit. "I am underwater, and my heartbeats make circles on the surface"; this line represented the adolescent trembling in front of the bathroom door, but at the same time his features, in this line, slowly became blurred; this line surpassed and transcended him. "Ah, my aquatic love," another line said, and Jaromil knew that the aquatic love was Magda, but he also knew that no one could recognize her behind these words, that she was lost, invisible, buried there; the poem he had written was absolutely autonomous, independent, and incomprehensible as reality itself, which is no one's ally and content simply to *be*; the poem's autonomy provided Jaromil a splendid refuge, the ideal possibility of a *second life*; he found that so beautiful that the next day he tried to write more poems, and little by little he gave himself over to this activity.

11

Even now that she was up and about the house like a convalescent, she was not cheerful. She had rejected the painter's love, but without regaining her husband's love in exchange. Jaromil's father was so rarely at home! They were used to his coming home late at night, they even got used to his often announcing absences of several days, for he was often away on business, but this time he had said nothing at all, he didn't return to the house in the evening, and Mama had no news of him.

Jaromil saw his father so rarely that he didn't even notice his absence as he thought in his room about his poems: for a poem to be a poem it must be read by someone other than the author; only then can it be proved that the poem is something more than simply a private diary in code and that it is capable of living its own life, independent of whoever has written it. His first thought was to show his poems to the painter, but they were too important for him to risk submitting them to such a severe judge. He needed someone who would be as enthusiastic about the poems as he was, and he soon realized who this first reader, this predestined reader of his poetry was; he saw this reader moving around the house with sad eyes and a sorrowful voice as if she were moving toward a meeting with his lines; gripped by great emotion, he therefore gave Mama several carefully typed poems and ran for refuge to his room, where he waited for her to read them and to call him.

She read them and she cried. Maybe she didn't know why she was crying, but it's not difficult to guess; flowing from her eyes were four kinds of tears: first of all, she was struck by the resemblance between Jaromil's poems and the poems the painter had lent her, and the tears poured forth, tears for a lost love;

then she felt a vague sadness emanating from her son's lines, recalling that her husband had been absent from the house for two days without having said a word, she shed tears of offended humiliation;

but soon there were tears of consolation flowing from her eyes, for her son, rushing to her with so much confidence and emotion to show her his poems, had spread a balm on all her wounds;

and finally, after reading the poems several times, she shed tears of admiration, because Jaromil's lines seemed unintelligible to her, and she therefore told herself that his poems contained much that she couldn't understand and that, as a consequence, she was the mother of a child prodigy.

Then she called him in, but when he stood before her she felt as if she were standing before the painter when he would question her about the books he had lent her; she didn't know what to say about the poems; she saw his lowered head eagerly waiting, and she could only hug and kiss him. Jaromil was nervous and hence glad to hide his head on Mama's shoulder, and Mama, feeling the fragility of his child's body in her arms, drove the painter's oppressive specter far away from her, regained her courage, and began to speak. But she was unable to rid her voice of its quaver and her eyes of their moisture, and for Jaromil these were more important than the words she was uttering; this tremor and this teariness were a sacred guarantee of his poems' power; of their real, physical power.

It was nightfall, Papa was not coming home, and Mama told herself that Jaromil's face had a delicate beauty neither her husband nor the painter could match; and this unseemly thought was so persistent that she couldn't free herself from it; she started to tell him that when she was pregnant she would look imploringly at the statuette of Apollo. "And you see, you really are as beautiful as that Apollo, you look just like him. They say that something of what a woman thinks about during her pregnancy always stays with the child, and it's not only a superstition. It's from him that you have your lyre."

Then she told him that literature had always been her greatest love, that she had gone to the university to study literature and it was only marriage (she didn't say pregnancy) that had prevented her from devoting herself entirely to that vocation; and now that she had found out that Jaromil was a poet (yes, she was the first to stick this great label on him), it was obviously a surprise but at the same time something she had long expected.

They talked for a long while that evening, and thus both mother and son, these disappointed lovers, at last found consolation, each in the other.

PART TWO

Xavier

1

The noise of the recreation period about to end reached him from inside the building; the old math teacher would be entering the classroom to plague the students with numbers chalked on the blackboard; the buzz of a stray fly would fill the vast duration between the teacher's question and a student's answer. . . . But by then he would already be far away!

The war had ended the year before; it was spring, and the sun was shining; he went down the streets to the Vltava and walked along the embankment. The five-hour galaxy of classes was far away, and only a small brown schoolbag containing notebooks and a textbook still connected him to it.

He reached the Charles Bridge. The double row of statues over the water beckoned him to cross to the other bank. When he absented himself from his high school (he was absent gladly and often!), he was almost always drawn to the Charles Bridge and to cross it. He knew that today too he would cross it, and that today too he would stop at the place where, having left the river behind, the bridge passed an old yellow house on the riverbank; its fourth-floor window was almost level with the bridge's parapet and just an arm's length away; he liked to gaze at it (it was always closed) and to wonder who lived behind it.

Now, for the first time (probably because it was so unusually sunny), the window was open. A cage with a canary was hanging at one side. He stopped, watched the small, elegantly wrought white rococo wire cage, and noticed a figure in the room's half-light: he saw its back, which he recognized as a woman's, and he longed for her to turn around so that he could see her face.

The figure moved, but in the opposite direction; she disappeared into the darkness. The window was open, and he was convinced that this was an invitation, a silent, private sign meant only for him.

He couldn't resist. He climbed up on the parapet. The window was separated from the bridge by a deep gap that ended in cobblestones. The schoolbag would hamper him. He hurled it through the open window into the murky room and jumped.

2

By extending his arms Xavier could touch both sides of the high rectangular window frame he had jumped into, and he entirely filled its height. He examined the room beginning at the far end (like people who always start by concentrating on the distant) and initially saw a door, then a big-bellied wardrobe along the left wall, on the right a wooden bed with carved posts, and in the middle of the room a round table with a crocheted cover on which stood a vase of flowers; and finally he noticed his schoolbag lying on the fringed edge of a cheap rug.

Most likely at the moment he noticed it and was about to hop down to pick it up, the door at the dark far end of the room opened, and the woman appeared. She saw him at once; the room was actually so dim that the window rectangle shone as if it were night inside and day outside; from the woman's viewpoint, the man standing in the window frame seemed like a black silhouette against a background of golden light; it was a man between day and night.

While the woman dazzled by the light was unable to make out the man's features, Xavier was a bit luckier; his eyes had already become accustomed to the dimness and he could at least see the softness of the woman's features and the melancholy of her face, the light of whose pallor would radiate to a distance even in deepest darkness; she stayed at the door, scrutinizing him;

she was neither spontaneous enough to express her fear aloud nor quick-witted enough to address him.

Only after long moments of gazing at each other's indistinct face did Xavier speak: "My schoolbag is here."

"Your schoolbag?" she asked, and as if the sound of Xavier's words had rid her of her initial amazement, she closed the door behind her.

Xavier squatted on the windowsill and pointed at the schoolbag lying on the floor below him: "I have important things in it. My math notebook, my science textbook, and also the notebook with my Czech homework. It's the one with my newest composition, 'The Coming of Spring.' It was a lot of work, and I'd hate to have to rack my brains with it again."

The woman took a few steps into the room, so that Xavier now was able to see her in better light. His first impression had been correct: softness and melancholy. He saw two big eyes floating in the indistinct face, and still another word occurred to him: "fright"; not a fright caused by his unexpected arrival, but an old fright that had remained with the woman in the form of the two big motionless eyes, in the form of her pallor, in the form of gestures that seemed to be asking forgiveness.

Yes, the woman was really asking forgiveness! "I'm sorry," she said, "but I don't understand how your schoolbag got here. I was just cleaning here a while ago, and I didn't see anything that doesn't belong here."

"All the same," said Xavier, still squatting on the windowsill and pointing at the rug, "I'm really glad it's here."

"I'm very pleased too that you found it," said the woman with a smile.

They were now face to face with nothing between them but the table with the crocheted cover and the vase filled with paper flowers.

"Yes, it would have been annoying to lose it," said Xavier. "My Czech teacher hates me, and she might flunk me if I lost my notebook."

Compassion appeared in the woman's face; her eyes suddenly became so big that Xavier could no longer make out anything else, as if the rest of her face and her body were merely their accompaniments, their containers; he didn't even know what the various features of the woman's face and the proportions of her body were like, all that remaining on the periphery of his vision; his impression of her figure was really only the impression made by her enormous eyes, whose brown light inundated all the rest of her body.

It was therefore toward her eyes that Xavier now moved, going around the table. "I'm an old flunker," he said, grasping the woman by the shoulder (that shoulder was as soft as a breast!). "Believe me, there's nothing sadder than to find yourself back again in the same class a year later, to sit down again at the same desk. . . ."

Then he saw the brown eyes raised toward him, and a wave of happiness engulfed him; Xavier knew that he could now slide his hand lower and touch her breast and belly and anything else he wanted to because the fright that supremely dominated this woman had dropped her, docile, into his arms. But he did nothing; he held his hand on her shoulder, that beautiful rounded height, and he found this beautiful enough, exhilarating enough; he wanted nothing more.

For a few moments they stood motionless, then the woman seemed to be alerted by something: "You have to leave. My husband's back!"

Nothing could have been simpler than for Xavier to pick up the schoolbag and jump onto the windowsill and from there over to the bridge, but he did not do it. The delightful feeling took hold of him that the woman was in danger and that he had to stay with her. "I can't leave you alone here!"

"My husband! Go away!" the woman pleaded with anguish.

"No, I'm going to stay with you! I'm not a coward!" said Xavier, while footsteps were already resounding clearly from the stairway.

The woman tried to push Xavier toward the window, but he knew that he had no right to abandon this woman when she was in danger. A door opening at the other end of the apartment could already be heard, and at the last moment, Xavier flung himself down and slid under the bed.

3

The space between the floor and his ceiling consisted of five boards supporting a torn mattress and was hardly bigger than a coffin; but, unlike a coffin, the space was fragrant (the good smell of the mattress straw), very resonant (the floor clearly transmitted every footstep), and full of visions (just above him he saw the face of the woman he knew he must never abandon, a face projected against the dark fabric of the mattress, a face pierced by three wisps of straw protruding through the ticking).

The footsteps he heard were heavy, and when he turned his head he saw a pair of boots tramping into the room. Then he heard a female voice, and he couldn't help experiencing a vague yet heartbreaking feeling of regret: the voice was as melancholy, frightened, and entrancing as it had been a few moments before when she was speaking to Xavier. But Xavier was reasonable and controlled his sudden impulse of jealousy; he understood that the woman was in danger and that she was defending herself with what she had: her face and her sadness.

Then he heard a male voice, and he thought that this voice was like the boots he saw moving across the floor; then he heard the woman saying "No, no, no," and then footsteps staggering toward his hiding place and then the low ceiling under which he was lying dropped still lower, nearly touching his face.

Again he heard the woman saying, "No, no, not now, please, not now," and he saw the vision of her face on the coarse ticking a centimeter from his eyes, and he thought the face was confiding its humiliation to him.

He wanted to stand up in his coffin, he wanted to save this woman, but he knew that he had no right to do it. The woman's face was so close to his, it bent over him, it pleaded with him, and it bristled with three wisps of straw like three arrows piercing it. The ceiling above Xavier started to sway rhythmically, and the wisps of straw, the three arrows piercing the woman's face, brushed rhythmically against Xavier's nose and tickled it so that he unexpectedly sneezed.

The movement stopped short. The bed became motionless, not even breathing could be heard, and Xavier too was as if paralyzed. Then, after a moment, he heard: "What was that?" "I didn't hear anything, darling," the woman's voice answered. Then there was another moment of silence and the male voice asked: "Whose bag is that?" Then heavy steps resounded through the room and the boots could be seen moving across the floor.

I'll be damned, that guy was in bed with his boots on! thought Xavier indignantly; he realized that he had to act immediately. Using his elbows, he slid out from under the bed far enough to see what was going on in the room.

"Who've you got here? Where did you hide him?" shouted the male voice, and Xavier saw that above the black boots was a pair of dark blue riding breeches and the dark blue jacket of a police uniform. The man inspected the room with a probing look and then threw himself at the big-bellied wardrobe, whose depth fostered the suspicion that a lover was hiding inside.

In a moment Xavier bounded out from under the bed, silent as a cat and agile as a panther. The man in uniform had opened the wardrobe, filled with clothes, and was starting to grope around inside. But Xavier was already there behind him, and when the man again plunged his hands into the darkness of clothing to search for the hidden lover, Xavier grabbed him by the collar and violently threw him into the wardrobe. He closed the door, locked it, put the key in his pocket, and turned to the woman.

4

He stood before the big brown eyes, and behind him he heard the pounding from inside the wardrobe, the racket and the shouts so muffled by the clothing there that the words were unintelligible.

He sat down near the big eyes, gripped a shoulder, and only then, with the touch of bare skin under his palm, did he realize that the woman was wearing only a flimsy slip, under which her bare, soft, supple breasts swelled.

The drumming from the wardrobe didn't stop, and Xavier held the woman's shoulders with both hands, trying hard to discern the clarity of her contours, which had disappeared in the flooding immensity of her eyes. He told her not to be afraid, he showed her the key to prove to her that the wardrobe was really locked, he reminded her that her husband's prison was made of oak and that the prisoner could neither open it nor break it open. And then he began to kiss her (his hands were still on her soft, naked shoulders, so boundlessly voluptuous that he was afraid to let his hands slip lower and touch her breasts, as if he were not strong enough to resist being overcome by vertigo), and as he put his lips to her face he thought he was going to drown in immense waters.

He heard her voice: "What are we going to do?"

He caressed her shoulders and told her not to worry, that they were all right here for now, that he was happier than he had ever been, and that the pounding from the wardrobe troubled him no more than the sound of a storm coming from a record player or the barking of a chained-up dog at the other end of the city.

To show her that he was in control of the situation, he stood up and examined the room. Then he laughed, because he saw a black nightstick lying on the table. He picked it up, went over to the wardrobe, and, in response to the pounding from inside, he rapped the wardrobe door a few times with the nightstick.

"What are we going to do?" the woman asked again, and Xavier replied: "We'll go away."

"And what about him?" the woman asked, and Xavier said: "A man can survive two or three weeks without food. When we come back next year there'll be a skeleton wearing a uniform and boots in the wardrobe," and once more he went over to the noisy wardrobe, gave it a rap with the nightstick, laughed, and looked at the woman in the hope that she would laugh with him.

But the woman didn't laugh, asking instead: "Where will we go?"

Xavier told her where they would go. She replied that this room was her home, while the place Xavier wanted to take her to had neither her linen closet nor her bird in its cage. Xavier replied that a home is not a linen closet or a bird in a cage but the presence of the person we love. And then he told her that he himself had no home, or rather, to put it another way, that his home was in his pace, in his walk, in his journeys. That his home was wherever new horizons opened. That he could only live by going from one dream to another, from one landscape to another, and that if he stayed too long in the same setting he would die, as her husband would die if he stayed in the wardrobe more than a couple of weeks.

When he had said this, they both suddenly noticed that the wardrobe had become silent. That silence was so striking that it roused them both. It was like the moment after a storm; the canary in the cage began to sing its head off, and through the window the setting sun glowed yellow. It was as beautiful as an invitation to a journey. It was as beautiful as great forgiveness. It was as beautiful as the death of a cop.

This time the woman caressed Xavier's face, and it was the first time she had touched him; it was also the first time that Xavier saw her not blurred but with firm contours. She said: "Yes. We'll go away; and we'll go wherever you wish. Wait a moment, I'll just get a few things for the journey."

She caressed him once more, smiled at him, and headed for the door. He looked at her with eyes full of sudden peace; he saw her stride, supple and flowing like the stride of water transformed into a human body.

Then he sat down on the bed feeling wonderful. The wardrobe was silent, as if the man inside had fallen asleep or hanged himself. The silence was filled with the space that entered the room through the window with the murmur of the Vltava and the distant shout of the city, a shout so distant that it resembled the voices of a forest.

Xavier once again felt that he was filled with journeys. And there is nothing more beautiful than the moment before a journey, the moment when tomorrow's horizon comes to visit us and makes us its promises. Xavier was lying on the rumpled bedspread and everything seemed to merge into a wonderful unity: the soft bed resembled a woman, the woman seemed just like water, the water he pictured outside below the window resembled an aquatic bed.

Then he again saw the door open, and the woman entered. She was wearing a blue dress. Blue like water, blue like the horizons he was going to rush toward, blue like the sleep he was slowly but irresistibly sinking into.

Yes. Xavier fell asleep.

5

Xavier doesn't sleep in order to gather strength for being awake. No, that monotonous pendulum movement, wakefulness-sleep, accomplished 365 times a year, is unknown to him.

For him sleep is not the opposite of life; for him, sleep is life, and life is a dream. He goes from dream to dream as if he were going from one life to another.

It is night, it is a dark night, but here are luminous disks coming down from above. They are lights given off by lanterns; in these circles carved from the darkness snowflakes falling thick and fast are to be seen.

He rushed through the door of a low building, quickly crossed the waiting room, and went onto the platform, where a train, its windows lit, was about to depart; an old man, a lantern in his hand, went by closing the doors of the cars. Xavier jumped nimbly aboard the train, the old man raised his lantern high, the slow call of a signal bugle answered from the other end of the platform, and the train began to move.

6

As soon as he entered the front of the car, he stopped to catch his breath. Once more he had arrived only at the last moment, and arriving at the last moment was a pride of his: everyone else had arrived at the pre-arranged time, living their whole lives without surprise, as if they were copying texts assigned by their teacher. He imagined them in the train compartments, in their prearranged seats, conducting prearranged conversations about the mountain chalet where they were going to spend a week, about the daily schedule they had learned at school so that they would be able to live blindfolded, by heart, without the slightest error.

Xavier, however, had arrived unprepared, at the last moment, led by a sudden impulse and by an unexpected decision. Now, in the railroad car, he was wondering what could have prompted him to join in a school excursion with boring schoolmates and bald teachers whose mustaches crawled with lice.

He went through the car: boys were standing in the corridor breathing on the frosty windowpanes and then gluing their eyes to the circular peepholes; others were stretched out lazily on the compartment seats, their crossed skis in the luggage racks overhead; some were playing cards, and in another compartment they were singing an endless student song made up of a primitive melody and a few words tirelessly repeated hundreds and thousands of times: "The old yellow canary is now quite dead, the old yellow canary is now quite dead, the old yellow canary is now quite dead. . . ."

He stopped at the door to that compartment and looked inside: in it were three older boys and, next to them, a blond girl from his class, who blushed when she saw him but said nothing, as if she were afraid to be caught, and with her mouth wide open and her eyes fixed on Xavier, she continued to sing: "The old yellow canary is now quite dead, the old yellow canary is now quite dead, the old yellow canary is . . . "

Xavier withdrew from the blond girl and passed another compartment, from which other student songs and the racket of clowning around resounded, and then he saw a man in a conductor's uniform moving toward him, stopping at each compartment door, and asking for tickets; the uniform didn't fool him, under the peak of the cap he recognized the old Latin teacher, and he immediately realized that he must avoid him, first of all because he had no ticket and then because it had been a long time (he couldn't remember how long) since he had gone to Latin class.

He took advantage of a moment when the Latin teacher had his head in a compartment to slip behind him to the front of the car, with its doors leading to the washroom and to the toilet. He opened the washroom door, surprising in a gentle embrace the Czech teacher, an austere woman in her fifties, and one of his class-mates, who sat in the first row and whom Xavier haughtily scorned during his infrequent appearances in class. When they caught sight of him, the surprised lovers quickly moved apart and bent over the washstand, feverishly rubbing their hands under the trickle of water coming out of the faucet.

Xavier didn't want to disturb them, and he went back out to the front of the car; there he found himself face to face with the blond classmate, who fixed her big blue eyes on him; her lips were no longer moving, no longer singing the song about the canary, which Xavier had thought would never end. Ah, what naïveté, he reflected, to believe in the existence of a song that never ends! As if everything here in this world, from the very beginning, has been anything other than betrayal!

Fortified by this thought, he took a look at the blond girl's eyes and knew that he must not take part in the rigged game in which the ephemeral passes for the eternal and the small for the big, that he must not take part in the rigged game called love. So he turned on his heels and went back into the little washroom in which the stocky Czech teacher was again planted in front of Xavier's schoolmate, her hands on his hips.

"Oh, no, please don't start washing your hands again," Xavier said to them. "It's my turn to wash my hands," and then he went discreetly past them, turned on the faucet, and bent over the washstand, seeking thus some relative solitude for himself and for the embarrassed lovers standing behind him. Then he heard the Czech teacher's urgent whisper: "Let's go next door," and the click of the door and the steps of two pairs of feet heading for the adjoining toilet. When he was alone, he leaned with satisfaction against the wall, abandoning himself to sweet reflections on the pettiness of love, to sweet reflections behind which gleamed two big imploring blue eyes.

7

Then the train stopped, a bugle call rang out, and there was a youthful din, banging and stamping; Xavier left his shelter and joined his schoolmates in their rush to the platform. And then the mountains, an enormous moon, and sparkling snow could be seen; they were walking in a night that was as clear as day. It was a long procession, in which the pairs of skis pointed upward like devotional accessories instead of crosses; like the symbol of a pair of fingers taking an oath.

It was a long procession, and Xavier walked along with his hands in his pockets because he was the only one without skis, the symbol of the oath; he walked and he listened to the remarks of his already tiring schoolmates; then he turned around and saw the blond girl, who was small and slender, stumbling in the rear and sinking into the snow under the weight of her skis, and when he turned around again a moment later he saw the old math teacher taking the skis from the girl and putting them on her shoulder along with her own and then taking the girl's arm in her free hand and helping her to walk. It was a sad scene, needy old age pitying needy youth; he looked at the scene and felt good.

After a while the sound of dance music reached them from afar, becoming gradually louder as they reached the restaurant surrounded by the wooden chalets in which the students would be staying. But Xavier had no room reservation, no skis to put away, no clothes to change into. So he went right into the dining room, where there was a dance floor, a band, and guests sitting at tables. He immediately noticed a woman in a thick, dark red sweater and ski pants; there were several men at her table with beer steins, but Xavier realized that the woman was elegant and proud, and that she was bored with them. He went over to her and asked her to dance.

They were the only dancers on the floor, and Xavier saw that the woman's neck was magnificently withered, that the skin around her eyes was magnificently wrinkled, and that two magnificently deep wrinkles made furrows at her mouth; he was happy to have so many years of life in his arms, happy that a high school student could have in his arms a life that was almost completed. He was proud to be dancing with her, and he thought that the blond girl could come in any minute and see him high above her, as if the age of his partner were a towering mountain and the youth of the adolescent girl stood at the foot of this mountain like a lowly blade of grass.

And so it was: the dining room began to fill with boys and girls, who had changed their ski pants for skirts, and they were sitting down at the free tables so that a large audience now surrounded Xavier as he danced with the woman in dark red; he noticed the blond girl, and he was satisfied; she was dressed with much greater care than the others; she was wearing a pretty dress totally inappropriate to the grubby room, a thin white dress in which she looked even more frail and vulnerable. Xavier knew that she had put it on for his sake, and he firmly decided that he must not lose her, that he must live this evening with her and for her.

8

He told the woman in the dark red sweater that he didn't want to dance anymore; that he was disgusted by those oafs staring at them from behind their beer steins. The woman agreed with a laugh; and even though the band was still playing and they were alone on the dance floor, they stopped dancing (everyone could see this) and went off hand in hand, passing along the tables and out onto the snow-covered plain.

They felt the icy air, and Xavier thought that the frail, sickly girl in the white dress would soon come out to join them in the cold. He seized the woman in dark red by the arm and led her across the sparkling plain, and he thought of himself as the legendary Pied Piper and of the woman beside him as the fife he was playing.

In a moment the door of the restaurant opened, and the blond girl emerged. She was even more frail than she had been before, her white dress merging with the snow so that it was like snow moving through snow. Xavier pressed the woman in the dark red sweater—who was warmly clothed and magnificently old—to himself, he kissed her, put his hands under the sweater, and out of the corner of his eye watched the snowlike girl gazing at them in torment.

Then he tipped the old woman over onto the snow, and he sprawled on top of her and knew that time was passing and that it was getting cold, that the girl's dress was thin, and that the frost was touching her calves and knees and reaching up to her thighs and caressing her higher and higher to touch her groin and belly. Then they got up, and the old woman led him to one of the chalets, where she had a room.

The room was on the first floor and the window, a meter above the snow-covered plain, allowed Xavier to see the blond girl only a few steps away and watching him through it; not wanting to leave this girl whose image filled him entirely, he turned on the light (the old woman greeted his need for light with a lascivious laugh), took the woman by the hand, and went with her to the window, where he embraced her, lifted the plush sweater (a warm sweater for a senile body), and thought about the girl, who must have been so chilled that she could no longer feel her own body, that she was no more than a soul, a sad, sorrowful soul barely afloat in a body so frozen that it felt nothing, had already lost the sense of touch, and was merely a dead envelope for the floating soul Xavier boundlessly loved, ah, yes! he boundlessly loved.

But who could bear such boundless love? Xavier felt his hands grow weak, no longer strong enough even to lift the plush sweater high enough to bare the old woman's breasts, and he felt a torpor throughout his body and sat down on the bed. It's hard to describe how good he felt, how satisfied and happy. When a man is excessively satisfied, sleep comes as a reward. Xavier smiled and fell into a deep sleep, into a beautiful sweet night in which gleamed two chilled eyes, two frozen moons. . . .

9

Xavier didn't merely live a single life that extended from birth to death like a long, filthy string; he didn't live his life, he slept it; in this life-sleep he leaped from dream to dream; he dreamed, fell asleep while dreaming, and dreamed another dream, so that his sleep was like a box into which another box is fitted, and in that one still another box, and in this one another still, and so on.

For example, at this moment he is sleeping at the same time in a house by the Charles Bridge and in a mountain chalet; these two sleeps resound like two prolonged organ tones; and now these two tones are joined by a third:

He is standing and looking around. The street is deserted, with once in a long while a shadow passing and vanishing around a corner or into a doorway. He too doesn't want to be noticed; he follows suburban side streets as the sound of gunfire is heard from the other end of the city.

At last he enters a house and descends the stairs; there are several doors in the basement; after a brief search for the right one, he knocks; three times, then once, then three times more.

10

The door opened and a young man in blue overalls invited him in. They went through several rooms filled with odds and ends, clothes on hangers, as well as rifles propped in corners, and then down a long passage (they must have gone far beyond the building's perimeter) into a small subterranean room, where twenty or so men were seated.

He sat down on an empty chair and scrutinized them; he knew some of them. Three men sat at a table near the door; one of them, wearing a peaked cap, was speaking; he was saying something about an approaching secret date when everything would be decided; according to plan, everything had to be ready by then: leaflets, newspapers, radio, post office, telegraph, weapons. Then he asked each man whether, to ensure success that day, he had executed the task assigned to him. Finally he turned to Xavier and asked him if he had brought the list.

That was an excruciating moment. In order to make sure that it would not be discovered, Xavier a while ago had copied the list on the last page of his Czech notebook. This notebook was in his schoolbag, along with his other notebooks and his textbooks. But where was the schoolbag? He didn't have it with him!

The man in the peaked cap repeated his question.

My God, where was that schoolbag? Xavier thought feverishly, and then from the back of his mind a vague and elusive memory emerged, a sweet breath of happiness; he wanted to seize this memory in flight, but there was no time because all the faces were turned toward him waiting for his answer. He had to admit that he didn't have the list.

The faces of the men he had come to as a companion among companions hardened, and the man in the peaked cap said to him icily that if the enemy were to get hold of the list, the date on which they had placed all their hopes would be ruined and be just another date: a date empty and dead.

But Xavier had no time to respond. The door discreetly opened, and a man appeared and whistled. It was the alarm signal; before the man in the peaked cap could give an order, Xavier spoke up: "Let me go first," he said, knowing that the route awaiting them now was dangerous and that the first one out would be risking his life.

Xavier knew that because he had forgotten the list he must atone for his guilt. But it was not only a feeling of guilt which drove him into danger. He detested the pettiness that made life semilife and men semimen. He wished to put his life on one of a pair of scales and death on the other. He wished each of his acts, indeed each day, each hour, each second of his life to be measured against the supreme criterion, which is death. That was why he wanted to march at the head of the column, to walk on a tightrope over an abyss, to have a halo of bullets around his head and thus to grow in everyone's eyes and become unlimited as death is unlimited . . .

The man in the peaked cap looked at him with cold, severe eyes in which there was a glimmer of understanding. "All right, get going!" he said to him.

11

He went through a metal door and found himself in a narrow courtyard. It was dark, the crackle of distant gunfire could be heard, and when he raised his eyes he saw the beams of searchlights wandering above the rooftops. Facing him was a narrow metal ladder leading to the roof of a six-story building. He began to climb up quickly. The others rushed into the courtyard behind him and hugged the walls. They were waiting for him to reach the roof and signal them that the way was clear.

Once on the rooftops, they crept along cautiously, with Xavier always in the lead; he was risking his life to protect the others. He moved alertly, he moved slowly, he moved like a feline, his eyes penetrating the darkness. At one point he stopped and gestured to show the man in the peaked cap the figures in black running around far below them, with short-barreled weapons in their hands and peering into the shadows. "Keep on leading us," the man said to Xavier.

And Xavier went on, jumping from one rooftop to another, climbing short metal ladders, hiding behind chimneys to escape the maddening searchlights ceaselessly sweeping the buildings, the rooftop edges, and the street canyons.

It was a beautiful journey of silent men turned into a swarm of birds passing through the sky to evade the enemy that was looking for them, crossing the city on wings of rooftops to escape being trapped. It was a beautiful, long journey, but a journey already so long that Xavier was beginning to feel fatigue; the fatigue that muddles the senses and fills the mind with hallucinations; he thought he heard a funeral march, the famous Chopin Funeral March played by brass bands in cemeteries.

He didn't slow down, trying with all his might to stay alert and get rid of the deadly hallucination. In vain; the music continued as if it were proclaiming his imminent end, as if at this moment of struggle it were pinning the black veil of coming death.

But why was he so strongly resisting this hallucination? Did he not wish that the grandeur of death would make his passage on the rooftops unforgettable and immense? Was not the funeral music that was coming to him like an omen the most beautiful accompaniment to his courage? Was it not sublime that his battle was also his funeral rite and that his funeral rite was a battle, that life and death were so magnificently joined?

No, what frightened Xavier was not that death had proclaimed itself but rather that he could no longer trust his own senses, could no longer (he, on whom the safety of his companions depended!) perceive the enemy's sly traps now that his ears had been clogged by the liquid melancholy of a funeral march.

But is it in fact possible that a hallucination can seem so real that one hears Chopin's march with all the faulty rhythms and the false notes of the trombone?

12

He opened his eyes and saw a room furnished with a scarred wardrobe and the bed he was lying on. He noted with satisfaction that he had been sleeping with his clothes on, so there was no need to change; he merely put on the shoes thrown off at the foot of the bed.

But where was that sad brass music coming from, its tones seeming so real?

He went over to the window. A few steps away, in a landscape from which the snow had nearly vanished, a group of men and women in black stood motionless with their backs to him. The group was desolate and sad, sad like the landscape surrounding them; all that remained of the dazzling snow was dirty bits and pieces on the wet ground.

He opened the window and leaned out. Now he understood the situation better. The people in black were gathered around an open grave with a coffin beside it. On the far side of the grave men in black were holding to their mouths brass instruments with tiny music holders clipped to them which the musicians' eyes were riveted on; they were playing Chopin's Funeral March.

The window was barely a meter above the ground. He stepped through it and went over to the group of mourners. At that moment, two sturdy workers slipped ropes under the coffin, lifted it up, and let it slowly down. An old couple among the mourners in black broke into sobs, and the others took them by the arms and tried to comfort them.

The coffin was set down at the bottom of the grave, and the people in black, one after another, went over to toss handfuls of earth on its lid. Xavier was the last to lean over the coffin and throw a lump of earth and clumps of snow into the grave.

He alone was unknown to all the others, and he alone knew everything that had happened. He alone knew how and why the blond girl had died, he alone knew that the icy hand had come to rest on her calf so as to climb up her body to her belly and between her breasts, he alone knew who had caused her death. He alone knew why she had asked to be buried here, for it was here that she had suffered most and had wished to die for having seen love betray and escape her.

He alone knew everything; the others were there as an uncomprehending audience or as uncomprehending victims. He saw them against the background of the distant mountainous landscape and it seemed to him that they were lost in immense distances as the girl was lost in immense earth; and that he himself (because he knew everything) was even more immense than the misty landscape, and that all of it—the mourners, the dead girl, the gravediggers with their shovels, and the countryside and mountains—entered him and vanished in him.

He was inhabited by the landscape, by the sadness of the mourners, and by the death of the blond girl, and he felt filled with their presence as if a tree were growing inside him; he felt himself grow, and his own real person seemed to be no more than an impersonation, a disguise, a mask of modesty; and it was under the mask of his own person that he approached the dead girl's parents (the father's face reminded him of the blond girl's features; it was red with weeping) and offered his condolences; they absently gave him their hands and he felt their fragility and insignificance in the palm of his hand.

Then he remained for a long while leaning with his back against the wall of the chalet in which he had slept for so long watching the people who had attended the funeral separate into small groups and slowly vanish into the misty distance. Suddenly, he felt a caress: yes, he felt the touch of a hand on his face. He was sure that he understood the meaning of that caress, and he accepted it gratefully; he knew that it was the hand of forgiveness; that the blond girl was letting him know that she had not stopped loving him and that love lasts beyond the grave.

13

He was falling from one dream into another.

The most beautiful moments were those when he was still in one dream while another into which he was awakening was beginning to dawn.

The hands that caressed him as he stood motionless in the mountainous landscape belonged to a woman in another dream into which he was about to fall again, but Xavier didn't know this yet, and for the moment the hands existed alone, by themselves; they were miraculous hands in an empty space; hands between two adventures, between two lives; hands unspoiled by a body or a head.

If only that caress of disembodied hands would last as long as possible!

14

Then he felt not only the caress of the hands but also the touch of soft, ample breasts pressing against his chest, and he saw the face of a dark-haired woman and heard her voice: "Wake up! My God, wake up!"

He was on a rumpled bed in a grayish room with a massive wardrobe. Xavier remembered that he was in the house at the Charles Bridge.

"I know you want to go on sleeping," said the woman, as if to excuse herself, "but I really had to wake you. I'm terribly afraid."

"What are you afraid of?"

"My God, you don't know anything," said the woman. "Listen!"

Xavier made an effort to listen attentively: he heard the sound of distant gunfire.

He jumped out of bed and ran to the window; groups of men in blue overalls with submachine guns slung across their shoulders were passing along the Charles Bridge.

It was like searching for a memory through several walls; Xavier was quite aware of the meaning of these groups of armed men guarding the bridge, but there was something he couldn't remember, something that would clarify his own link to what he was seeing. He was aware that he had a part to play in this scene and that he was not in it because of a mistake, that he was like an actor who has forgotten to make his entrance and the play, oddly crippled, goes on without him. And suddenly he remembered.

As he was remembering, he ran his eyes over the room and felt relieved: the schoolbag was still there, propped against the wall in a corner, no one had taken it. He leaped over to it and opened it. Everything was there: the math notebook, the Czech notebook, the science textbook. He took out the Czech notebook, opened it from the back, and again felt relief: the list that the man in the peaked cap had demanded of him had been carefully written out in a small but legible hand, and Xavier was thrilled by his idea of hiding this important document in a school notebook, the front of which was devoted to a composition on the theme "The Coming of Spring."

"What are you looking for in there, for goodness' sake?"

"Nothing," said Xavier.

"I need you, I need your help. You can see what's happening. They're going from house to house, arresting people and shooting them."

"Don't worry," he said, laughing. "They can't shoot anybody!"

"How can you know that?" the woman asked.

How could he know that? He knew it very well: the list of all the enemies of the people, who were to be executed on the first day of the revolution, was in his notebook; it was really true that the executions couldn't take place. Anyway the beautiful woman's anxiety mattered little to him; he heard gunfire, he saw the men guarding the bridge, and he thought that the day he had been enthusiastically preparing for alongside his companions in the struggle had finally come, and that he had been asleep; that he had been elsewhere, in another room and in another dream.

He wanted to leave, he wanted immediately to rejoin these men in overalls, to return to them the list only he had and without which the revolution was blind, not knowing whom to arrest and shoot. But then he realized that it was impossible: he didn't know the day's password, he had long been regarded as a traitor, and nobody would believe him. He was in another life, he was in another adventure, and he was unable to save from this life the other life in which he no longer was.

"What's the matter with you?" the woman insisted anxiously.

And Xavier thought that if he couldn't save that lost life, he would have to make great the life he was living at the moment. He turned to the beautiful, generously curved woman and understood that he must leave her, for it was over there that life was—outside, on the other side of the window, over there from where the rattling gunfire reached him like a nightingale's trill.

"Where are you going?" the woman shouted.

Xavier smiled and pointed at the window.

"You promised to take me with you!"

"That was a long time ago."

"Are you going to betray me?"

She fell to her knees before him and clasped his legs. He looked at her and thought about how beautiful she was and how hard it was to leave her. But the world on the other side of the window was still more beautiful. And if he was abandoning a beloved woman for it, that world was even more costly by the price of his betrayed love.

"You are beautiful," he said, "but I must betray you." He tore himself out of her embrace and moved toward the window.

PART THREE

The Poet Masturbates

1

The day Jaromil showed his poems to Mama, she waited in vain for her husband, and she also waited in vain the next day and the following days.

She received instead an official notification from the Gestapo telling her that her husband had been arrested. Toward the end of the war she received another official notification that he had died in a concentration camp.

Her marriage had been joyless, but her widowhood was grand and glorious. She found a large photograph of her husband from their early days together, and she put it into a gilded frame and hung it on the wall.

Soon the war ended with great jubilation in Prague, the Germans withdrew from Bohemia, and Mama began a life that enhanced the austere beauty of renunciation; the money she had inherited from her father having been used up, she dismissed the maid, after Alik's death she refused to buy a new dog, and she had to look for a job.

There were still other changes: her sister decided to give the apartment in the center of Prague to her newly married son, and to move with her husband and younger son into the ground floor of the family villa, while Grandmama settled into a room on the widow's floor.

Mama had been contemptuous of her brother-in-law ever since she had heard him assert that Voltaire was a physicist who had invented volts. His family was noisy and indulged in crude entertainments; the jolly life resounding throughout the rooms of the ground floor was separated by an impassable border from the melancholy terrain of the upper floor.

And yet Mama at that time stood up straighter than in the past. It was as if she carried on her head (like Dalmatian women carrying baskets of grapes) her husband's invisible urn.

2

In the bathroom small bottles of perfume and tubes of creams stand on the shelf beneath the mirror, but Mama hardly ever uses them for skin care. She often lingers over these objects, but only because they remind her of her late father, his cosmetics shop (long since the property of the detested brother-in-law), and the long years of carefree life in the villa.

Her past life with parents and husband are illuminated by the nostalgic light of a sun that has already set. This nostalgic glow breaks her heart; she realizes that, now that they are gone, it is too late to appreciate the beauty of those years, and she reproaches herself for having been an ungrateful wife. Her husband had exposed himself to great dangers and been burdened with cares, but in order to leave her tranquillity undisturbed he had never breathed a word of it to her, and to this day she is unaware of the reason for his arrest, which resistance group he had belonged to, and what role he played in it; she knows nothing at all about it, and she thinks of that as a humiliating punishment inflicted on her for having been a narrow-minded woman who merely saw in her husband's behavior a sign of indifference. The thought that she had been unfaithful to him at the very moment he was running the greatest risks brings her close to self-contempt.

Now she looks at herself in the mirror and notes with surprise that her face is still young, and even, it seems to her, needlessly young, as if time has mistakenly and unjustly forgotten her. Recently she had learned that someone saw her in the street with Jaromil and had taken them for brother and sister; she finds that comical. All the same it pleases her; since then it has been a still greater pleasure for her to go to the theater or a concert with her son.

Besides, what else was left to her?

Grandmama had lost much of her health, staying home to darn Jaromil's socks and iron her daughter's dresses. She was filled with regrets and caring concern. Around her she created a melancholically loving atmosphere, intensifying the feminine character of the milieu (a milieu of double widowhood) in which Jaromil lived.

3

The walls of Jaromil's room were no longer decorated by his childhood sayings (with regret, Mama put them away in a drawer), but by twenty small reproductions of cubist and surrealist paintings he had cut out of magazines and pasted on cardboard. On the wall with them was a telephone receiver with a severed end of wire coming out of it (a telephone repairman had been in the villa some time ago, and Jaromil had seen in the defective receiver the kind of object that, removed from its usual context, creates a magical impression and can rightly be called a *surrealist object*). But the image he most often examined was in the mirror hanging on the same wall. He studied nothing more carefully than his own face, nothing that tormented him more, and nothing (even if it was at the cost of strenuous effort) in which he invested more hope:

This face resembled Mama's, but because Jaromil was a man, the delicacy of its features was more striking: he had a good-looking, narrow nose and a small, slightly receding chin. This chin worried him a lot; he had read in a famous passage by Schopenhauer that a receding chin is a particularly repulsive feature because it is precisely his prominent chin that distinguishes man from ape. But then he came across a photograph of Rilke and saw that Rilke, too, had a receding chin, and this gave him priceless comfort. He would look at himself in the mirror for a long time, deperately struggling in the immense space between ape and Rilke.

His chin in fact was only moderately receding, and Mama rightly regarded her son's face as having the charm of a child's. But that tormented Jaromil even more than his chin: the delicacy of his features made him seem a few years younger, and because his classmates were a year older than he, the childishness of his looks was striking, obvious, and a subject daily of numerous comments Jaromil was unable to forget for even an instant.

Oh, what a burden it was to bear such a face! How heavy it was, this fine drawing of features!

(Jaromil sometimes had terrible dreams: he dreamed that he had to lift some extremely light object—a teacup, a spoon, a feather—and he couldn't do it, that the lighter the object, the weaker he became, that he *sank under its lightness;* he experienced his dreams as nightmares and would wake up bathed in sweat; it seems to me that these dreams were about his fragile face, patterned in needlepoint lace he tried in vain to lift off and throw away.)

4

Poets come from homes where women rule: the sister of Trakl and those of Yesenin and Mayakovsky, the aunts of Blok, the grandmother of Hölderlin and that of Lermontov, the nurse of Pushkin, and above all of course, the mothers, the poets' mothers, behind whom the fathers' shadows pale. Lady Wilde and Frau Rilke dressed their sons like little girls. Are you wondering why the child looked so anxiously at himself in the mirror? "It is time to become a man," Jiri Orten* wrote in his diary. During his entire life the poet searches for masculinity in the features of his face.

When he looked at himself in the mirror for a very long time, he succeeded in finding what he was looking for: a hard eye or a severe line of the mouth; but to do that it was of course essential to show a certain smile, or rather a certain grin that ferociously drew back his upper lip. He also sought a way to wear his hair that would alter his features: he tried to put his hair up above his forehead so as to give the impression of a thick, wild undergrowth; but alas, his hair, which Mama so cherished that she kept a bit of it in a locket, was the worst he could imagine: yellow as the down of a newly hatched chick and fine as dandelion fluff; it was impossible to shape; Mama often stroked his head and told him he had the hair of an angel. But Jaromil hated

---

*Czech poet who died in 1941 at the age of twenty-two.

angels and loved devils; he longed to dye his hair black, but he didn't dare do it because dyeing his hair would be even more effeminate than being blond; all he could do was let it grow very long and shaggy.

He never lost an opportunity to check and correct his appearance; he never passed a shop window without a glance at himself. But the more he watched over his appearance, the more he became aware of it and the more troubling and painful it seemed. For example:

He is coming home from high school. The street is deserted, but far off he catches sight of a young woman coming toward him. They are unavoidably nearing each other. Jaromil is thinking about his face because he has seen that the woman is beautiful. He tries to put on his well-prepared tough-guy smile, but he senses that he won't manage it. He can think only of his face, whose childish femininity makes him ridiculous in the eyes of women, he is completely incarnated in that pathetic, sweet facelet, which stiffens, petrifies, and (calamity!) blushes! So he quickens his pace to reduce the risk of the woman casting her eyes on him, for if he were to allow a pretty woman to surprise him the moment he blushes, the shame would be unbearable!

5

The hours spent in front of the mirror made him touch the depths of despair; fortunately there was another mirror that took him to the stars. That exalting mirror was his poetry; he yearned for the poems he had not yet written, and those he had already written he remembered with the delectation men get from remembering women; he was not only the poems' author but also their theoretician and historian; he wrote reflections on what he had written, and he divided his output into different periods to which he gave names, so that in the course of two or three years he came to regard his poetic works as a historical process worthy of a historian's efforts.

This gave him solace: *down below*, where he lived his everyday life, where he went to his classes, where he had lunch with Mama and Grandmama, an unarticulated emptiness stretched out before him; but *up above*, in his poems, he showed the way, installing inscribed signposts; there time was articulated and differentiated; he went from one poetic period to another, enabling him (looking out of the corner of his eye at the appalling, uneventful stagnation down below) to anticipate, with exalted ecstasy, the advent of a new era that would open his imagination to undreamed-of horizons.

And he was also firmly and quietly confident that, despite the insignificance of his face (and of his life), he had within him exceptional riches; in other words, confidence in becoming one of the *elect*.

Let's stop at this word:

Jaromil continued to see the painter, not very often of course, because Mama was unenthusiastic about these visits; he had long since stopped drawing, but one day he gathered enough courage to show the painter some of his poems and after that brought him the rest. The painter read them with ardent interest and sometimes kept them to show his friends, which thrilled Jaromil because the painter, who had once showed such skepticism about his drawings, remained for Jaromil a steadfast authority; Jaromil was convinced that there exists an objective criterion (carefully maintained in the minds of initiates) for evaluating artistic values (just as the Sèvres museum maintains a platinum standard meter), and that the painter knew what that criterion was.

But all the same there was something irritating about this: Jaromil had never been able to discern beforehand what the painter would like in his poems and what he would dislike; he would sometimes praise poems Jaromil had written in haste, and at other times he would sullenly dismiss poems Jaromil had great regard for. What did this mean? If Jaromil himself was incapable of understanding the value of what he had written, didn't he have to conclude that he was creating values mechanically, fortuitously, unknowingly, and unwittingly, and thus with no merit attached to it (just as he had once charmed the painter with a world of dog-headed people he had discovered quite by chance)?

"Surely you believe, don't you," the painter said to him one day when they had touched on this subject, "that a fantastic image you've put into your poem is the result of rational thought. Not so: it came to you out of nowhere; suddenly; unexpectedly; the author of that image is not you but rather someone inside you, someone who wrote your poem inside you. And that someone who wrote your poem is the omnipotent stream of the unconscious that flows through each of us; it's not due to your merits that this stream, to which we're all the same, has chosen to make you its violin."

The painter thought of these words as a lesson in modesty, but they instantly kindled Jaromil's pride; all right then, it wasn't he who had created the images in his poem; but it was something mysterious that had chosen precisely his writing hand; he could thus take pride in something greater than *merit*; he could take pride in *being elected*.

Besides, he had never forgotten what the lady in the little spa had said: "This child has a great future ahead of him." He believed these words as if they were prophecies. The future consisted of unknown distances in which a vague image of revolution (the painter often spoke of its inevitability) merged with a vague image of the bohemian freedom of poets; he knew that he would fill that future with his glory, and this knowledge gave him the certainty that (free and independent) lived in him alongside the uncertainties that tormented him.

6

Ah, the long misery of afternoons when Jaromil is shut up in his room and looking, one after the other, into his two mirrors!

How is it possible? He has read everywhere that youth is the most plentiful period of life! Where then does such nothingness, such dispersal of living matter come from? Where does such *emptiness* come from?

That word was as unpleasant as the word "failure." And there were other words not to be said in his presence (at least in the house, that metropolis of emptiness). For example, the word "love" or the word "girls." How he hated the three people who lived on the villa's ground floor! They often had guests who stayed late into the night, and one could hear drunken voices, among them the shrill ones of women, that tore at Jaromil's soul as he lay huddled under his blanket, unable to sleep. His cousin was only two years older than he, but those two years stood between them like Pyrenees separating one century from another; his cousin, a university student, brought pretty girls to the villa (with the amused complicity of his parents) and was vaguely contemptuous of Jaromil; his uncle was seldom there (he was absorbed in the shops he had inherited), but his aunt's voice thundered through the house; whenever she met Jaromil, she asked him her stereotypical question: "So, how's it going with the girls?" Jaromil wanted to spit in her face, because her condescendingly jovial question completely

bared his misery. Not that he didn't go out with girls, but
his dates were so rare that they were as far apart as the
stars in the universe. The word "girls" sounded as sad to
his ear as the word "yearning" and the word "failure."

Though his time was scarcely taken up by dates with
girls, it was entirely occupied with the anticipation of
dates, an anticipation that was no mere contemplation of
the future but rather preparation and study. Jaromil was
convinced that, for a date to succeed, it was essential not
to fall into embarrassed silence, essential to know how to
speak. A date with a girl was first of all the art of conversation. He therefore kept a special notebook in which he
wrote down stories worth telling; not jokes, because they
don't reveal anything personal about the teller. He wrote
down his own adventures; but since he had not had any,
he made them up; in this he showed good taste; the
adventures he made up (or remembered reading or hearing about) and of which he was the hero didn't show him
in a heroic light but only conveyed him delicately, almost
imperceptibly, from the world of stagnation and emptiness into the world of activity and adventure.

He also wrote down quotations from various poems
(incidentally, not poems he himself admired), in which
the poets dealt with feminine beauty and that could pass
for spontaneous repartee. For example, he wrote down in
his notebook the line: "On your face, components of a tricolor: your eyes, your mouth, your hair . . ." Of course he
had to free the line of its rhythmic devices and say it to the
girl as if it were a sudden and natural idea, a compliment
both spontaneous and witty: "Your face has a tricolor on

it! Eyes, mouth, hair. It's the only flag I'm going to honor!"

On every date Jaromil thinks about his prepared lines, worrying that his voice will seem unnatural, that his words will sound as if they were learned by heart and that his expression will be that of a talentless amateur. So he doesn't dare use them, but because they preoccupy him, he has nothing else to say. The date passes in painful silence. Jaromil senses the irony in the girl's look, and when they part he leaves with a feeling of failure.

When he gets home he angrily sits down at his desk and writes rapidly and with hatred: "Looks run out of your eyes like urine / I fire my rifle at those scared sparrows, your idiot thoughts / Between your legs, a pond jumping with armies of toads . . . "

He writes on and on, and then reads his lines several times over, greatly satisfied with his fantasy, which seems to him marvelously diabolical.

I'm a poet, I'm a great poet, he tells himself, and then writes it down in his diary. "I am a great poet, I have a diabolical imagination, I feel what others do not feel . . . "

Meanwhile, Mama comes home and goes into her room . . .

Jaromil goes over to the mirror and looks for a long time at his childish, hated face. He looks at it so long that at last he sees the glow of an exceptional being, of one of the elect.

And in the next room, Mama stands on tiptoe to take her husband's gilt-framed picture off the wall.

7

She had just learned that, starting well before the war, her husband had been having an affair with a young Jewish woman; when the Germans occupied Bohemia and Jews had to wear the degrading yellow star on their coats, he didn't leave her, continued to see her, and did his best to help her.

Then she was deported to the Theresienstadt ghetto, and he did something insane: with the help of some Czech policemen, he succeeded in getting into the closely guarded town and seeing his mistress for a few minutes. Tempted by his success, he again went to Theresienstadt and this time was caught, and neither he nor his mistress ever returned.

The invisible urn Mama carried on her head has been put behind the wardrobe, along with her husband's picture. She no longer needs to walk with her head upright, she no longer has anything left to make her stand up straight, because all the moral grandeur belongs to others:

She can still hear the voice of the old Jewish woman, a relative of her husband's mistress, who told her everything: "He was the bravest man I ever knew." And: "I'm all alone in the world. My whole family died in the concentration camp."

The Jewish woman sat facing her in all the glory of her pain, while the pain Mama experienced at that moment had no glory to it; she felt the pain bowing her miserably down.

8

O you haystacks vaguely smoking
Smoking perhaps the tobacco of her heart

he wrote, imagining a girl's body buried in a field.

Death often appeared in his poems. But Mama was wrong (she was still the first reader of all his verse) when she tried to ascribe this to the precocious maturity of her son, who had been captivated by the tragedy of life.

Death in Jaromil's poems had little in common with real death. Death becomes real when it begins to penetrate a person through the fissures of aging. For Jaromil it was infinitely far away; it was abstract; for him it was not a reality but a dream.

But what was he looking for in that dream?

He was looking for immensity. His life was hopelessly small, everything surrounding him was nondescript and gray. And death is absolute; it is indivisible and indissoluble.

The presence of a girl was pathetic (a few caresses and a lot of meaningless words), but her absolute absence was infinitely grand; when he imagined a girl buried in a field, he suddenly discovered the nobility of pain and the grandeur of love.

But it was not only the absolute but also bliss he was looking for in his dreams of death.

He dreamed of a body slowly dissolving in the earth,

seeing this as a sublime act of love in which the body at length and voluptuously is transformed into earth.

The world was constantly wounding him; he blushed when he faced women, he was ashamed, and he saw ridicule everywhere. In his dreams of death he found silence; one could live there slowly, mutely, and happily. Yes, death, as Jaromil imagined it, was a *lived* death: it was oddly like that period when a person has no need to enter the world because he is a world unto himself, when he has above him, like a protective vault, the internal arch of a mother's belly.

In this kind of death, which resembles endless bliss, he longed to be united with a beloved woman. In one of his poems the lovers embrace until they merge into each other, becoming a single paralyzed being that slowly changes into a mineral and lives forever, withstanding the ravages of time.

Or else he imagined two lovers locked together for so long that they are overgrown by moss and turned into moss themselves; then someone accidentally steps on them, and (it was in an era when moss bloomed) like pollen they rise up into space, indescribably happy, as only a flight can be happy.

9

Do you think that the past, because it has already occurred, is finished and unchangeable? Oh, no, it is clothed in mutable taffeta, and whenever we look back at it we see it in another color. Not long ago Mama was reproaching herself for having betrayed her husband with the painter, and now she is tearing her hair because she betrayed her only love for her husband's sake.

What a coward she had been! Her engineer had been experiencing a great romantic love, while she was the servant who was left only the crusts of everyday life. And she had been so fearful and repentant that the tide of her adventure with the painter had rolled over her before she had the time to experience it. Now she could see this clearly: she had rejected the only great opportunity life had offered her heart.

She began to think about the painter with mad persistence. Remarkably her memories didn't bring back the setting of the Prague studio where she had experienced interludes of sensual love with him, but rather the background of a pastel landscape with the river, boat, and Renaissance colonnade of a small spa. She found her heart's paradise in the tranquil vacation weeks when love had not yet been born but only conceived. She longed to see the painter, so as to ask him to go back there with her and begin again to live their love story, to live it in that pastel setting, freely, lightheartedly, with no restraint.

One day she climbed the stairs to his top-floor apartment. But she didn't ring the bell because she heard a talkative female voice coming from inside.

She took to pacing back and forth in front of the building until she finally saw him; as usual, he was wearing his leather coat, and he was arm in arm with a young woman he was accompanying to the streetcar stop. On his way back she came toward him. He recognized her and greeted her with surprise. She pretended that she, too, was surprised by the unexpected encounter. He asked her to come upstairs. Her heart started to pound; she knew that at the first furtive touch she would melt in his arms.

He offered her some wine and showed her his new paintings; he smiled at her in the friendly way we smile at the past; he never touched her, and he accompanied her to the streetcar stop.

10

One day, when the students leaving for the recreation break were crowded at the blackboard, he thought the moment had finally come; he made his way unnoticed to a girl sitting alone at her desk; he had liked her for a long time, and they often exchanged long looks; he sat down beside her. When the students, always mischievous, saw them together, they seized the opportunity for a practical joke; giggling, they left the room and locked the door behind them.

While he was surrounded by his classmates, Jaromil had felt inconspicuous and at ease, but now that he was alone in the classroom with the girl it seemed as though he was on a brightly lit stage. He tried to conceal his awkwardness with witty remarks (he had finally learned to talk without recourse to prepared phrases). He said that what their classmates had done was an example of the worst possible action; it was disadvantageous for the perpetrators (out in the corridor their curiosity remained unsatisfied) and advantageous for the supposed victims (they were alone together just as they had wished). The girl agreed and said that they should make the most of the opportunity. A kiss hung in the air. All he had to do was lean closer to the girl. And yet the route to her lips seemed to him to be immensely long and difficult; he talked—talked and didn't kiss.

The bell rang, which meant that the teacher was about to arrive at any moment and compel the students gathered at the door to open it. That excited them. Jaromil said that the best way to revenge themselves on their classmates would be to make them envy their kisses. He brushed the girl's lips (where did he find such audacity?) and said that a kiss by lips so heavily made up would surely leave a very noticeable mark on his face. The girl agreed again, saying it was too bad that they hadn't kissed, and just then the teacher's angry voice could be heard behind the door.

Jaromil said it was too bad that neither the teacher nor the students would see the mark of a kiss on his face, and again he wanted to lean closer to the girl, and again her lips seemed as inaccessible as the peak of Mount Everest.

"Yes, we have to make them envy us," said the girl, and she took a lipstick and a handkerchief out of her bag, smeared the lipstick on the handkerchief, and daubed Jaromil's face with it.

The door opened and the furious teacher rushed into the classroom, followed by the students. Jaromil and the girl stood up, as students must when the teacher enters; they stood alone amid rows of empty desks, facing a crowd of spectators whose eyes were fixed on Jaromil's face, with its glorious red stains. Happy and proud, he presented himself to everyone's gaze.

11

A colleague in her office was pursuing her. He was married and trying to persuade her to invite him to her place.

She sought to find out how Jaromil would respond to her erotic freedom. She began cautiously and indirectly by speaking about war widows and the difficulties they experienced in starting a new life.

"What do you mean, a new life?" he said irritably. "Do you mean life with another man?"

"That's part of it, certainly. Life goes on, Jaromil, life has its requirements . . . "

A woman's faithfulness to a fallen hero was one of Jaromil's sacred myths; it assured him that the absolute of love was not only an invention of poets but also a reality that made life worth living.

"How can a woman who has had a great love wallow in bed with someone else?" he shouted with indignation at faithless widows. "How can they even touch someone else when they remember a husband who was tortured and murdered? How can they torture the victim yet again, put him to death a second time?"

The past is clothed in mutable taffeta. Mama rejected her likable colleague and her past took on still another light:

It isn't true that she betrayed the painter for her husband's sake. She left him for Jaromil's sake, in order to safeguard the tranquillity of her home! If her nakedness made her anxious to this day, it was because of Jaromil, who had made her belly ugly. And it was also because of him that she had lost her husband's love, by stubbornly insisting on having the child!

From the very beginning, he had taken everything away from her.

12

One day (by then he had already had many real kisses) he was walking along the deserted paths of Stromovka Park with a girl he had met at dancing class. After a while their conversation flagged, and their footsteps resounded in the silence, their footsteps in tandem suddenly making them realize what they had not dared give a name to: they were walking together, and if they were walking together, they probably loved each other; the footsteps resounding in the silence gave them away, and their pace became slower and slower, until the girl put her head on Jaromil's shoulder.

This was extremely beautiful, but before he was able to savor that beauty, Jaromil felt that he was becoming aroused, and in a very visible manner. He took fright. The only thing he wished was that the visible proof of his arousal would vanish as quickly as possible, but the more he thought about it the less his wish was granted. He was frightened by the thought that the girl would lower her eyes and see the compromising gesture of his body. He tried his best to entice her to look upward by talking about the clouds and the birds in the trees.

That walk was filled with bliss (it was the first time a woman had put her head on his shoulder, a gesture he saw as the sign of lifelong devotion), but at the same time also filled with shame. He was afraid that his body would repeat the inopportune indiscretion. After much thought he took a long, wide ribbon out of Mama's linen closet and before his next date tied it under his trousers in such a way that the possible proof of his excitement would remain chained to his leg.

13

I've chosen this episode among dozens of others in order to show that the greatest happiness Jaromil had experienced up to this point in his life was having a girl's head on his shoulder.

A girl's head meant more to him than a girl's body. He knew almost nothing about the body (what exactly are pretty legs? what does a pretty rump look like?), whereas the face was comprehensible to him, and in his eyes it alone decided whether a woman was beautiful.

I don't mean that he was indifferent to the body. The thought of female nakedness made him giddy. But let's carefully note this subtle distinction:

He didn't long for the nakedness of a girl's body; he longed for a girl's face lighted by the nakedness of her body.

He didn't long to possess a girl's body; he longed to possess the face of a girl who would yield her body to him as proof of her love.

That body was beyond the limits of his experience, and precisely for this reason he devoted countless poems to it. How many times did the female genitals figure in his poems of that time? But through a miraculous effect of poetic magic (the magic of inexperience), Jaromil made of these copulatory and reproductive organs a chimerical object and a theme of playful dreams.

For instance, in one poem he wrote about a "small watch ticking away" in the center of her body.

In another he wrote about her groin as the "home of invisible creatures."

In still another he let himself be carried away by the image of an opening and thought of himself as a child's marble falling through this opening so endlessly that he turned into a fall, "a fall forever falling through her body."

And in another poem her legs turned into two rivers joining; at this confluence he imagined a mysterious mountain for which he invented a name with a biblical sound: Mount Hanina.

In still another he wrote about the long wanderings of a velocipedist (this word seemed as beautiful to him as a twilight) riding wearily through a landscape; that landscape is her body, and the two haystacks in which he wants to sleep are her breasts.

It was so beautiful to wander over a female body, an unknown, unseen, unreal body, a body with no odor, no blackheads, no small flaws or illnesses, an imaginary body, a body that was the playground of his dreams!

It was so enchanting to write about female breasts and groins in the same tone used in telling fairy tales to children; yes, Jaromil was living in the land of tenderness, which is the land of *artificial childhood*. I say "artificial" because real childhood is no paradise, nor is it so tender.

Tenderness comes into being at the moment when life propels a man to the threshold of adulthood, and he anxiously realizes all the advantages of childhood he had not appreciated as a child.

Tenderness is the fear instilled by adulthood.

Tenderness is the attempt to create a tiny artificial space in which it is mutually agreed that each will treat the other like a child.

Tenderness is also fear of the physical consequences of love; it is an attempt to take love out of the world of adults (where it is insidious, coercive, heavy with flesh and responsibility) and to consider a woman as a child.

"Softly beat the heart of her tongue," he wrote in a poem. He thought that her tongue, her little finger, her breasts, her navel were autonomous beings who conversed in inaudible voices; he thought that a girl's body consisted of thousands of such creatures, and that loving that body meant listening to its creatures and hearing "its two breasts speaking a secret language."

14

The past tormented her. But one day, as she was taking a long look back at it, she found the area of paradise in which she had lived with the newborn Jaromil, and she had to correct her verdict: no, it was not true that Jaromil had taken everything away from her; on the contrary, he had given her much more than anyone else ever had. He had given her a piece of life unsoiled by lies. No Jewish woman from a concentration camp could tell Mama that her happiness had been based merely on hypocrisy and emptiness. That area of paradise was her only truth.

And the past (it was like turning a kaleidoscope) again looked different to her: Jaromil had never taken anything of value from her, he had merely torn the gilded mask away from an error and a lie. He was still unborn when he helped her find out that her husband didn't love her, and thirteen years later he had saved her from a mad adventure that could only bring her further grief.

She told herself that the shared experience of Jaromil's childhood was a commitment and a sacred pact between them. But more and more often she became aware that her son was not honoring that pact. When she spoke to him she saw that he wasn't listening and that his head was full of thoughts he didn't wish to confide to her. She noticed that he was ashamed before her, that he was jealously keeping his little secrets of body and mind to himself, and that he was wrapping himself in veils she couldn't see through.

She was hurt and irritated by this. Was it not part of the sacred pact they had drawn up together when he was a child that he would always confide in her without shame?

She had hoped that the truth they had experienced together would last forever. As she had when he was small, she told him every morning what he should wear, and by laying out his underwear for him she was a presence all day long beneath his clothing. When she sensed that this had become disagreeable to him, she took her revenge by deliberately scolding him for small stains on his underwear. She enjoyed lingering in the room where he dressed and undressed, to punish him for his insolent modesty.

"Jaromil, come here and let me see you," she said to him one day when there were guests in the house. "My God, what a mess!" she announced indignantly when she saw his carefully disheveled hair. She went off for a comb and without interrupting her conversation with the guests she took hold of his head and began to comb him. And the great poet, who had a diabolical imagination and looked like Rilke, sat quietly, crimson with fury, letting himself be combed; all he could do was wear his cruel grin (the one he had been practicing for years) and let it harden on his face.

Mama stepped back to appraise her work with the comb, then, turning to her guests: "Good God, can you tell me why this child is making such a nasty face?"

And Jaromil swore that he would always be on the side of those who want radically to change the world.

15

When Jaromil arrived the discussion was already at its height; it was about the meaning of progress and whether it in fact existed. He looked around and noticed that the gathering of the Marxist youth circle he had been invited to by one of his classmates consisted of young people you could see in any Prague high school. Attentiveness was probably better sustained here than it was during the discussions his Czech teacher had tried to organize in the classroom, but here too there were troublemakers; one of them was holding a lily that he kept sniffing, which caused so much laughter that the dark-haired fellow in whose apartment the meeting was taking place at last confiscated the flower.

Then he pricked up his ears, because someone asserted that you can't talk about progress in art; you can't say, he explained, that Shakespeare is inferior to contemporary playwrights. Jaromil wanted very much to join the discussion, but he hesitated to address people he didn't know; he was afraid that everyone would see his face turn red and his hands shake nervously. And yet he wished strongly to *bind* himself to this small group, and he knew that he couldn't do so unless he spoke up.

To give himself courage, he thought of the painter and of his great authority, which he had never doubted, reassuring himself that he was his friend and disciple. This thought gave him the strength to join the debate and to repeat the ideas he had heard during his visits to the painter's studio. The fact that he was making use of ideas that were not his own is much less remarkable than the fact that he was expressing them in a voice that was not his own. He himself was a bit surprised to notice that the voice coming from his mouth resembled the painter's, and that this voice also induced his hands to make the painter's gestures.

That there was progress in the arts, he said, was indisputable: the trends of modern art represented a total upheaval in a thousand-year evolution; they had finally liberated art of the obligation to propagate political and philosophical ideas and to imitate reality, and one could even say that modern art was the beginning of the true history of art.

Several people now wanted to speak, but Jaromil refused to yield the floor. At first it was unpleasant to hear the painter's words and intonation coming from his own mouth, but he soon found this borrowing reassuring and protective; he hid behind this mask as if behind a shield; he stopped feeling shy and self-conscious; he was satisfied that his phrases sounded good in this setting, and he went on:

He referred to Marx's idea that until now mankind had been living in its prehistory, and that its true history only began with the proletarian revolution, which was the transition from the realm of necessity to the realm of freedom. The corresponding decisive moment in the history of art was when André Breton and the other surrealists discovered automatic writing and along with it the miraculous wealth of the human unconscious. The fact that this discovery occurred at almost the same time as the socialist revolution was highly significant because liberating the imagination represented for mankind the same leap into the realm of freedom as the abolition of economic exploitation.

Now the dark-haired fellow spoke up; he approved of Jaromil's defense of the principle of progress but questioned his putting surrealism on the same level as the proletarian revolution. Instead, he expressed the opinion that modern art was decadent and that the era in art which corresponded to the proletarian revolution was socialist realism. Not André Breton but Jiri Wolker,* the founder of Czech socialist poetry, must be their model. Jaromil had heard about such ideas from the painter, who had ridiculed them. Jaromil, too, now tried to sound sarcastic, saying that socialist realism was nothing new in art, that it was difficult to tell it apart from the old bourgeois kitsch. The dark-haired fellow replied that the only art that was modern was the art that helps in the fight for a new world, which was not the case with surrealism because the masses do not understand it.

The discussion was interesting: the dark-haired fellow developed his argument with charm and without raising his voice, so that the discussion never degenerated into a quarrel, even when Jaromil, intoxicated by being the center of attention, resorted to somewhat edgy irony; moreover, no one announced a definitive verdict, others

---

*Czech poet who died in 1924 at the age of twenty-four.

joined the debate, and the idea Jaromil was defending was soon submerged by new topics of discussion.

But was it so important to ascertain whether progress existed or not, whether surrealism was bourgeois or revolutionary? Was it so important whether it was Jaromil or the others who were right? What was important to him was that he was bound to them. He argued with them, but he felt warmly drawn to them. No longer even listening to them, he was only thinking how happy he was: he had found a society of people with whom he was not merely his Mama's son or his classroom's student but also his own self. And he reflected that one cannot completely become his own self until one is completely among others.

The dark-haired fellow now got up, and everyone understood that it was time to head for the door because their leader had work to do, which he had referred to in a deliberately vague manner indicating something important and impressive. When they were at the door, ready to leave, a girl wearing glasses approached Jaromil. Let me say at once that Jaromil had not even noticed her during the meeting; anyway, there was nothing noticeable about her, she was rather nondescript; not ugly, only a little slovenly; without makeup; with her hair, untouched by any hairdresser, falling smoothly over her forehead; and wearing the kind of clothes one wears only to avoid going around naked.

"What you said was really very interesting to me," she said to him. "I'd very much like to discuss it some more with you. . . ."

16

There was a garden square not far from the dark-haired fellow's apartment; they went toward it, constantly talking; Jaromil learned that the girl was a university student and that she was two years older than he (this piece of news filled him with pride); they went along the square's winding path, both making erudite conversation as they hurried to disclose what they believed, what they thought, what they were (the girl was more scientific, Jaromil more literary); they reeled off lists of the great names they admired, and the girl repeated that she was very interested in Jaromil's unusual opinions; then, after a moment's silence, she called him an ephebus; yes, when he came into that room she felt she was seeing a graceful ephebus. . . .

Jaromil didn't know exactly what the word meant, but he thought it beautiful to be designated by a word, whatever it meant, and a Greek one at that; moreover, he guessed that the word "ephebus" was applied to someone young and that the youth it referred to was not the awkward and degrading kind he had until now experienced but rather a youth both vigorous and worthy of admiration. With her use of the word "ephebus" the student did have his immaturity in mind, but at the same time she relieved it of its ineptness and turned it into a superiority. This was so comforting that, on their sixth circuit of the square, Jaromil dared to make the gesture he had been contemplating from the beginning but had been unable to find the courage for: he took the student by the arm.

To say that he "took" her by the arm isn't quite right; it would be more accurate to say that he "insinuated" his hand under her arm; he insinuated it there very discreetly, as if he hoped that the girl would not even notice; she actually didn't react at all to the gesture, so that Jaromil's hand remained insecurely slipped between her elbow and side like some foreign object, a bag or package its owner has forgotten and is about to let drop. But soon the hand began to sense that the arm under which it had inserted itself was aware of its presence. And his legs began to sense that the student was slowing down somewhat. He recognized this slowing and knew that something irrevocable was in the air. Ordinarily when something irrevocable is about to happen, people (perhaps to prove that they have some power over events) speed up the inevitable. Thus Jaromil's hand, which had been motionless all this time, suddenly came to life and squeezed the student's arm. She stopped, raised her glasses toward Jaromil's face, and let her briefcase drop to the ground.

Jaromil was dumbfounded by this; at first, in his awe, he had not even noticed that the girl was carrying a briefcase; now that it had fallen, the briefcase appeared on the scene like a message from heaven. And when he considered that the girl had come to the Marxist gathering directly from the university, and that her briefcase probably contained duplicated copies of course materials and important scientific works, his intoxication increased: she had let the university drop to the ground in order to clasp him in her unburdened arms.

The fall of the briefcase was really so affecting that they began to kiss in a glorious bewitchment. They kissed for a long time, and when the kissing was finally over and they were unsure what to do next, she again raised her glasses toward him and, anxious agitation in her voice, said: "You probably think I'm like all the other girls. But that's not so. I'm not at all like them."

These words were perhaps more affecting than the fall of the briefcase, and Jaromil realized with amazement that he was with a woman who loved him, that she had loved him at first sight, miraculously, and without his knowing why. And he noted in passing (in the margin of his consciousness, so as to reread it carefully later on) that the student spoke of other women as if she saw in him a man who was already so experienced with women that any woman who loved him could only suffer.

He told the girl that he didn't consider her at all like other women; the girl picked up her briefcase (now Jaromil could get a better look at it: it was really large and heavy, filled with books) and they set off on their seventh circuit of the square; when they stopped to kiss again, they suddenly found themselves in a cone of glaring light. Two cops were facing them, demanding their identity cards.

Embarrassed, the two lovers looked for their cards; with trembling hands they gave them to the policemen, who were either cracking down on prostitutes or only looking for some amusement during a long tour of duty.

In any case they provided the two young people with an unforgettable experience: for the rest of the evening (Jaromil accompanied the girl to her door) they talked about love persecuted by prejudice, morality, the police, the old generation, stupid laws, and the rottenness of a world that deserved to be swept away.

17

The day had been beautiful and the evening too, but it was nearly midnight when Jaromil returned home, and Mama was nervously pacing through the rooms of the villa.

"I've been so anxious about you! Where were you? You have no regard for me!"

Jaromil was still bursting with his great day and started to answer her in the voice he had used at the Marxist youth circle; he was imitating the painter's self-assured tone.

Mama immediately recognized that voice; she saw her son's face with her lost lover's voice coming out of it; she saw a face that didn't belong to her; she heard a voice that didn't belong to her; her son stood before her like the image of a double repudiation; that seemed intolerable to her.

"You're killing me! You're killing me!" she shouted hysterically, and she ran off into the next room.

Frightened, Jaromil stood rooted to the spot, and a sensation of great guilt spread through him.

(Ah, my boy, you'll never rid yourself of that feeling. You are guilty, you are guilty! Every time you leave the house you will sense behind you a reproachful look that will shout out to you to come back! You will walk in the world like a dog on a long leash! And even when you are far away you will always feel the contact of the collar on the nape of your neck! Even when you are with women, even when you are in bed with them, there will be a long leash attached to your neck, and somewhere far away your mother will be holding the other end and feeling through the spasmodic movements of the cord the obscene movements to which you have abandoned yourself!)

"Mama, please don't be angry, Mama, please forgive me!" He is now timidly kneeling at her bedside and caressing her wet cheeks.

(Charles Baudelaire, you'll be forty and still afraid of your mother!)

And Mama puts off forgiving him in order to feel as long as possible the touch of his fingers on her skin.

18

(This is something that could never have happened to Xavier, because Xavier has no mother, and no father either, and not having parents is the first precondition of freedom.

But please understand, it's not a matter of losing one's parents. Gérard de Nerval's mother died when he was a newborn, and yet he lived his whole life under the hypnotic gaze of her wonderful eyes.

Freedom does not begin where parents are rejected or buried, but where *they do not exist:*

Where man is brought into the world without knowing by whom.

Where man is brought into the world by an egg thrown into a forest.

Where man is spat out on the ground by the sky and puts his feet on the world without feeling gratitude.)

19

What was brought into the world during the first week of love between Jaromil and the student was Jaromil himself; he learned that he was an ephebus, that he was beautiful, that he was intelligent, and that he had imagination; he realized that the girl with glasses loved him and feared the moment when he would leave her (it was, she said, when they parted that evening in front of her house and she watched him airily leave that she had the feeling of seeing him as he really was: a man going away, getting away, vanishing . . .). He had finally found the image he had sought so long in his two mirrors.

That first week they saw each other every day: they took four long evening walks through the city and went to the theater once (they sat in a box, kissed, and ignored the performance) and to the movies twice. On the seventh day they again went for a walk: it was freezing cold, and Jaromil was wearing only a light topcoat with nothing between his shirt and jacket (because the gray cardigan Mama told him to wear seemed to him better suited to a retired provincial), no hat or cap (because on the second day the girl with glasses had praised his hair, which he had formerly hated, by asserting that it was as untamable as he himself), and since the elastics of his knee socks had worn out and were always sliding down his calves and into his shoes, short gray socks.

They met at seven and started on a long walk

through suburbs where the snow on vacant lots crunched under their feet and where they could periodically stop to kiss. What fascinated Jaromil was the docility of the girl's body. Until then his advance toward the female body had been like a long journey with one stage after another: it took time before a girl let him kiss her, it took time before he could put his hand on her breast, and when he touched her rump he thought he was already far along the way—never having gone any farther. This time, from the very first, something unexpected happened: the student was totally submissive in his arms, defenseless, ready for anything, he could touch her wherever he wanted. He considered this a great proof of love, but at the same time he was embarrassed about it because he didn't know what to do with this sudden freedom.

And that day (the seventh day) the girl told him that her parents were often away from home and that she was looking forward to inviting Jaromil to her house. The radiant explosion of these words was followed by a long silence; both of them knew what a meeting in an empty apartment would mean (let's recall that when the girl with glasses was in Jaromil's arms she didn't refuse him anything); they remained silent for quite a while, and then the girl serenely said: "I believe that when it comes to love there's no such thing as compromise. When you're in love you must give everything."

Jaromil agreed with this statement wholeheartedly because for him, too, love meant everything; but he didn't know what to say; by way of an answer he stopped, with pathos fixed his eyes on the girl (forgetting that it was night and that the pathos of a look was barely perceivable), and began to hug and kiss her frantically.

After fifteen minutes of silence, the girl resumed the conversation, telling him that he was the first man she had ever invited to her house; she said that she had many men friends, but they were only friends; they had become used to this and nicknamed her the Stone Virgin.

Jaromil was very pleased to learn that he was to be the student's first lover, but at the same time he was struck by stage fright: he had heard a lot about the act of love and he knew that defloration was generally considered a difficult matter. So he was unable to join the student in her effusiveness, finding himself beyond the present moment; in his mind he was experiencing the voluptuous pleasures and torments of that promised great day (Marx's well-known idea about mankind's leap from prehistory into history had always inspired him) when the true history of his life would begin.

Not talking much, they walked through the streets for a very long time; as the evening went on it grew colder, and Jaromil felt the cold on his thinly clad body. He suggested they find a place to sit down somewhere, but they were too far from the center of town and there was no café or tavern in the area. By the time he came home he was chilled to the bone (toward the end of the walk it had been an effort for him to keep her from hearing the chattering of his teeth), and when he woke up the next morning he had a sore throat. Mama took his temperature and confirmed that he had a fever.

20

Jaromil's sick body was in bed, but his soul was experiencing the long-awaited great day. His idea of this day consisted, on the one hand, of abstract happiness and, on the other, of concrete worries. For Jaromil absolutely could not imagine in precise detail what going to bed with a woman really involved; he knew only that it required preparation, skill, and knowledge; he knew that behind physical love the threatening specter of pregnancy grinned, and he also knew (it had been the subject of innumerable conversations among his classmates) that there were ways to prevent this danger. In those barbarous times men (like knights donning armor before a battle) slipped onto their love-leg a translucent sock. Theoretically Jaromil was thoroughly informed about all this. But how could he procure that sock? Jaromil would never overcome his shyness and go into a pharmacy to buy one! And how could he actually put it on without the girl seeing it? The sock seemed ridiculous to him, and he couldn't bear the idea that the girl would know about it! Could he put it on in advance, at home? Or did he have to wait until he was naked in front of the girl?

These were questions he couldn't answer. Jaromil had no trial (training) sock, but he decided to get one at all costs and practice putting it on. He thought that speed and dexterity played a decisive role in this area, and that these couldn't be acquired without training.

But other things, too, tormented him: What exactly was the act of love? What did it feel like? What happened in your body? Was the pleasure so great that you started to scream and lose control of yourself? Didn't screaming make you look ridiculous? How long did the whole thing actually take? Ah, my God, was it even possible to embark on something like that without preparing for it?

Until then Jaromil had never masturbated. He had considered this activity to be something shameful, which a real man should guard against; it was a great love he felt destined for, not onanism. But how do you achieve a great love without some preparation? Jaromil realized that masturbation was indispensable to such preparation, and he abandoned his principled feeling of hostility toward it: it was no longer a wretched substitute for physical love but a necessary step toward it; it was not a confession of poverty but a rung on the ladder to riches.

And so he performed (with a fever of thirty-eight and two tenths) his first imitation of the act of love, which surprised him by its extreme brevity and by its inability to induce screams of sensual pleasure. Thus he was both disappointed and reassured: during the next few days he repeated the experiment several times, learning nothing new; but he was convinced that he was becoming increasingly seasoned in this way, and that he would be able to face his beloved without fear.

He had been in bed for three days with compresses around his neck when Grandmama rushed into the

168

room in the morning and said: "Jaromil! Everybody's in a panic downstairs!" "What's happened?" he asked her, and Grandmama explained that they were listening to the radio at his aunt's downstairs, and there had been a revolution. Jaromil jumped out of bed and ran into the next room. He turned on the radio and heard the voice of Klement Gottwald.

He quickly understood what was going on, for in the past few days he had heard talk (though the matter didn't interest him much, for—as we have just seen—he had more serious worries) that the non-Communist ministers had threatened the Communist prime minister Gottwald that they would resign. And now he heard Gottwald addressing a crowd in Old Town Square, denouncing the traitors who were plotting to oust the Communist Party from the government and obstruct the people's march to socialism; Gottwald called on the people to insist on and accept the ministers' resignations and to set up everywhere new, revolutionary organs of power under the leadership of the Communist Party.

Static crackled on the old radio, mingling Gottwald's words with the tumult of the crowd, which inflamed Jaromil and filled him with enthusiasm. He was in his pajamas with a towel around his neck, standing in Grandmama's room and shouting: "At last! It had to come! At last!"

Grandmama was not quite sure that Jaromil's enthusiasm was justified. "Do you really think this is good?" she asked him anxiously. "Yes, Grandmama, it's good.

It's even excellent!" He took her into his arms; then he started to pace vigorously up and down the room; he reflected that the crowd gathered in Old Town Square had launched today's date into the skies, where it would shine like a star for centuries; and then that it was really a shame to be spending such a great day at home with his grandmother instead of being in the streets with the crowd. Before he had time to think this through, the door opened and his uncle came in, flushed and furious, shouting: "Do you hear them? The scum! The scum! It's a putsch!"

Jaromil looked at his uncle, whom along with his wife and their conceited son he had always hated, and he thought that his moment to defeat the man had finally come. They stood face to face: the uncle had the door at his back, and at Jaromil's back was the radio, which made him feel linked to a crowd of a hundred thousand people, and he now spoke to his uncle like a hundred thousand people speaking to one man: "It's not a putsch, it's a revolution," he said.

"Fuck off with your revolution," the uncle said. "It's easy to make a revolution when you've got the army and the police and a certain big country behind you."

When he heard his uncle's self-assured voice talking to him as if he were a stupid kid, Jaromil's hatred went to his head: "The army and the police are trying to prevent a handful of hooligans from oppressing us again."

"You little moron," said the uncle. "The Communists had most of the power already, and they made this putsch so they could have all of it. I always knew you were a little idiot."

"And I always knew that you were an exploiter and that the working class would wring your neck."

Jaromil made this assertion in a fit of anger, in fact without much thought; all the same, it's worth our attention for a moment: he used words frequently seen in the Communist press and heard in the speeches of Communist orators, but he had been rather repelled by them, just as he was repelled by all stereotypical language. He always considered himself a poet first, and so, even though he made revolutionary speeches, he was unwilling to abandon his own language. And yet he had said: "The working class will wring your neck."

Yes, it was strange: in a moment of excitement (thus at a moment when an individual acts spontaneously and reveals his true self), Jaromil abandoned his language and chose to be a medium for someone else. And not only did he do this, he did it with a feeling of intense pleasure; it seemed to him that he was part of a thousand-headed crowd, one of the heads of the thousand-headed dragon of a people on the march, and he found that glorious. He suddenly felt strong and with the power to laugh openly at a man who used to make him blush with timidity. The harsh simplicity of the assertion ("the working class will wring your neck") gave him pleasure because it placed him in the ranks of those wonderfully simple men who laugh at nuances and whose entire wisdom consists of the essential, which is always insolently simple.

Jaromil (in pajamas and with a towel around his neck) stood, legs apart, in front of the radio, which right behind his back had just resounded with tremendous applause, and it seemed to him that this din was entering and expanding him so that he stood facing his uncle like an immovable tree, like a laughing rock.

And his uncle, who believed that Voltaire had invented volts, came forward and slapped his face.

Jaromil felt a sharp pain on his cheek. He was humiliated, and because he felt as big and powerful as a tree or a rock (the thousands of voices were still resounding from the radio behind him), he wanted to throw himself at his uncle and slap him back. But since it took him a moment to decide, his uncle had time to turn around and leave the room.

Jaromil shouted: "I'll get him for this! The bastard! I'll get him!" and headed toward the door. But Grandmama grabbed him by the pajama sleeve and begged him to calm down, which made Jaromil content himself with repeating "the bastard, the bastard, the bastard" as he returned to the bed in which, less than an hour ago, he had left his imaginary lover. He was now unable to think about her. He saw his uncle before him and felt the slap and heaped endless reproaches on himself for not having acted swiftly, like a man; he reproached himself so bitterly that he began to cry and wet his pillow with angry tears.

Late that afternoon Mama came home and anxiously told him that the director of her department, a very respected man, had already been dismissed and that all the non-Communists in the office feared they would soon be arrested.

In bed Jaromil propped himself up on his elbow and began to talk passionately. He explained to Mama that what was happening was a revolution, and that a revolution is a brief period when recourse to violence is necessary in order to hasten the arrival of a society in which violence is forbidden. Mama should understand that!

She, too, put her heart and soul into the debate, but Jaromil managed to refute her objections. He said that the rule of the rich and of that whole society of entrepreneurs and shopkeepers was stupid, and he cleverly reminded Mama that she herself, in her own family, was the victim of such people; he reminded her of the arrogance of her sister and the ignorance of her brother-in-law.

This made her waver, and Jaromil was pleased by the success of his arguments; he felt that he had taken revenge for the slap he had been given a few hours before; but when he thought of that, he felt his anger return, and he said: "And you know, Mama, I want to join the Communist Party too."

He read the disapproval in Mama's eyes, but he persisted with his assertion; he said that he was ashamed he had not joined earlier, that only the burdensome legacy of the house in which he had grown up separated him from those with whom he had long known he belonged.

"Are you saying you're sorry you were born here and that I'm your mother?"

Mama's tone showed that she was hurt by this, and Jaromil had to add quickly that she had misunderstood; in his opinion Mama, as she really was, had basically nothing in common with her sister or brother-in-law or the world of rich people.

But Mama told him: "If you love me at all, don't do it! You know how hellish your uncle already makes my life. If you join the Party it'll be absolutely intolerable. Be sensible, I beg you."

A tearful sadness clutched Jaromil's throat. Instead of returning his uncle's slap, he had just received from him a second one. He turned away from Mama and waited for her to leave the room. Then he again began to cry.

21

It was six o'clock in the evening, and the student greeted him at the door in a white apron and led him into a tidy kitchen. Dinner was nothing special, scrambled eggs with diced sausage, but it was the first dinner a woman (except for Mama and Grandmama) had ever prepared for Jaromil, and he ate with the pride of a man whose mistress takes care of him.

Then they went into the next room; it contained a round mahogany table with a crocheted cover on which there stood, like a weight, a massive crystal vase; the walls were decorated with hideous paintings, and one corner was occupied by a couch heaped with countless cushions. Everything had been determined and agreed in advance for this evening, and all they had to do was to sink into the pillows' soft swells; but the student, oddly enough, sat down on a hard chair at the round table and he sat down facing her; then, still sitting on those hard chairs, they talked about one thing and another for a long, long time, until Jaromil felt his throat tighten.

He had to be home by eleven; he had of course asked Mama to let him stay out all night (he invented a party organized by his classmates), but he came up against such vigorous resistance that he didn't dare insist and thus could only hope that the five hours between six and eleven would be sufficient for his first night of love.

But the student chattered on and on, and the five

hours rapidly dwindled; she talked about her family, about her brother who had once attempted suicide over an unhappy love affair: "That marked me. I can't be like other girls. I can't take love lightly," she said, and Jaromil felt that these words were meant to put the imprint of seriousness on the physical love that had been promised him. And so he got up from his chair, bent over the girl, and said in a very serious voice: "I understand, yes, I understand you"; he then helped her up from her chair, led her to the couch, and sat her down.

Then they kissed, caressed, necked. That lasted for a long while, until Jaromil thought it was probably time to undress the girl, but never having done such a thing before, he didn't know how to begin. First of all he didn't know whether he should or shouldn't turn off the light. According to all the reports he had heard about situations of this kind, he supposed that he should turn it off. Somewhere in his jacket pocket he had a little packet containing the translucent sock, and if at the decisive moment he was to put it on discreetly and secretly, darkness was absolutely essential. But he couldn't just decide to get up in the midst of the caresses and head for the light switch, which seemed to him rather out of place (let's not forget that he was well brought up), for he was a guest here and it was up to the hostess to turn the switch. Finally he dared to ask shyly: "Shouldn't we turn off the light?"

The girl answered: "No, no, please." Jaromil wondered whether this meant that the girl didn't want darkness because she didn't want to make love or whether the girl wanted to make love but not in the dark. He could of course have asked her, but he was ashamed to say out loud what he thought.

Then he recalled that he had to be home by eleven, and he made an effort to overcome his shyness; he unbuttoned the first female button of his life. It was a button on her white blouse and he unbuttoned it with fearful expectation of what she might say. She said nothing. So he continued unbuttoning, lifted her blouse out of the waistband of her skirt, and then took her blouse off entirely.

She was now lying on the cushions in her skirt and brassiere, and then astonishingly, although she had been kissing Jaromil avidly just moments before, now that he had taken her blouse off, she seemed to have fallen into a stupor; she didn't move; she slightly thrust out her chest, like a condemned man offering himself to the gun barrels.

There was nothing else he could do but go on undressing her: he found the zipper at the side of her skirt and opened it; the poor innocent didn't know about the fastener that held the skirt at the waist, and he tried stubbornly but in vain to pull it down over the girl's hips; she thrust out her chest, facing the invisible firing squad and not even noticing his difficulties.

Ah, let's pass over in silence Jaromil's fifteen or so minutes of trouble! He finally succeeded in undressing the student completely. When he saw her obediently lying on the cushions, awaiting the long-awaited moment, he realized that he now had to undress as well. But the ceiling light was glaring and Jaromil was ashamed to take his clothes off. Then he had a saving idea: next to the living room he had noticed the bedroom (an old-fashioned bedroom with twin beds); the light was off there; he could undress in the dark there and even hide under the covers.

"Aren't we going to the bedroom?" he asked her shyly.

"To the bedroom? What for? Why do you need a bedroom?" said the girl, laughing.

It's hard to say why she was laughing. It was gratuitous, embarrassed, thoughtless laughter. But Jaromil was wounded by it; he feared that he had said something stupid, as if his suggestion of going to the bedroom exposed his ridiculous inexperience. He was disconcerted; he was in a strange apartment, under a revealing light he couldn't turn off, with a strange woman who was making fun of him.

He instantly realized that they wouldn't be making love that evening; he felt offended and sat silently on the couch; he regretted what had happened, but at the same time he was relieved; he no longer had to wonder whether he should or shouldn't turn off the light or how to undress; and he was glad it wasn't his fault; she had reason to laugh so stupidly!

"What's wrong?" she asked.

"Nothing," said Jaromil, and he knew that he would look even more ridiculous if he were to tell the girl the reason for his touchiness. He therefore made an effort

178

to control himself, lifted her from the couch, and began conspicuously to examine her (he wanted to dominate the situation, and he thought that the one who examines dominates the one who is being examined); then he said: "You're beautiful."

Risen from the couch on which she had been lying in motionless expectation, the girl seemed suddenly freed; she was again talkative and sure of herself. She was not at all embarrassed to be examined by a boy (perhaps she thought that the one being examined dominated the one who examines), and she asked: "Am I more beautiful naked or dressed?"

There are a number of classic female questions that every man encounters sooner or later and that the educational institutions should prepare young males for. But Jaromil, like all of us, attended bad schools and didn't know how to answer; he tried to guess what the girl wanted to hear, but he was at a loss: most of the time, when she is with others, a girl is dressed, and so she is probably glad to be more beautiful with clothes on; but since nakedness is the body's truth, Jaromil was probably just as glad to tell her she was prettier when she was naked.

"You're beautiful naked and dressed," he said, but the student was not at all satisfied with that answer. She pranced around the room, posed for the young man, and demanded a straight answer. "I want to know which way you like me more."

When the question was put so precisely, it was easier to answer. Since other people knew her only when she was dressed, he thought it would be tactless to say that she was less beautiful dressed than naked; but because she had asked for his personal opinion, he could boldly answer that personally he preferred her naked, as this showed more clearly that he loved her as she was, for herself alone, and that he didn't care about anything that was merely added to her person.

Evidently he had not misjudged, for when the student heard that she was more beautiful naked she reacted very favorably. She didn't put her clothes back on until after he left, she kissed him many times, and on the doorstep, as he was leaving (it was a quarter to eleven, Mama would be satisfied), she whispered in his ear: "Today you showed me that you love me. You're very nice; you really love me. Yes, it's better this way. We'll save it for later."

At around that time he began to write a long poem. It was a story poem about a man who suddenly realized that he was old; that he was "where fate no longer builds its rail stations"; that he was abandoned and forgotten; that around him

> They're whitewashing the walls they're removing
> the movables
> They're changing everything in his room

So he rushes out of his house and goes back to where he experienced the most intense moments of his life:

> Rear of the house fourth floor rear door at left in
> the corner
> With a name on the card unreadable in the
> darkness
> "Moments have passed since twenty years ago
> please take me in!"

An old woman opens the door, disturbed out of the careless apathy she has been immersed in during long years of solitude. Quickly, quickly she bites her bloodless lips to give them back a bit of color; quickly, with a gesture from long ago, she tries to put a bit of order into her sparse wisps of unwashed hair, and with an embarrassed air she waves her arms to hide from him the photographs of former lovers hanging on the walls. But then she feels that all is well in this room, and that appearances don't matter; she says:

> *"Twenty years And yet you've come back*
> *As the last important thing I'll ever meet*
> *I have no chance of seeing anything*
> *If I try to peer over your shoulder into the*
>   *future."*

Yes, all is well in this room; nothing matters any longer, neither wrinkles nor shabby clothes nor yellow teeth nor sparse hair nor pale lips nor a sagging belly.

> *Certainty certainty I no longer move and I'm*
>   *ready*
> *Certainty Compared to you beauty is nothing*
>   *Compared to you youth is nothing*

And he wearily crosses the room, "wipes fingerprints of strangers off the table with his glove," and realizes that she had lovers, crowds of lovers who

> *Squandered all the glow of her skin*
> *Even in the dark she is no longer beautiful*
> *A worthless coin worn out by fingers*

And an old song clings to his soul, a forgotten song, my God, what is that song?

You're drifting away, you're drifting away on the
        sand of beds
And your appearance is fading
You're drifting away, you're drifting away and of
        you nothing remains
But the center nothing but the center of you

And she knows that she no longer has anything
youthful for him. But:

In the moments of weakness that now assail me
My fatigue my withering that process so
        important and so pure
Belong only to you

Their wrinkled bodies touch each other with emotion, he says "little girl," she says "my darling," and
they start to cry.

And there was no go-between between them
Not a word not a gesture Nothing behind which
        to hide
Nothing to disguise their misery from each other

Because it is exactly that mutual misery they seize full
on the lips, they greedily drink one from the other. They
caress each other's miserable bodies and already hear,
under each other's skin, the engines of death softly
purring. And they know that they are definitively and
totally pledged to each other; that this is their last and also

their greatest love, because the last love is the greatest.
The man thinks:

> *This is love with no way out This is love like a*
> *wall*

And the woman thinks:

> *Here is death distant perhaps in time but*
> *already so near in its likeness*
> *So near in being so like the two of us deeply*
> *sunk in our armchairs*
> *Here is the goal attained and the legs so happy*
> *they no longer even try to take a step*
> *And the hands so certain they no longer even*
> *seek a caress*
> *There is nothing more to do but wait for the*
> *saliva in our*
> *mouths to turn into dewdrops*

When Mama read this strange poem, she was as
usual stunned by the precocious maturity that allowed
her son to understand a time of life so far off from his
own; she didn't understand that the characters in the
poem had no connection with the real psychology of
old age.

No, this poem was not at all about an old man and an
old woman; if Jaromil had been asked the age of the
characters in the poem, he would have hesitated and
then replied that they were between forty and eighty; he

was unaware of old age, which to him was a distant, abstract notion; what he knew of old age was that it is a time of life where the adult age already belongs to the past; where one's destiny is already completed; where one no longer fears that terrible unknown called the future; where love, when we encounter it, is certain and final.

For Jaromil was filled with anxiety; he moved toward the undressed body of a young woman as if he were treading on thorns; he desired this body and he was afraid of it; that is why, in his poems of tenderness, he fled from the tangibility of the body to take refuge in the world of childish imagination; he deprived the body of its reality and imagined the female groin as a mechanical toy; this time, he had taken refuge on the opposite side: the side of old age; where the body is no longer proud and dangerous; where it is miserable and pitiful; the misery of a decrepit body more or less reconciled him to the pride of a youthful body that must age in its turn.

His poem was filled with naturalistic ugliness; Jaromil had forgotten neither the yellow teeth nor the pus at the corners of eyes nor the sagging belly; but behind the coarseness of these details was the touching desire to limit love to the eternal, to the indestructible, to that which can replace the motherly embrace, to that which is not subject to time, to that which is "the center nothing but the center," to that which can overcome the power of the body, of the perfidious body whose universe was stretched out before him like unknown territory inhabited by lions.

He wrote poems about the artificial childhood of tenderness, he wrote poems about an unreal death, he wrote poems about an unreal old age. These were the three blue flags under which he fearfully advanced toward the immensely real body of an adult woman.

23

When she arrived at his house (Mama and Grandmama were away from Prague for two days), he made sure not to turn on the lights, even though darkness was slowly falling. They finished dinner and were sitting in Jaromil's room. At about ten (that was when Mama ordinarily sent him to bed), he uttered the sentence he had mentally been repeating many times in order to be able to enunciate it easily and naturally: "What about going to bed?"

She agreed, and Jaromil turned down the bed. Yes, everything happened as he had anticipated, and everything happened without difficulty. The girl undressed in a corner and Jaromil undressed (much more hastily) in another corner; he immediately put on his pajamas (in the pocket of which he had carefully deposited the packet containing the sock), then rapidly slipped under the covers (he knew that the pajamas didn't suit him, that they were too large for him and made him look small) and gazed at the girl who had kept nothing on and came naked (ah! in the darkness she seemed to him even more beautiful than last time) to stretch out beside him.

She pressed up against him and started to kiss him furiously; after a moment Jaromil decided it was high time to open the packet. So he plunged his hand into his pocket and tried to lift it out discreetly. "What have you got there?" asked the girl. "Nothing," he answered, and he hastily placed on the student's breast the hand that was about to grasp the packet. Then he thought that he would have to excuse himself and go to the bathroom for a moment to get himself discreetly ready. But while he was considering this (the girl kept on kissing him), he noticed that the arousal he had felt at the beginning in all its physical obviousness had vanished. Noticing this threw him into a new plight, for he knew that under these conditions there was no point in opening the packet. So he tried to caress the girl with passion while he waited anxiously to regain the vanished arousal. In vain. Under his attentive gaze his body seemed to be seized with dread; rather than expand, it shrank.

The caresses and kisses no longer brought him pleasure or satisfaction; they were no more than a screen behind which the boy tormented himself and desperately demanded his body's obedience. These were interminable caresses and embraces and endless torture, torture in total silence, for Jaromil didn't know what to say and had the feeling that any word would reveal his shame; the girl was silent too, probably because she too began to suspect something shameful, without knowing exactly whether the failure was Jaromil's or hers; in any case, something was happening that she was unprepared for and that she was afraid to name.

But then, when the intensity of this terrible pantomime of caresses and kisses diminished and no longer had the strength to continue, both rested their heads on pillows and tried to sleep. It's hard to say if they slept or not and for how long, but even if they didn't sleep, they pretended, so as to hide, to get away from each other.

When they got up in the morning, Jaromil was afraid to look at the student's body; she seemed painfully beautiful to him, all the more beautiful because he had not possessed her. They went into the kitchen, made breakfast, and tried to talk naturally.

But then the student said: "You don't love me."

Jaromil tried to assure her that it wasn't true, but she didn't let him speak: "No, it's not worth the trouble of looking for a way to persuade me. It's stronger than you are, and it was easy to see it last night. You don't love me enough. Last night you yourself noticed quite clearly that you don't love me enough."

Jaromil wanted to explain to the girl that what happened had nothing to do with the extent of his love, but he said none of this. The girl's words had actually offered him an unexpected opportunity to hide his humiliation. It was a thousand times easier to take the reproach of not loving the girl than to admit the thought that his body was defective. He therefore didn't answer and lowered his head. And when the girl repeated the accusation, he said in a deliberately vague and unconvincing tone of voice: "Of course I love you."

"You're lying," she said. "There's someone else in your life that you love."

That was even better. Jaromil bowed his head and sadly shrugged his shoulders, as if to acknowledge some truth to this reproach.

"It makes no sense if it isn't real love," said the student morosely. "I warned you that I can't take these things lightly. I can't stand the thought that I'm replacing someone else for you."

The night he had just lived through had been cruel, and there was only one way out for Jaromil: to start afresh and erase his failure. He thus found himself forced to reply: "No, you're being unfair. I love you. I love you tremendously. But I did hide something. It's true that there's another woman in my life. That woman loved me, and I treated her badly. There's now a shadow over me that weighs on me and that I'm helpless against. Please understand me. It would be unfair of you not to see me anymore because of that, because I love only you, only you."

"I didn't say I didn't want to see you anymore, I only said that I can't stand the thought of another woman, even if it's just a shadow. Please understand me too, to me love is an absolute. In love I don't compromise."

Jaromil looked at the face of the girl with glasses, and his heart was wrung by the thought that he might lose her; it seemed that she was close to him, that she could understand him. But despite that, he didn't want to, he couldn't confide to her that he had to pass himself off as a man over whom a fateful shadow hung, a man torn and worthy of pity. He replied: "Doesn't absolute love mean above all that you can understand the other and love everything about him, even his shadows?"

That was well said, and the student appeared to be reflecting on it. Jaromil thought that perhaps all was not lost.

24

He had not yet shown her his poems; the painter had promised to have them published in an avant-garde magazine, and he counted on the prestige of the printed word to dazzle the girl. But now he needed his poems to come quickly to his aid. He was convinced that once the student read them (particularly the one about the old couple), she would understand and be moved. He was wrong; she thought she had to give her young friend a critical opinion, and she chilled him with the terseness of her remarks.

What had become of the marvelous mirror of her enthusiastic admiration in which he had first discovered his uniqueness? Now every mirror presented him with the grinning ugliness of his immaturity, and that was intolerable. It was then that he thought of the name of a famous poet who wore the halo of acceptance by the European avant-garde and of involvement in Prague scandals, and although he didn't know him and had never seen him, Jaromil had the same blind faith in him that a simple believer has in a high-ranking dignitary of his church. He sent him his poems along with a humble, pleading letter. He dreamed about a friendly, admiring response, and this dream spread like a balm over his dates with the student, which were getting rarer and rarer (she claimed that the approaching university exams left her little time) and sadder and sadder.

So he was back to the period (not very long ago)

when any conversation with any woman was difficult for him and required preparation at home; again he experienced every date several days in advance, spending long evenings in imaginary conversations with the student. Appearing in these unspoken monologues more and more clearly (and yet mysteriously) was the other woman about whose existence the student had expressed her suspicions during breakfast at Jaromil's house; that woman gave Jaromil the glow of a past, awakening jealous interest and explaining his body's failure.

Unfortunately she appeared only in these unspoken monologues, for she had quickly and discreetly vanished from the real conversations between Jaromil and the student; the student had lost interest in her as unexpectedly as she had started talking about her existence. How disappointing this was to Jaromil! All his little allusions, his carefully calculated slips of the tongue and sudden silences designed to indicate that he was thinking of another woman went by without prompting the slightest attention.

Instead she talked to him at length (alas, very cheerfully) about the university, and she described some of her fellow students in so lively a fashion that they seemed much more real to Jaromil than he was to himself. The two of them were back to what they had been before they knew each other: the shy little boy and the Stone Virgin who carried on learned conversations. Only now and then (Jaromil greatly cherished those moments and didn't let go of them) did she suddenly

fall silent or point-blank say something sad and yearning to which Jaromil tried in vain to link words of his
own, for the girl's sadness was turned inward and had
no wish to be in harmony with Jaromil's sadness.

What was the source of her sadness? Who knows?
Maybe she missed the love she saw disappearing;
maybe she was thinking about someone else whom she
desired. Who knows? One day that moment of sadness
was so intense (they had left a movie theater and were
walking down a dark, silent street) that she put her
head on his shoulder.

My God! This had happened before! It had happened
the evening he was walking in Stromovka Park with the
girl from his dancing class! This gesture of the head,
which had aroused him that evening, again had the
same effect on him: he was aroused! He was immensely
and conspicuously aroused! But this time he was not
ashamed, on the contrary, this time he was desperately
hoping that the girl would notice his arousal!

But the girl's head was resting sadly on his shoulder,
and God knows what she was looking at through her
glasses.

Jaromil's arousal persisted, victoriously, proudly,
steadily, visibly, and he wanted her to see and appreciate it! He wanted to seize the girl's hand and put it on
his body, but this was only a thought that seemed crazy
and impractical to him. Then he realized that if they
stopped and kissed, the girl's body would feel his
arousal.

But when his slowing steps made her perceive that he

was going to stop to kiss her, she said: "No, no, please don't . . ." and she said this so sadly that Jaromil silently obeyed. And that creature between his legs seemed to him to be a prancing buffoon, a clown, an enemy making fun of him. He was walking with a sad strange head on his shoulder and a strange mocking clown between his legs.

25

Perhaps he imagined that sadness and the craving for consolation (the famous poet had still not answered) justified some kind of unusual gesture, so he dropped in on the painter unexpectedly. When he reached the entrance he realized from the sound of voices that there were a number of people inside, and he tried to excuse himself and leave; but the painter cordially invited him into the studio, where he introduced him to his guests, three men and two women.

Jaromil felt his cheeks flushing under the gaze of five strangers, but at the same time he was flattered; the painter introduced him as the author of excellent poetry and spoke of him as if his guests had already heard of him. That was a pleasant feeling. As he sat in the armchair looking around, he noticed with great pleasure that the two women were prettier than his student. Such natural elegance as they crossed their legs, flicked ashes from their cigarettes into the ashtray, and combined erudite terms and obscene words into bizarre sentences! Jaromil had the impression that he was in an elevator taking him to beautiful heights where the torturing voice of the girl with glasses would not reach his ears.

One of the women turned to him and amicably asked him what kind of poetry he wrote. "Just poetry," he said, shrugging his shoulders in embarrassment. "Remarkable poetry," the painter added, and Jaromil lowered his head; the other woman looked at him and said in an alto voice: "Here with us, he makes me think of Rimbaud with Verlaine and his friends in the painting by Fantin-Latour. A child among men. They say that Rimbaud at eighteen looked thirteen. And you too," she said, turning to Jaromil, "look like a child."

(I can't resist observing that this woman leaned over Jaromil with the same cruel tenderness as when the sisters of Rimbaud's teacher Izambard, the famous "lice hunters," leaned over Rimbaud upon his return from one of his extended adventures and washed, cleaned, and deloused him.)

"Our friend," said the painter, "has the good fortune, which won't last long, of no longer being a child and not yet being a man."

"Puberty is the most poetic age," said the first woman.

"You'd be astonished," the painter said with a smile, "at how perfect and mature the poems of this imperfect and immature virgin are."

"That's right," one of the men agreed, showing by this that he knew Jaromil's poetry and approved of the painter's praise.

"Are you going to publish them?" the woman with the alto voice asked Jaromil.

"I doubt that the era of positive heroes and busts of Stalin is auspicious for his poetry," said the painter.

The mention of positive heroes again steered the conversation back to the course it had been on before Jaromil's arrival. Jaromil was familiar with such issues and could easily have participated in the discussion, but he was no longer listening to what they were saying. Echoing endlessly through his head was that he looked thirteen, that he was a child, that he was a virgin. He knew, of course, that no one here wished to offend him and that the painter sincerely liked his poems, but that only made things worse: at the moment his poems meant nothing to him. He'd give up their maturity a thousand times over in exchange for his own maturity. He'd give up all his poems for one single coition.

An animated debate ensued, and Jaromil wanted to leave. But he felt so weighed down he had trouble finding the words to announce his departure. He was afraid to hear his own voice; he was afraid that it would shake or crack and once more expose his childish immaturity to the light of day. He wanted to become invisible, to tiptoe far away and disappear, to doze off and sleep a long time and wake up dozens of years later, when his face had aged and would be showing masculine creases.

The woman with the alto voice again turned to him: "Why are you so quiet, my child?"

He mumbled that he preferred listening to talking (though he hadn't been listening at all), and he thought that it was impossible for him to escape the sentence the student had passed on him and that the verdict of virginity rendered against him, which he bore like a mark (my God, just looking at him everyone could see that he'd never had a woman!), had been confirmed once more.

And because he knew that everyone was looking at

him, he was bitterly aware of his face and felt, nearly with dread, that on that face was his Mama's smile! He clearly recognized that delicate, bitter smile, he felt it stuck on his lips and he had no way to get rid of it. He felt that Mama was glued on his face, that she swathed him as a chrysalis swathes a larva, denying it the right to its own look.

There he was, among adults and inside Mama's chrysalis, and Mama was holding him tight in her arms, pulling him away from a world he wanted to belong to and that behaved kindly toward him and yet as one behaves toward someone who still has no place in that world. This situation was so intolerable that Jaromil gathered all his strength to throw off the mother mask, to escape it; he tried hard to listen to the debate.

It focused on an issue that at the time was being passionately debated by all artists. In Bohemia modern art had always called for a Communist revolution; but when the revolution came, it had proclaimed a program of unconditional adherence to a popular realism comprehensible to everyone and had rejected modern art as a monstrous manifestation of bourgeois decadence. "That's our dilemma," said one of the painter's guests. "Should we betray the modern art we grew up with or the revolution we called for?"

"The question is badly put," said the painter. "A revolution that resurrects academic art and manufactures thousands of copies of politicians' busts betrays not only modern art but first of all betrays itself. Such a revolution doesn't want to change the world, but rather the contrary: it wants to preserve the most reactionary spirit of history, the spirit of fanaticism, discipline, dogmatism, faith, and conventionality. For us there's no dilemma. As true revolutionaries we cannot agree to this betrayal of the revolution."

Jaromil would not have found it difficult to elaborate on the painter's idea, the logic of which he knew very well, but he was loath to appear here in the role of the touching pupil, the obedient, praiseworthy boy. He was overcome by the desire to rebel, and turning to the painter, he said:

"You're always quoting Rimbaud: 'It is necessary to be absolutely modern.' I agree completely. But the absolutely modern isn't what we've been anticipating for fifty years, but, on the contrary, what shocks and surprises us. The absolutely modern isn't surrealism, which has been around for a quarter of a century, but the revolution that's taking place at the moment under our eyes. The very fact that you don't understand this is quite simply proof that it's really new."

Someone interrupted him: "Modern art was a movement directed against the bourgeoisie and against its world."

"Yes," said Jaromil, "but if it had really been logical in its negation of the contemporary world, it would have had to reckon with its own disappearance. It would have had to know—and it would have had to wish—that the revolution would create a totally new kind of art, an art in its own image."

"So you approve," said the woman with the alto

voice, "of pulping Baudelaire's poetry, prohibiting all modern literature, and shoving the cubist paintings in the National Gallery into the cellar?"

"A revolution is an act of violence," said Jaromil, "that's well known, and surrealism itself knew very well that old-timers have to be brutally kicked off the stage, but it didn't suspect that it was one of them."

In a fury of humiliation, he expressed his ideas, as he himself was aware, precisely and spitefully. Only one thing unsettled him from his very first words on: once again he was hearing the painter's distinctive, authoritative tone in his own voice, and he was unable to prevent his right hand from describing in the air the painter's characteristic gestures. It was actually a strange debate between the painter and the painter, between the man painter and the child painter, between the painter and his rebellious shadow. Jaromil was aware of this, and he felt even more humiliated; thus his formulations became more and more harsh, so as to revenge himself on the painter, who had imprisoned him in his gestures and his voice.

The painter twice replied to Jaromil with rather lengthy explanations, but the third time he remained silent. He merely looked at him with severity, and Jaromil knew that he would never again enter his studio. Everyone was silent until the woman with the alto voice (this time she no longer spoke leaning over him tenderly like Izambard's sister leaning over Rimbaud's deloused head, but on the contrary seeming to withdraw from him sadly and with surprise): "I don't know your poetry, but from what I've heard about it, it might be difficult to publish under the regime you've just defended with such vehemence."

Jaromil thought of his latest poem, about the two old people and their last love; he was aware that this poem, which he liked immensely, could never by published in this era of optimistic slogans and propaganda poems, and that by renouncing it now he would be renouncing what he held most dear, renouncing his only riches, without which he would be all alone.

But there was something more precious than his poems; something far away he didn't yet possess and longed for—manliness; he knew that it could only be attained by action and courage; and if courage meant courage to be rejected, rejected by everything, by the beloved woman, by the painter, and even by his own poems—so be it: he wanted to have that courage. And so he said:

"Yes, I know that the revolution has no need for my poems. I regret that, because I like them. But unfortunately my regret is no argument against their useless-ness."

Again there was silence, and then one of the men said: "This is dreadful," and he actually shuddered as if a chill had run down his spine. Jaromil felt the horror his words had produced in everyone there, that they were seeing in him the living disappearance of every-thing they loved, everything that made life worthwhile.

It was sad but also beautiful: within the space of an instant, Jaromil lost the feeling of being a child.

26

Mama read the poems Jaromil silently put on her table and tried to read the life of her son between the lines. If only the poems were written in plain language! Their sincerity was deceptive; they were full of puzzles and hints; Mama knew that her son's head was full of women, but she knew nothing about what he did with them.

So she ended up opening Jaromil's desk drawer and rummaging in it for his diary. She knelt on the floor and leafed through it emotionally; the entries were terse, but even so she could discern that her son was in love; because he designated his beloved only with an initial, Mama was unable to tell who the woman was; on the other hand, with a passion for detail Mama found repugnant, he gave the date of their first kiss and the dates when he first touched her breasts and her buttocks.

Then she came to a date written in red and decorated with numerous exclamation marks; the entry read: "Tomorrow! Tomorrow! Ah, dear bald-headed old Jaromil, when you read this many years from now, remember that on this day began the real history of your life!"

Thinking quickly, she recalled that this was the day she had left Prague with Grandmama; and she recalled that on her return she had found her precious little perfume bottle unstoppered in the bathroom; she had asked Jaromil what he had been doing with her perfume, and he answered, embarrassed: "I was playing with . . ." Oh, how stupid she had been! She remembered that when Jaromil was small he wanted to be an inventor of perfumes, and this memory was touching. Therefore she merely said: "You're a bit too big to be playing such games!" But now everything was clear: a woman had been in the bathroom, the woman with whom Jaromil had spent that night in the villa and with whom he had lost his virginity.

She imagined his naked body; she imagined next to this body the naked body of a woman, she imagined that this female body was perfumed with her perfume and that therefore the woman's odor was the same as her own; that disgusted her. She looked again at the diary and noticed that the entries ceased after the date with the exclamation marks. There it is, it's all over for a man after he goes to bed with a woman for the first time, she thought bitterly, and her son seemed contemptible to her.

For a few days she avoided him. Then she observed that he was pale and had lost weight; because of too much lovemaking, she was sure.

A few days later she noticed not only fatigue but also sadness in her son's dejection. That reconciled her somewhat with him and gave her hope: she told herself that girlfriends wound and mothers comfort; she told herself that girlfriends are many and a mother is one and only. I must fight for him, I must fight for him, she repeated, and from that moment on she began circling him like a vigilant, compassionate tigress.

27

That's how things were when he successfully passed his high school final examinations. He took leave with great sadness of the classmates with whom he had spent eight years, and his officially confirmed adulthood seemed to stretch before him like a desert. Then one fine day he learned (by chance: he ran into a boy he had seen at the meetings in the dark-haired fellow's apartment) that the girl with the glasses had fallen in love with another student.

He made a date with her; she told him that she was going on vacation in a few days; he took down her address; he didn't tell her what he had learned; he was afraid that talking about it would only hasten their break-up; he was glad that she hadn't dropped him completely, even though she had someone else; he was glad that she sometimes let him kiss her and that she at least treated him as a friend; he was terribly attached to her and was ready to relinquish all pride; she was the only living creature in the desert he saw before him; he clung to the hope that their barely surviving love might still be revived.

The student went away, leaving behind her a scorching summer like a long, stifling tunnel. A letter (whining and imploring) fell into that tunnel and was lost there without an echo. Jaromil thought of the telephone receiver hanging on the wall of his room; alas, that receiver had suddenly taken on a meaning: a receiver with a severed wire, a letter without an answer, a conversation with someone who isn't listening . . .

And women in flimsy dresses glided through the streets, hit tunes floated out of the open windows, streetcars were crammed with people carrying bags of towels and bathing suits, and excursion boats on the Vltava made their way south to the forests . . .

Jaromil was forlorn, and only Mama's eyes watched him and remained faithful to him; but it was intolerable to him to have these eyes lay bare his forlornness, which wanted to remain invisible and hidden. He couldn't bear Mama's gaze or her questions. He would flee the house, returning late in the evening and going right to bed.

I've noted that he was not born for masturbation but for a great love. During these weeks, however, he masturbated desperately and with frenzy, as if he wanted to punish himself by an activity so vile and humiliating. Afterward he would have a headache for the rest of the day, but this almost made him happy because the pain shielded him from the beauty of women in flimsy dresses and muffled the brazenly sensual melodies of the hit tunes; thus the victim of a pleasant stupor, he could more easily get through the endless surface of the day.

There was no letter from the girl. If only there had at least been a letter from anybody! If only someone had agreed to enter his nothingness! If only the famous poet to whom he had sent his poems had finally written him a few lines! Oh, if only he had written him a few friendly words! (Yes, I did say that he would have given all his poetry to be considered a man, but I must add here: if he was not to be considered a man, only one thing could bring him some consolation: at least to be considered a poet.)

He wanted once more to attract the attention of the famous poet. Not by means of a letter, but by a gesture laden with poetry. One day he left the house with a sharp knife. He walked for a long time around a telephone booth, and when he was certain that no one was nearby he went inside and cut off the receiver. He managed to cut off a receiver a day for twenty days (he still had no letter either from the girl or the poet), collecting twenty receivers with severed wires. He put them into a box that he wrapped with paper and tied with string, addressed it to the famous poet, and wrote his own name as the sender. Quite excited, he took the package to the post office.

As he was leaving the counter, someone slapped him on the shoulder. He turned around and recognized his old friend from school, the school janitor's son. Jaromil was happy to see him (the slightest event was welcome in this emptiness where nothing happened!); he entered into the conversation gratefully, and when he learned that his old classmate lived nearby, he almost compelled him to invite him over.

The janitor's son no longer lived in the school building with his parents, but had his own one-room apartment. "My wife has gone out," he explained as they entered. Jaromil had not suspected that his friend was married. "Yes, a year ago," said the janitor's son, and he said this so naturally and with such confidence that Jaromil felt envious.

They sat down and Jaromil noticed a baby's crib across the room; he reflected that his old classmate was a father and he himself was merely an onanist.

The janitor's son took a bottle of liqueur out of a cabinet and filled two glasses while Jaromil reflected that he couldn't have such a bottle in his room because Mama would have asked him a thousand questions about it.

"What are you up to these days?" asked Jaromil.

"I'm with the police," said the janitor's son, and Jaromil recalled the day he had spent with his neck wrapped in compresses, listening on the radio to the din of the chanting crowd. The police gave the most solid support to the Communist Party, and his old classmate had surely been in the roaring crowd while Jaromil was home with his grandmother.

Yes, the janitor's son had actually spent those days in the streets, speaking about it proudly but cautiously, and Jaromil thought it necessary to make him understand that they shared the same convictions; he told him about the meetings in the dark-haired fellow's apartment. "That Yid?" said the janitor's son without enthusiasm. "Watch yourself with him! He's a strange bird!"

The janitor's son kept eluding him, was always a step ahead of him, and Jaromil hoped to find common ground; he said sadly: "I don't know if you know that my father died in a concentration camp. Since then I've realized that the world has to be radically changed, and I know where my place is."

The janitor's son finally seemed to understand, nodding in agreement; after this they talked for a long while, and when they came to their future Jaromil suddenly asserted: "I want to be in politics." He was himself surprised to have said this; as if the words had preceded the thought; as if the words themselves, not he, had decided his future for him. "You know," he went on, "my mother wants me to study the history of art or French literature or something like that, but I'm not interested. Those things aren't life. Real life—that's what you're immersed in."

As he was leaving the janitor's son's place he reflected that he had just experienced a decisive illumination. A few hours earlier he had mailed a package containing twenty telephone receivers, convinced that this was a fantastic plea that he was addressing to a great poet so that he would respond to him. That he was thus making a gift to him of the fruitless wait for his words, a gift to him of the longing for his voice.

But the conversation with his old classmate right afterward (he was certain it wasn't by chance!) gave his poetic act an opposite meaning: it was no longer a gift and a plea; not at all; he was proudly *returning* to the poet his fruitless wait; the receivers with severed wires were the severed heads of his veneration, and Jaromil was sending them to the poet with contempt, like a

Turkish sultan returning to a Christian commander the severed heads of Crusaders.

Now he understood everything: his whole life had merely been a long wait in an abandoned telephone booth with a dead phone. Now there was only one solution: to leave the abandoned booth as quickly as possible!

28

"What's wrong, Jaromil?" The warmth of this sympathetic question brought tears to his eyes; he couldn't get away, and Mama went on: "You're my child all the same. I know you inside out. I know everything about you, even though you don't confide in me."

Jaromil looked away, ashamed. Mama kept talking: "Don't think of me as your mother, think of me as an older friend. If you confided in me, maybe you'd feel better. I know you're tormenting yourself." And she added softly: "And I also know that it's on account of a woman."

"Yes, Mama, I'm sad," Jaromil admitted, because the warm atmosphere of mutual understanding surrounded him, and he couldn't get away from it. "But it's hard for me to talk about it . . . "

"I understand. Besides, I don't want you to tell me what it is right now, I just want you to know that you can tell me anything whenever you want to. Listen. It's a beautiful day. I'm going out on a boat ride with some friends. Come along with us. You need a bit of diversion."

The idea didn't attract Jaromil much, but he had no excuse handy; and then was too weary and sad that he didn't have the energy to refuse, and so without quite knowing how, he suddenly found himself on the deck of an excursion boat with four ladies.

The other ladies were Mama's age, and Jaromil provided them with an ideal subject for conversation; they

were very surprised to learn that he had already finished high school; they declared that he looked like his
mama; they were astonished to hear that he had
decided to study political science (they thought the field
unsuitable for such a sensitive young man), and of
course they asked him suggestively whether he already
had a girlfriend; Jaromil hated them in silence, but he
saw that Mama was having a good time, and for her
sake he kept smiling obligingly.

The boat docked and the ladies and their young man
disembarked on a shore covered with half-naked bodies
and looked for a spot where they could sunbathe; only
two of them had brought swimsuits, the third bared her
fat, white body down to her bra and underpants
(unashamed of showing her underwear, perhaps feeling
her modesty preserved by her ugliness), and Mama
announced that she would only tan her face and turned,
squinting, toward the sun. All four urged that their young
man should undress, sunbathe, and go into the water.
Mama had remembered to bring Jaromil's swim trunks.

Hit tunes reached them from a nearby café, filling
Jaromil with an unappeased languorous desire; tanned
girls and boys went by them, clad only in bathing
suits, and Jaromil had the impression that they were
all focusing on him; he was enveloped by their gaze as
though by fire; he tried desperately to prevent people
from seeing that he was with four middle-aged ladies;
but the ladies noisily surrounded him and behaved
like one mother with four cackling heads; they insisted
he go into the water.

He objected: "There's no place to change."

"Silly boy, nobody's going to look at you, just put a towel around you," suggested the fat lady in the bra and pink underpants.

"He's shy," said Mama, laughing, and the other ladies laughed with her.

"We should respect his modesty," said Mama. "Come on, change behind the towel and nobody'll see you." She held up a large white towel in her extended hands as a partition to shield him from the eyes of the people on the shore.

He backed away, and Mama followed him with the towel. He backed away from her and she kept following him like a huge white-winged bird pursuing its fleeing prey.

Jaromil backed away, backed away and then turned and ran.

The ladies looked at him in surprise, Mama still held the white towel between her extended hands, and he ran, threading his way among bare young bodies until he was out of sight.

PART FOUR

The Poet Runs

1

The time must come when a poet tears himself away from his mother's arms and runs.

Until recently he was still walking obediently two abreast: his sisters Isabelle and Vitalie up ahead, he behind them with his brother, Frédéric, and, like a captain bringing up the rear, his mother, who once a week took her children this way through Charleville.

When he was sixteen, he tore himself away from his mother's arms for the first time. In Paris he was arrested by the police, his teacher Izambard and Izambard's sisters (yes, the ones who leaned over him to delouse his hair) sheltered him for a few weeks, and then, after two slaps in the face, the cold maternal embrace closed on him again.

But Arthur Rimbaud ran away again and again; he ran with a collar fastened to his neck, writing his poems as he ran.

2

The year is 1870, and the cannons of the Franco-Prussian War can be heard in Charleville from afar. That is a particularly favorable situation for running away, because the din of battle has a nostalgic allure for poets.

His squat body with its crooked legs is strapped up tight in a hussar's uniform. At eighteen Lermontov has become a soldier so as to run away from his grandmother and her burdensome maternal love. He has exchanged the pen, which is the key to his soul, for the pistol, which is the key to the world's doors. For when we send a bullet into a man's chest it is as if we are entering that chest ourselves; and another man's chest—that is the world.

From the moment he tore himself away from Mama's arms, Jaromil has not stopped running, and it seems that the sound of his footsteps mingles with still another sound, which resembles the roar of cannon. It is not the detonations of shellfire but rather the tumult of political upheaval. At such a time the soldier is mere decoration, and the politician takes the soldier's place. Jaromil no longer writes poetry but diligently studies political science at the university.

3

Revolution and youth are a pair. What can a revolution promise to adults? To some, disgrace; to others, favor. But that favor is not worth much, for it affects only the more miserable half of life and, along with advantages, brings uncertainty, exhausting activity, and disruption.

Youth is more fortunate: it is not burdened by guilt, and the revolution can take it entirely under its wing. The uncertainty of revolutionary times is an advantage for youth, for it is the world of the fathers that is being hurled into uncertainty. Oh, how beautiful it is to enter adulthood when the ramparts of the adult world are crumbling!

In the first years after 1948, Communist professors were a minority in Czech higher education. To maintain its grip on the university, the revolution had to give power to the students. Jaromil was a militant in his faculty's Youth Union, and as such he was an observer at examinations. He then submitted a report to the faculty's political committee indicating how this or that professor behaved during examinations, the questions he asked, and the opinions he expressed, so that it was actually the examiner rather than the examined who was being subjected to an examination.

4

But Jaromil was himself subjected to an examination when he presented his report to the committee. He had to answer the questions of stern young people, and he wanted to speak in a way that would please them: When young people's education is at stake, compromise is a crime. We must guard against teachers with outdated ideas: the future will be new, or it will not exist. And we can no longer trust teachers who change their ideas from one day to the next: the future will be pure, or it will be tarnished.

Now that Jaromil has become a rigorous militant whose reports affect the destiny of adults, can I still maintain that he is on the run? Doesn't it seem instead that he has reached his goal?

Not at all.

When he was six years old, Mama had put him in the position of being a year younger than his classmates; he is still a year younger. When he is reporting on a professor who has bourgeois opinions, it is not the professor he is thinking about but rather the young people whose eyes he is anxiously watching to see his own image in them; just as he checks his smile and hair in the mirror at home, so he checks in their eyes the firmness, manliness, and harshness of his words.

He is always surrounded by a wall of mirrors, and he cannot see beyond it.

For adulthood is indivisible; adulthood is total, or it doesn't exist. As long as Jaromil remains a child, his presence at the examination board and his reports on professors will merely be a variant route of his run.

5

Because he is always running away from her, and always without success; he has breakfast and dinner with her, he says goodnight and good morning to her. Every morning she hands him the shopping bag; Mama doesn't care that this household emblem is ill suited to an ideological supervisor of professors, and she sends him off to do the day's marketing.

Look: he is on the same street we saw him walk at the beginning of the preceding part, when he blushed at the sight of a woman coming toward him. Several years have passed, but he still blushes, and in the store to which Mama sends him he is afraid to meet the eyes of a girl in a white smock.

He is mad about this girl, who spends eight hours a day in the cashier's cage. The softness of her features, the slowness of her gestures, her imprisonment—all this seems mysteriously close to him and predestined. Moreover, he knows why: this girl resembles the maid whose fiancé was shot; Magda: sadness-beautiful face. And the cashier's cage in which she is sitting resembles the bathtub in which he saw the maid.

6

He is bent over his desk and and trembling at the thought of his exams; he is just as afraid of them at the university as he was in high school, because he is used to showing his mother his perfect grades and he doesn't wish to disappoint her.

But how unbearable the airlessness of this tiny Prague bedroom when the air outside is filled with echoes of revolutionary songs and the windows admit the shadows of vigorous men with hammers in their hands!

It is 1922, five years after the great Russian revolution, and he is forced to bend over a textbook and tremble with fear because of an exam! What a penalty!

At last he pushes the book aside (it is late at night) and he dreams about the poem he is writing: the poem is about a worker who wants to kill his dream about the beauty of life by making it come true; holding a hammer, he gives his other arm to his beloved, and marches with a multitude of comrades to make a revolution.

And the law student (yes, of course, it's Jiri Wolker) sees blood on the desk; much blood, for

when we kill great dreams
much blood is spilled

but he is not afraid, for he knows that if he wants to be a man, he must not be afraid of blood.

7

The store closes at six, and he positions himself at the opposite corner. He knows that the cashier always quits work a little after six, but he also knows that she is always accompanied by one of the salesgirls.

This friend is much less pretty, seeming almost ugly to Jaromil; the two are exact opposites: the cashier is dark haired, the other is a redhead; the cashier is buxom, the other skinny; the cashier is quiet, the other noisy; he feels mysteriously close to the cashier, repelled by the other.

He often returned to his observation post in the hope that the girls might leave the store separately so that he could speak to the dark-haired one. But that never happened. One day he followed them; they went down several streets and entered a building; he remained near the door for almost an hour, but neither one of them came out.

8

She has come to Prague from the provinces to see him, and she listens to him reading his poems to her. She is tranquil; she knows that her son is still hers; neither women nor the world have taken him away from her; on the contrary, women and the world have entered the magical circle of poetry, and this is a circle she herself has drawn around her son, a circle inside which she secretly rules.

He is reading her a poem he has written in memory of his grandmother, his mother's mother:

> *since I go into battle*
> *Grandmother*
> *for the beauty of this world*

Mrs. Wolker is tranquil. Her son can go into battle in his poems, holding a hammer in his hand and giving his arm to his girlfriend; that doesn't trouble her; because in his poems he has retained his mother and his grandmother, the family meal, and all the virtues she has inculcated in him. Let the world see him march by, hammer in hand! No, she doesn't want to lose him, but she knows very well that she has nothing to fear: *to show himself* to the world is an entirely different thing from *going into* the world.

But the poet also knows this difference. And he alone knows how sad he is in the house of poetry!

9

Only a true poet can speak of the immense longing not to be a poet, the longing to leave that house of mirrors where deafening silence reigns.

> *Banished from the land of dreams*
> *I seek shelter in the crowd*
> *And wish to change my song*
> *To insults*

But when Frantisek Halas* wrote these lines he wasn't with the crowd in the streets; the room he wrote in, bent over his desk, was silent.

And it's not at all true that he was banished from the land of dreams. The crowd he speaks of in his poems was in fact the land of his dreams.

And he didn't succeed in changing his song to insults; it was, on the contrary, his insults that always changed into song.

Well, is there really no way out of the house of mirrors?

---

*Czech poet (1905–1952).

10

> *But I*
> *Have tamed*
> *Myself*
> *I have stomped*
> *On the throat*
> *Of my own song*

wrote Vladimir Mayakovsky, and Jaromil understands him. Poetic language seems to him like the lace in Mama's linen closet. He has written no poetry for several months, and he has no desire to write any. He is on the run. Of course, he goes marketing for Mama, but he keeps his desk drawers locked. He has removed all the reproductions of modern paintings from the walls of his room.

What did he put up instead? A photo of Karl Marx?

Not at all. On the bare wall he hung up a photograph of his father. It was a picture taken in 1938, at the time of the sad mobilization, and his father is dressed in his officer's uniform.

Jaromil loved this photograph of a man he hardly knew and whose image was beginning to blur in his mind. He yearned more and more for this man, who had been a soccer player, soldier, and concentration camp prisoner. He missed this man very much.

11

The political science faculty auditorium was packed, and there were several poets sitting on the podium. A young man in a blue shirt (worn in those days by members of the Youth Union) and with an enormous mop of hair was standing at the front of the podium and speaking:

Poetry's role is at its most important in revolutionary times; poetry gave the revolution its voice, and in exchange the revolution freed poetry from its isolation; today the poet knows that he is understood by the people and especially understood by young people because youth, poetry, and revolution are one and the same!

The first of the poets to speak now got up and recited a poem about a girl who broke up with her boyfriend, who worked at the milling machine next to hers, because he was lazy and failed to meet his production goals; but the boyfriend didn't want to lose his girlfriend, and so he set about working so diligently that the red flag of a shock worker was soon attached to his machine. Following this, other poets got up and recited poems about peace, Lenin and Stalin, martyrs in the antifascist struggle, and workers who exceed their norms.

12

Youth is unaware of the great power being young confers, but the poet (in his sixties) who now rises to recite his poem knows this.

That person is young, he proclaims in a melodious voice, who is with the youth of the world, and the youth of the world is socialism. That person is young who plunges into the future and never looks back.

In other words: according to the poet in his sixties, the word "youth" does not designate a specific period of life but a *value* above age and unconnected with it. This idea, elegantly versified, had at least a double objective: it flattered the young audience, and it magically rid the poet of his wrinkles and assured him (for he made it clear that he was on the side of socialism and that he would never look back) of a place beside the boys and girls.

Jaromil was in the audience and watched the poets with interest, even though it seemed that he was on the other side, like someone who was no longer one of them. He listened to their poems as coldly as he had listened to the words of the professors he reported on to the committee. What interested him more was the famous poet who was now getting up from his chair (the applause for the poet in his sixties had died down) and heading toward the center of the podium. (Yes, he is the one who not long ago had received a package containing twenty telephone receivers with severed wires.)

13

"Dear Master, We are now in the month of love; I am seventeen years old. The age of hopes and chimeras, as they say. . . . I am sending you some of this verse because I love all poets, all good Parnassians. . . . Don't make too many faces when you read this verse: . . . . You would render me deliriously happy and hopeful if you could *make* a small place among the Parnassians for the poem 'Credo in Unam'. . . . I am unknown; does that matter? Poets are brothers. These verses believe; they love, they hope: that is everything. My dear Master: raise me up a little: I am young; give me your hand. . . ."

Anyway, he is lying; he is fifteen years and seven months old; he has not yet run away from Charleville to escape from his mother. But this letter would long remain in his head as a litany of shame, as proof of weakness and servility. He would get even with this dear master, this old idiot, this bald-headed Théodore de Banville! A year later he would cruelly ridicule all his work, all the hyacinths and languid lilies that fill his verse, sending his sarcasms in a letter like a registered slap in the face.

But at the moment the dear master as yet has no idea of the hatred lying in wait for him as he recites a poem about a Russian town that had been leveled by the fascists rising from its ruins; a town decorated with magical surrealist garlands; the breasts of young Soviet women float through the streets like small colored balloons; a kerosene lamp hanging below the sky lights up the white town on whose rooftops helicopters settle like angels.

14

Captivated by the charm of the poet's personality, the audience applauded. There was, however, among this unthinking majority a thoughtful minority who knew that a revolutionary audience ought not to wait like a humble beggar for whatever the podium deigns to give it; on the contrary, nowadays it is the poems that are the beggars; they are begging to be admitted to the socialist paradise; but the young revolutionaries who guard the gates of this paradise must be stern: for the future will be new, or it will not exist; the future will be pure, or it will be tarnished.

"What is this nonsense he's feeding us?" Jaromil shouted, and others joined him. "He's hitching social-ism to surrealism! He's hitching a cat to a horse, the future to the past!"

The poet understood what was happening, but he was proud and had no intention of giving in. Since his youth he had been accustomed to being provocative before bourgeois narrow-mindedness, and he was unabashed by being one against many. His face flushed and he decided to recite as his final poem a different one from the one he had originally chosen: it was a poem full of violent metaphors and unbridled erotic images; there was hooting and shouting when he finished.

The students whistled derisively at the old man standing before them, who had come there because he loved them; in their angry rebellion he saw the radiance of his own youth. He believed that his love for them gave him the right to tell them what he thought. It was the spring of 1968 in Paris. Alas! The students were incapable of seeing the radiance of their youth in the wrinkles of his face, and the old scholar watched with surprise as he was whistled at by those he loved.

15

The poet raised his hand to quell the din. And then he started to shout that the students were like puritan schoolmarms, dogmatic priests, and bigoted cops; that they protested against his poem because they hated freedom.

The old scholar silently listened to the whistling and reflected that when he was young he too had been part of a group, that he too had eagerly whistled, but the group had long since scattered, and now he was alone.

The poet shouted that freedom was poetry's duty, and that even a metaphor was worth fighting for. He shouted that he would go on hitching a cat to a horse and modern art to socialism, and if this was quixotic he wanted to be a Don Quixote, because for him socialism was an era of freedom and joy, and he rejected any other kind of socialism.

The old scholar was watching the noisy young people around him, and it suddenly occurred to him that he was the only one in the whole audience who had the privilege of freedom, for he was old; when he is old a man is no longer obliged to care about his group's opinions, about the public, and about the future. He is alone with approaching death, and death has neither eyes nor ears, he has no need to please death; he can do and say what he pleases.

And they whistled and demanded the floor in order to answer him. Jaromil got up in his turn; he had black before his eyes and the crowd behind him; he said that only the revolution was modern and that decadent eroticism and unintelligible images were musty old poetizing that meant nothing to the people. "What's really modern," he asked the famous poet, "your unintelligible poems, or we who are building a new world? The only thing that's absolutely modern," he said, answering himself, "is the people building socialism." Thunderous applause greeted these words.

The applause was still ringing as the old scholar departed through the corridors of the Sorbonne, reading the inscriptions on the walls: *Be realistic, demand the impossible.* And a bit farther on: *The emancipation of man will either be total or nothing at all.* And a bit farther still: *Above all, no remorse.*

16

The seats in the large classroom have been pushed against the walls and brushes and paint pots and long streamers strewn across the floor, where several political science students are painting slogans for the May Day procession. Jaromil, the author and editor of the slogans, is standing behind them and consulting a notebook.

What is this? Have we got the wrong year? The slogans he is dictating to his fellow students are exactly the same as those the old scholar who was jeered at read a moment ago on the walls of the insurgent Sorbonne. No, we're not wrong; the slogans Jaromil is having inscribed on the streamers are exactly the same as those the French students scrawled twenty years later on the walls of the Sorbonne, the walls of Nanterre, the walls of Censier.

He gives the order to write on a streamer: *Dream is reality*; on another one: *Be realistic, demand the impossible*; and nearby: *We decree a state of permanent happiness*; and a bit farther: *Cancel churches* (he is particularly pleased with this slogan, consisting of two words and rejecting two millennia of history); and more: *No freedom for freedom's enemies*; and still another: *Power to the imagination!* And then: *Death to the lukewarm!* And: *Revolution in politics, in the family, in love!*

The students paint the letters and Jaromil proudly

goes from one to the other like a field marshal of words. He is happy to be useful, happy that his gift for language has found a use. He knows that poetry is dead (for *Art is dead*, a Sorbonne wall proclaims), but it died in order to rise again from its grave and become the art of propaganda and slogans inscribed on streamers and on the walls of cities (for *Poetry is in the street*, proclaims a wall of the Odéon).

17

"Don't you read the newspaper? On the front page of *Rude Pravo* there was a list of a hundred slogans for May Day. It was drawn up by the propaganda section of the Party Central Committee. Couldn't you find one to suit you?"

Jaromil was facing a plump young fellow from the Party District Committee, who introduced himself as chairman of the university committee in charge of organizing the festivities for May 1, 1949.

"'Dream is reality.' That's idealism of the crudest kind. 'Cancel churches.' I agree with you, comrade. But for the moment that conflicts with the Party's policy on religion. 'Death to the lukewarm.' Since when do we threaten people with death? 'Power to the imagination,' what would that be like? 'Revolution in love.' Can you tell me what you mean by that? Do you want free love as against bourgeois marriage, or monogamy as against bourgeois promiscuity?"

Jaromil asserted that the revolution would transform all aspects of life, including love and the family, or it would not be a revolution.

"That might well be so," the plump young fellow admitted. "But it can be put much better: 'For a socialist politics, for a socialist family!' You see, and it's one of the *Rude Pravo* slogans. There was no need to rack your brains over it!"

18

Life is elsewhere, the students have written on the walls of the Sorbonne. Yes, he knows that very well, it is why he is leaving London for Ireland, where the people are rebelling. His name is Percy Bysshe Shelley, he is twenty years old, he is a poet, and he is bringing with him hundreds of copies of leaflets and proclamations that are to serve him as visas for entry into real life.

Because real life is elsewhere. The students are tearing up the cobblestones, overturning cars, building barricades; their irruption into the world is beautiful and noisy, illuminated by flames and greeted by explosions of tear-gas grenades. How much more painful was the lot of Rimbaud, who dreamed about the barricades of the Paris Commune and never got to it from Charleville. But in 1968 thousands of Rimbauds have their own barricades, behind which they stand and refuse any compromise with the former masters of the world. The emancipation of mankind will be total, or it will not exist.

But only a kilometer from there, on the other bank of the Seine, the former masters of the world continue to live their lives, and the din of the Latin Quarter reaches them as something far away. *Dream is reality*, the students wrote on the walls, but it seems that the opposite was true: that reality (the barricades, the trees cut down, the red flags) was a dream.

19

But we never know at the present moment whether reality is a dream or a dream is reality; the students who lined up with their placards at the university came gladly, but they also knew that they risked trouble if they stayed away. In Prague the year 1949 marked for Czech students a curious transition during which a dream was already no longer only a dream; their shouts of jubilation were still voluntary but already compulsory.

The procession marched through the streets with Jaromil alongside it; he was responsible not only for the slogans inscribed on the streamers but also for the rhythmic shouting of his comrades; this time he no longer invented beautiful provocative aphorisms but merely copied into a notebook some slogans recommended by the central propaganda section. He shouted them out loudly, like a priest leading a procession, and his comrades repeated them after him.

20

The processions had already passed the reviewing stand in Wenceslas Square, improvised bands had appeared on the street corners, and blue-shirted young people were starting to dance. Everyone was fraternizing here with both friends and strangers, but Percy Shelley is unhappy, the poet Shelley is alone.

He's been in Dublin for several weeks, he's passed out hundreds of leaflets, the police already know him well, but he hasn't succeeded in befriending a single Irish person. Life is elsewhere, or it is nowhere.

If only there were barricades and the sound of gunfire! Jaromil thinks that formal processions are merely ephemeral imitations of great revolutionary demonstrations, that they lack substance, that they slip through your fingers.

And suddenly he imagines the girl imprisoned in the cashier's cage, and he is assailed by a horrible longing; he sees himself breaking the store window with a hammer, pushing away the women shoppers, opening the cashier's cage, and carrying off the liberated dark-haired girl under the amazed eyes of the gawking onlookers.

And then he imagines that they are walking side by side through crowded streets, lovingly pressed against each other. And all at once the dance whirling around them is no longer a dance but barricades yet again, we are in 1848 and in 1870 and in 1945, and we are in

Paris, Warsaw, Budapest, Prague, and Vienna, and these yet again are the eternal crowds crossing through history, leaping from one barricade to another, and he leaps with them, holding the beloved woman by the hand. . . .

21

He was feeling the young woman's warm hand in his palm when he suddenly saw him. The man was coming toward him, broad-shouldered and sturdy, and a young woman was walking at his side; she was not wearing a blue shirt like most of the girls who were dancing along-side the streetcar tracks; she was as elegant as a fash-ion-show sylph.

The sturdy man was absentmindedly looking around and acknowledging people's greetings; when he was a few steps away from Jaromil, their eyes met and in a sudden instant of confusion (and following the example of the other people who had recognized and greeted the famous man) Jaromil nodded and the man greeted him in turn, but with an absent look (as we greet someone we don't know) and the woman gave him a distant nod.

Ah, that woman was immensely beautiful! And she was completely real! And the girl from the cashier's cage and the bathtub, who until just a moment ago had been pressed against Jaromil, began to fade away in the radiant light cast by that real body, and then she vanished.

He stood on the sidewalk in his ignominious solitude, turned around, and threw a look of hatred at the cou-ple; yes, it was he, the "dear master," the recipient of the twenty telephone receivers.

22

Dusk was slowly falling on the city, and Jaromil wanted to meet the dark-haired cashier. He followed several women who looked like her from the back. He found it beautiful to devote himself completely to the fruitless pursuit of a woman lost in a multitude of human beings. Then he decided to pace up and down in front of the building he had once seen her enter. There was little chance of meeting her, but he didn't want to go home before Mama went to bed. (The family home was bearable only at night, when Mama was asleep and his father's photograph awakened.)

And so he went back and forth on the deserted suburban street on which the flags and flowers of May Day had left no trace of gaiety. Lights began to go on in the building windows. Then a light went on in a basement window above sidewalk level. Inside he saw a girl who looked familiar!

No, it wasn't the dark-haired cashier. It was her friend, the skinny redhead; she was on her way to the window to lower the shade.

He couldn't bear the bitterness of this disappointment, and he realized that he had been seen; he blushed and he did just what he did the day the sad, beautiful maid looked up from the bathtub toward the keyhole:

He ran away.

23

It was six o'clock in the evening on May 2, 1949; the salesgirls hurriedly left the store, and something unexpected happened: the redhead left alone.

He tried to hide around the corner, but it was too late. The redhead saw him and came toward him: "Don't you know, sir, that it's not polite to spy on people through the window in the evening?"

He blushed and tried to cut the conversation short; he was afraid that the presence of the redhead might again spoil his chances when her dark-haired friend left the store. But the redhead was very talkative and didn't intend to leave Jaromil; she even suggested that he accompany her home (it's much more appropriate, she said, to accompany a girl home than to watch her through the window).

Jaromil looked desperately at the door of the store. "Where's your friend?" he finally asked.

"Wake up. She's been gone for days."

They walked together to the building, and Jaromil learned that the two girls had come from the country, got work in the store, and shared the room; but the dark-haired girl had left Prague to get married.

When they stopped in front of the building, the girl said: "Do you want to come in for a moment?"

Surprised and confused, he went into her small room. And then, without knowing how it happened, they were embracing and kissing, and a moment later they were sitting on the bed.

It was all so quick and simple! Without allowing him the time to think that he was about to undertake a difficult and decisive task, the redhead put her hand between his legs, and he experienced wild joy, for his body reacted in the most normal way.

24

"You're terrific, you're terrific," the redhead whispered into his ear as he was lying beside her, his head buried in the pillow; he was filled with fantastic joy; after a moment of silence he heard: "How many women have you had before me?"

He shrugged his shoulders and smiled enigmatically.

"You won't say?"

"Guess."

"I'd say between five and ten," she said knowledgeably.

He was filled with comforting pride; it seemed to him that he had just made love not only with her but also with the five or ten other women she attributed to him. She not only relieved him of his virginity, she suddenly brought him far into his adulthood.

He looked at her gratefully, and her nakedness filled him with enthusiasm. How could he have considered her unattractive? Weren't there two entirely unquestionable breasts on her chest and an entirely unquestionable cluster of hair on her lower belly?

"You're a hundred times more beautiful naked than dressed," he told her, and he went on praising her beauty.

"Have you wanted me for a long time?" she asked him.

"Yes, you know very well I wanted you."

"Yes, I know it. I noticed it when you came to the store. I know that you waited for me outside."

"Yes."

"You didn't dare talk to me, because I was never alone. But I knew that someday you'd be here with me. Because I wanted you too."

25

He looked at the girl as her last words died away; yes, that's how it was; during all that time when he was tormented by solitude, when he was desperately taking part in meetings and processions, when he kept running on and on, his life as an adult had already been prepared for him here: this basement room with walls stained by dampness had been patiently waiting for him, this room and this ordinary woman whose body had finally linked him in a completely physical way to the crowd.

The more I make love, the more I want to make a revolution—the more I make a revolution, the more I want to make love, a Sorbonne wall proclaims, and Jaromil entered the redhead's body a second time. Adulthood is total, or it doesn't exist. This time he made love to her long and marvelously.

And Percy Bysshe Shelley, who like Jaromil had a girlish face and looked younger than his age, ran through the streets of Dublin, he ran on and on because he knew that life was elsewhere. And Rimbaud, too, kept running endlessly, to Stuttgart, to Milan, to Marseilles, to Aden, to Harar, and then back to Marseilles, but by then he had only one leg, and it is hard to run on one leg.

Again he slid out of the girl's body, and as he lay stretched out beside her, it seemed to him that he was not resting after two acts of love but after months of running.

PART FIVE

The Poet Is Jealous

1

While Jaromil ran, the world changed; his uncle, who thought that Voltaire was the inventor of volts, was falsely accused of fraud (like thousands of other shop-keepers at that time), his two shops were confiscated (from then on they belonged to the state), and he was sent to prison for several years; his wife and son were expelled from Prague as class enemies. They left the villa in icy silence, determined never to forgive Mama, whose son had sided with the family's enemies.

A family to whom the local authorities had assigned the ground-floor rooms moved into the villa. They came from miserable lodgings in a converted basement and considered it unjust for anyone to have owned such a spacious and pleasant villa; they thought that they hadn't come to the villa merely to live in it but to redress a long-standing historical injustice. Without asking for permission, they took over the garden, and they demanded that Mama have the peeling plaster of the walls repaired to prevent their children from being hurt when they played outside.

Grandmama had aged; she lost her memory entirely, and one fine day (almost unnoticed) she turned into smoke at the crematorium.

It's no surprise that Mama found it hard to bear seeing her son escape her; he was studying subjects she disliked, and he had stopped showing her his poems, which she had become used to reading regularly. When she tried to open his drawer she found it locked; it was like a slap in the face; Jaromil suspected her of rummaging through his things! But when she opened it with an extra key Jaromil didn't know about, she found no new entries in his diary and no new poems. Then, seeing the photo of her uniformed husband on the wall of the little room, she recalled that long ago she had implored the statuette of Apollo to erase her husband's features from the fruit of her womb. Oh, no—did she still have to contend with her deceased husband over her son?

About a week after the evening at the end of the preceding part, when we left Jaromil in the redhead's bed, Mama again opened his desk drawer. She found in his diary several laconic remarks she didn't understand, but she also discovered something much more important: new poems. Apollo's lyre, she reflected, had again prevailed over her husband's uniform, and she quietly rejoiced.

After reading the poems she was still more favorably impressed, because she really liked them (actually for the very first time!); they rhymed (deep down, Mama always thought that an unrhymed poem was no poem at all) and, moreover, they were easily understandable and full of pretty words; there were no old people, no bodies rotting in the earth, no sagging bellies or pus at the corners of eyes; there were instead the names of flowers, the sky, clouds, and several times (something completely new in Jaromil's poems!) the word "mama."

Then Jaromil came home; when she heard his steps on the stairs, all the years of suffering rose to her eyes, and she couldn't hold back a sob.

"Mama, what's the matter—my God, what's wrong?" he asked, and she heard a tenderness in his voice that she had not sensed in a long time.

"Nothing, Jaromil, nothing," she answered, encouraged to sob all the more by her son's concern. Once again her tears were of several kinds: tears of sorrow, because she had been abandoned; tears of reproach, because her son had neglected her; tears of hope, because he might (by means of the new poems' melodious phrases) finally come back to her; tears of anger, because he was just standing there awkwardly, incapable even of stroking her hair; tears of deceit, expected to stir him and keep him near her.

After a moment of embarrassment, he ended up taking her hand; that was beautiful; Mama stopped crying, and words began to flow from her as generously as tears had moments before; she talked about everything that tormented her: her widowhood, her loneliness, the tenants trying to drive her out of her own house, her sister closing the door on her ("because of you, Jaromil!"), and then the main thing: the only human being in the world she had in this horrible loneliness turned his back on her.

"But that's not true, I'm not turning my back on you!"

She could not accept such easy assurances, and she laughed bitterly; as for not turning his back, he came home late at night; whole days went by without a word exchanged between them; and when they did manage to talk, she knew very well that he wasn't listening but thinking of something else. Yes, he treated her like a stranger.

"No, Mama, come on!"

Again she laughed bitterly. He didn't treat her like a stranger? She'd have to show him proof! She'd have to tell him what hurt her? She'd always respected his privacy; even when he was a little boy she had struggled with everyone to get him his own room; and now, what an insult! Jaromil couldn't imagine what she felt the day she learned (completely by chance, while dusting the furniture in his room) that he locked his desk drawers! Why did he lock them? Did he really think that she was going to stick her nose into his business like a busybody?

"Mama, that's a misunderstanding! I don't use that drawer anymore! If it's locked it's by chance!"

Mama knew that her son was lying, but that wasn't important; much more important than the lying words was the humility in his voice, which seemed to be offering reconciliation. "I want to believe you, Jaromil," she said, and she squeezed his hand.

As he looked at her, she became conscious of her teary face, and she left for the bathroom, where she was horrified by her reflection in the mirror; her tear-stained face seemed hideous to her; she even

254

reproached herself for still wearing the gray dress she had worn to the office. She quickly washed her face with cold water, put on a pink dressing gown, went to the kitchen, and came back with a bottle of wine. Then she began to talk effusively, saying that they should again trust each other, because they had no one else in this sad world. She talked on this theme for a long time, and the look in Jaromil's eyes seemed friendly and approving. She thus allowed herself to say that she had no doubt that Jaromil, now a university student, certainly had his personal secrets, which she respected; she only hoped that any woman in Jaromil's life would not disrupt their relationship.

Jaromil listened patiently and with understanding. He had avoided Mama for some time because his sorrow required solitude and murkiness. But since his landing on the sunny shore of the redhead's body, he had been longing for peace and light; disagreement with Mama troubled him. Feelings apart, there was also a more practical consideration: the redhead had a room of her own while Jaromil lived with Mama, and if he wanted to lead a personal life he could do so only through his girl's independence. He bitterly resented this inequality, and he was glad that Mama was now sitting beside him in a pink dressing gown and with a glass of wine, giving him the impression of a pleasant young woman with whom he could come to an amicable agreement regarding his rights.

He told her that he had nothing to hide from her (Mama felt her throat tighten), and he started to talk

about the redheaded girl. He didn't say, of course, that
Mama already knew her by sight from the store where
she shopped, but he did tell her that the girl was eighteen and that she was not a student but a simple girl (he
said this almost aggressively), earning her living with
her own hands.

Mama poured some more wine and thought that
things were taking a turn for the better. The picture of
the girl that her son, his tongue loosened, was drawing
for her allayed her anxiety: the girl was very young (the
horrifying vision of a depraved older woman happily
vanished), she wasn't overeducated (Mama thus had no
fear of the strength of her influence), and finally Jaromil
had so emphasized, in a nearly suspect manner, the
virtues of her simplicity and kindness that she concluded the girl was probably not much of a beauty
(enabling Mama to assume, to her secret satisfaction,
that her son's infatuation would not last very long).

Jaromil perceived that Mama didn't disapprove of
the person he had described, and this made him happy;
he imagined sitting at the same table with Mama and
the redhead, with the angel of his childhood and the
angel of his adulthood; that seemed to him as beautiful
as peace; peace between home and the world; peace
beneath the wings of two angels.

And so, after a long break, mother and son again
experienced a happy intimacy. They talked for a long
while, but Jaromil never lost sight of his modest practical objective: the right to bring his girlfriend to his room
whenever and for as long as he liked; for he understood

that the only true adult is someone who is the unrestrained master of a closed-off space where he can do what he wishes without being observed and watched over by anyone. He said this (cautiously and in a roundabout way) to Mama; he would feel more at home if he could consider himself his own master there.

Despite the wine haze, Mama was still the vigilant tigress: "Are you saying, Jaromil, that you're not your own master here?"

Jaromil replied that he liked his home very much but that he wanted the right to bring anyone here, to have the same independence here that the redhead had from her landlady.

Mama realized that Jaromil was offering her a great opportunity; she too had several admirers whom she had been compelled to turn away because she feared Jaromil's disapproval. Couldn't she, with a bit of cleverness, exchange Jaromil's freedom for a bit of freedom for herself?

But the thought that Jaromil could bring a woman into his childhood room filled her with insurmountable disgust: "You have to understand that there's a difference between a mother and a landlady," she said, offended, and at the same moment she realized that she was deliberately preventing herself from living the life of a woman again. She understood that the disgust aroused in her by her son's carnal life was stronger than her body's desire to live its own life, and she was terrified by this discovery.

Jaromil, stubbornly pursuing his objective, didn't

perceive Mama's state of mind and continued to pursue
a lost cause, raising further useless arguments. After a
while he noticed tears running down Mama's face. It
frightened him that he had offended the angel of his
childhood, and he fell silent. In the mirror of Mama's
tears he suddenly saw his demand for independence as
insolence, shamelessness, even obscene impudence.

Mama was in despair: she saw the abyss reopening
between her and her son. She had gained nothing, she
was going to lose everything once more! Thinking
quickly, she wondered what she could do to prevent a
complete break in the precious thread of understanding
between her and her son; she took his hand, and in
tears, said:

"Jaromil, please don't be angry! I'm so unhappy to
see how much you've changed. You've changed so
much recently."

"How have I changed? I haven't changed at all,
Mama."

"Yes, you've changed. And I'm going to tell you what
hurts me most. It's that you've stopped writing poetry.
You wrote such beautiful poems, and it hurts me that
you're not writing them anymore."

Jaromil was about to answer, but she didn't let him
speak: "Believe your mama. I know something about it;
you have immense talent; it's your vocation; you mustn't
abandon it: you're a poet, Jaromil, you're a poet, and it
makes me ill to see that you've forgotten it."

Jaromil heard Mama's words with near enthusiasm.
It was true, the angel of his childhood understood him

better than anyone else! Wasn't he himself also tormented by the thought that he was no longer writing?

"Mama, I've started writing poetry again, I've written it! I'll show it to you!"

"That's not true, Jaromil," Mama replied, shaking her head sadly. "Don't try to mislead me, I know very well that you're not writing."

"But I am! I'm writing! I'm writing!" Jaromil shouted, and he rushed over to his room, opened his drawer, and returned with his poems.

Mama read the same poems she had read a few hours earlier, kneeling in front of Jaromil's desk:

"Oh, Jaromil, these are such beautiful poems! You've made great progress, great progress. You're a poet, and I'm so happy . . . "

2

Everything seemed to indicate that Jaromil's immense desire for the new (the religion of the New) had merely been the desire for inconceivable, still unknown, coition, a desire projected into a foggy distance; the first time he landed on the shore of the redhead's body, the strange idea came to him that he finally knew what it meant to be absolutely modern; to be absolutely modern meant to lie on the shore of the redhead's body.

He was so happy and full of enthusiasm at this moment that he wanted to recite poetry to the girl; he thought about the poems he knew by heart (his own and other poets'), but he realized (with some amazement) that the redhead wouldn't like any of them, and he concluded that the only poems that were absolutely modern were those that the redhead, a girl of the crowd, could understand and appreciate.

It was like a sudden illumination: Why stomp on the throat of his own song? Why give up poetry for the sake of the revolution? Now that he had landed on the shore of real life (by "real life" he was referring to the density created by the fusion of the crowd, physical love, and revolutionary slogans), all he had to do was give himself up entirely to this life and become its violin.

He felt full of poetry and tried to write a poem the redheaded girl would like. That wasn't so simple; until now he had written unrhymed verse, and he now came up against the technical difficulties of regular verse, for it was certain that the redhead regarded a poem as something that rhymed. Besides, the victorious revolution was of the same opinion; let's recall that in those days no free verse was published; modern poetry as a whole was denounced as a product of the putrefying bourgeoisie, and free verse was the most obvious sign of the putrefaction of poetry.

Isn't the victorious revolution's love for rhyme merely a chance infatuation? Probably not. Rhyme and rhythm possess magical power: the formless world enclosed in regular verse all at once becomes limpid, orderly, clear, and beautiful. If in a poem the word "death" is in the same spot as the sound "breath" echoing in the preceding line, death becomes a melodious element of order. And even if the poem is protesting against death, death is automatically justified, at least as the theme of a beautiful protest. Bones, roses, coffins, wounds—everything in a poem changes into a ballet, and the poet and the reader are the dancers in this ballet. The dancers, of course, cannot disagree with the dance. By means of a poem, man achieves his agreement with being, and rhyme and rhythm are the most violent way to gain agreement. Doesn't a revolution that has just triumphed need a violent affirmation of the new order, and therefore poetry filled with rhyme?

"Join me in delirium!" Vitezslav Nezval cried out to his reader, and Baudelaire wrote: "One must always be drunk . . . on wine, on poetry, or on virtue, as you wish. . . ." Lyricism is intoxication, and man drinks in order to merge more easily with the world. Revolution has no desire to be examined or analyzed, it only desires that the people merge with it; in this sense it is lyrical and in need of lyricism.

The revolution, of course, had in mind poetry of a kind other than the poetry Jaromil used to write; at that time he was rapturously observing the quiet adventures and beautiful eccentricities of his own self; but now he emptied his soul as a hangar for the world's noisy brass bands to enter; he had exchanged the beauty of singularities that he alone understood for the beauty of generalities that everyone understood.

He passionately hoped to restore to favor the old beauties at which modern art (with its apostate's pride) had turned up its nose: sunsets, roses, dewy grass, the stars, darkness, a melody heard from afar, mama, and nostalgia; oh, how beautiful that world was, familiar and comprehensible! Jaromil was returning there with amazement and emotion, like a prodigal son returning after long years to the house he had abandoned.

Oh, to be simple, totally simple, simple like a folk song, like a nursery rhyme, like a brook, like a little redhead!

To be at the source of eternal beauties, to love the words "far away," "silver," "rainbow," "love," and even that much-despised little word "oh!"

Jaromil was also fascinated by certain verbs: above all those that represent simple forward movement: "run," "walk," and especially "sail" and "fly." In a poem he wrote for Lenin's birthday, he threw an apple branch into a stream (this gesture charmed him because it was linked to old popular customs like throwing wreaths of flowers into the current), so that it would be borne on the water to Lenin's country; not a single river runs from Bohemia to Russia, but a poem is a magical territory where rivers change their course. In another poem he wrote that "some day the world will be free like the fragrance of firs that spans the mountain ranges." In another he spoke of the fragrance of jasmine being so powerful that it becomes an invisible sailing ship floating in the air; he imagined himself on the bridge of this fragrance and that he was sailing far, far away, away to Marseilles, where (as he had read in *Rude Pravo*) the workers he wished to join as a comrade and brother had just gone on strike.

This is also why the most poetic instrument of motion, wings, appeared countless times in his poems: night was filled with a "silent beating of wings"; desire, sadness, even hatred, and of course time had wings.

What was hidden in all these words was the desire for a *boundless embrace*, which seemed to recall Schiller's famous lines: "*Seid umschlungen, Millionen! / Diesen Kuss der ganzen Welt!*" This boundless embrace encompassed not only space but also time; the destination of the flight was not only Marseilles on strike but also the *future*, that miraculous distant island.

Previously the future had above all been a mystery to Jaromil; everything unknown was hidden there; that was why it at once attracted and frightened him; it was the contrary of certainty, the contrary of home (this is why in times of anxiety he dreamed about the love of old people, who were happy because they no longer had a future). But the revolution gave the future an opposite meaning: the future was no longer a mystery; a revolutionary knew it by heart; he knew it from brochures, books, lectures, propaganda speeches; it didn't frighten, on the contrary, it offered certainty within an uncertain present, so that a revolutionary rushed to it for refuge like a child to its mama.

Jaromil wrote a poem about a Communist functionary asleep late at night on the couch in the secretariat, at the hour when "dawn is breaking on the thoughtful meeting" (at the time the idea of a Communist fighter was always expressed as a Communist at a meeting); the clang of the streetcar bell under the windows becomes in his dream a chiming of bells, the chiming of all the bells in the world announcing that there would be no more wars and that the globe belongs to the workers. He realizes that a miraculous leap has transported him to the distant future; he is somewhere in the countryside, and coming toward him on her tractor is a woman (on all the posters the woman of the future was depicted as a woman on a tractor) who recognizes him, with amazement, as a kind of man she has never seen before, a man of the past worn out by labor, a man who had sacrificed himself so that she would be able to work joyfully (and singing) in the fields. She descends from her machine to welcome him, saying: "This is your home, this is your world . . . ," and she wants to reward him (my God, how could this young woman reward an old militant worn out on the job?); at this moment the streetcar bells down in the street start clanging very loudly and the man sleeping on the narrow couch in a corner of the secretariat awakens. . . .

Jaromil had already written quite a few new poems, but he wasn't satisfied, because only he and Mama had read them. He sent all of them to *Rude Pravo*, and he bought the newspaper every morning; one day he finally found five quatrains on the top right of page three, with his name in boldface under the title. That same day he handed a copy of *Rude Pravo* to the redhead and told her to look through it carefully; she examined the paper for a long time without finding anything remarkable (as a rule she paid no attention to poetry, so she paid no attention to the names of its authors), and in the end Jaromil had to point his finger at the poem.

"I had no idea you were a poet," she said, looking into his eyes admiringly.

Jaromil told her that he had been writing poetry for a very long time, and he took some typed poems out of his pocket.

The redhead read them, and Jaromil told her he had stopped writing poetry some time ago, but that he had begun again after coming to know her. Meeting her was like meeting Poetry itself.

"Really?" asked the girl, and when Jaromil nodded she embraced and kissed him.

"What's extraordinary," Jaromil went on, "is that you're not only the queen of the poems I'm writing now but also of those that I wrote before I met you. When I saw you the first time, it seemed to me that my old poems had come back to life and turned into a woman."

He gazed eagerly at her curious and incredulous face and began to tell her that several years ago he had written a long piece of poetic prose, a kind of fantastic story about a young man named Xavier. Written? Not really. It was rather that he had dreamed his adventures and wanted to write them down someday.

Xavier lived in a competely different way from other people; his life was sleep; Xavier slept and had a dream; in that dream he fell asleep and had another dream and in that dream he slept again and had still another dream; he woke up from that dream and found himself in the preceding dream; he thus went from dream to dream and lived several successive lives; he lived in several lives and passed from one to the other. Wasn't it marvelous to live as Xavier lived? Not to be imprisoned in a single life? To be mortal, of course, and yet to have several lives?

"Yes, it would be nice . . . ," said the redhead.

And Jaromil told her that the day he first saw her in the store he had been dumbfounded because she looked exactly the way he had imagined Xavier's great love to look: a frail, redheaded woman, with a delicately freckled face. . . .

"I'm ugly!" said the redhead.

"No! I love your freckles and your red hair! I love them because they're my home, my homeland, my old dream!"

The redhead kissed Jaromil, and he went on: "Imag-

ine that the whole story started like this: Xavier likes to
walk through smoky suburban streets; he passes a
basement window, stops, and has a reverie about a
beautiful woman who perhaps lives behind that window. One day there is a light in that window and he sees
a tender, frail, redheaded girl. He can't resist—he opens
the shutters wide and jumps inside.

"But you ran away from my window!" said the redhead, laughing.

"Yes, I ran away," Jaromil admitted, "because I was
afraid of having that same dream again! Do you know
what it's like to find yourself suddenly in a situation
you've already experienced in a dream? It's something
so frightening that you want to escape!"

"Yes," the redhead happily agreed.

"So he jumps inside to get to the girl, but then her
husband comes in, and Xavier locks him into a heavy
oak wardrobe. The husband is there to this day, turned
into a skeleton. And Xavier takes the woman far away,
just as I'm going to take you."

"You're my Xavier," whispered the redhead gratefully in Jaromil's ear, and she improvised variations on
that name, turning it into Xavi, Xaxa, Xavipet, and she
called him by all these diminutives and kissed him for a
long, long time.

3

Among Jaromil's numerous visits to the redheaded girl's room, I wish to mention in particular the one when she was wearing a dress with a row of large white buttons all the way down its front. Jaromil began to unbutton them, and the girl burst out laughing because the buttons served only as decoration.

"Wait, I'll undress myself," she said, and she raised her arms to reach the zipper at the back of her neck.

Jaromil was irritated at having shown his ineptness, and at last understanding the way the garment was fastened, he quickly tried to nullify his failure.

"No, no, I'll undress myself, let me do it!" said the girl, backing away from him and laughing.

He couldn't keep insisting because he was afraid of seeming ridiculous, but it was utterly unpleasant to him that the girl wanted to undress herself. To his mind the difference between amorous undressing and ordinary undressing consisted precisely in the woman being undressed by the man.

This idea had not been instilled in him by experience, but by literature and its suggestive phrases: "he knew how to disrobe a woman"; or "he impatiently tore off her dress." He could not imagine physical love without a prologue of confused and eager gestures to undo buttons, pull down zippers, lift up sweaters.

He complained: "It's not as if you're at the doctor's, undressing yourself." But the girl had already taken off her dress and was wearing only her underwear.

"At the doctor's? Why?"

"Yes, you seem to me as if you're at the doctor's."

"Of course," said the girl. "It's just the way it is at the doctor's."

She took off her bra and stood in front of Jaromil, thrusting her small breasts at him. "I have a sharp pain here, Doctor, next to my heart."

Jaromil looked at her uncomprehendingly, and she said, by way of apology: "I'm sorry, Doctor, you're probably used to examining your patients lying down," and she lay down on the bed. "Please take a look! What's wrong with my heart?"

Jaromil had no choice but to go along with the game; he leaned over the girl's chest and put the side of his head over her heart; he touched the soft fullness of her breast with his ear and heard a regular beat. He thought that the doctor probably touched the redhead's breasts like this when he listened to the sounds in her chest behind the closed, mysterious doors of the examining room. He raised his head, looked at the naked girl, and felt a sharp pain, for he was seeing her just as another man, the doctor, saw her. He quickly placed both his hands on the redhead's chest (not the doctor's way but his own) so as to put an end to this painful game.

The redhead complained: "Now, now, Doctor, what are you doing? You're not allowed to do that! That's not part of the examination!" Jaromil flared up: he saw what his girlfriend's face expressed when a stranger's hands were touching her; he saw that she was complaining frivolously, and he wanted to hit her; but at that very moment he realized that he had become aroused, and he tore off the girl's underpants and entered her.

His arousal was so great that Jaromil's jealous rage quickly weakened, all the more when he heard the girl's moans (that splendid homage) and the words that had become a perpetual part of their intimate moments: "Xavi, Xaxa, Xavipet!"

Afterward he lay quietly beside her, tenderly kissed her on the shoulder, and felt good. But that scatterbrain was incapable of being satisfied with a beautiful *moment*; a beautiful moment was meaningful to him only if it was an emissary from a beautiful eternity; a beautiful moment that had fallen from a tarnished eternity was only a lie to him. He wanted therefore to be sure that their eternity was unblemished, and he asked, more pleadingly than aggressively: "Tell me that it's just a bad joke, that stuff with the doctor."

"Of course it is!" said the girl; what else could she say to such a stupid question? But Jaromil wasn't satisfied with that "Of course it is"; he went on:

"I couldn't bear it if anyone else's hands touched you. I couldn't bear it," and he caressed the girl's meager breasts as if his entire happiness depended on their inviolability.

The girl started to laugh (quite innocently): "But what do you want me to do when I get sick?"

Jaromil knew that it was hard to avoid medical

examinations and that his position was indefensible; but he also knew that if someone else's hands were to touch the girl's breasts, his whole world would crumble. And so he repeated:

"I couldn't bear it, do you understand, I couldn't bear it."

"Then what should I do if I'm sick?"

He said softly and reproachfully: "You could find a woman doctor."

"As if I have a choice! You know how it works," she answered, indignantly this time, "everybody is assigned a doctor! Don't you know what socialist medicine is? You have no choice and you have to obey! Take gynecological consultations, for instance. . . ."

Jaromil felt his heart skip a beat, but he said calmly: "Is something wrong with you?"

"No, it's just preventive medicine. Because of cancer. It's compulsory."

"Keep quiet, I don't want to hear about it," said Jaromil, and put his hand over her mouth; his gesture was so fierce that it nearly frightened him, for the redhead could think of it as a blow and become angry; but the girl's eyes looked at him so humbly that Jaromil felt no need to moderate the involuntary roughness of his gesture; he took pleasure in it, and he said:

"I want you to know that if anyone ever touches you, I'll never touch you again."

He was still holding his hand over the girl's mouth; it was the first time he had ever touched a woman roughly, and he found it intoxicating; he then put his hands around her throat, as though he were choking her; he felt the fragility of her neck under his fingers, and he thought that he only had to clench them in order to strangle her.

"I'll strangle you if anyone ever touches you," he said, and he still had his hands around the girl's throat; he was thrilled to feel the girl's possible nonexistence in this contact; he thought that, at least at this moment, the redhead really belonged to him, and a sensation of elated power intoxicated him, a sensation so beautiful that he began again to make love.

During the lovemaking he squeezed her roughly several times, put his hand on her neck (he thought it would be beautiful to strangle a beloved while making love), and also bit her several times.

Afterward they lay side by side, but the lovemaking had probably not lasted long enough to dissipate the young man's anger; the redhead, unstrangled, alive, was lying beside him, a naked body that went to gynecological consultations.

She caressed his hand: "Don't be angry with me."

"I'm telling you that a body other men have touched disgusts me."

The girl realized that Jaromil was serious; she said insistently: "Dammit, it was only a joke!"

"It was no joke! It was the truth."

"It wasn't the truth."

"Sure it was! It was the truth, and I know there's nothing to be done about it. Gynecological consultations are compulsory, and you have to go. I'm not blaming you. But a body other men touch is repellent to me. I can't help it, that's how it is."

"I swear to you there's no truth to it! I've never been sick except when I was a child. I never go to the doctor. I was summoned to a gynecological consultation, but I threw away the notification. I never went."

"I don't believe you."

It was an effort to convince him.

"And what will you do if they summon you again?"

"Don't worry, they're totally disorganized."

He believed her, but his bitterness couldn't be eased by practical arguments; it wasn't only a matter of medical examinations; the root of the problem was that she eluded him, that she was not totally his.

"I love you so much," she said, but he placed no confidence in that brief moment; he wanted eternity; he wanted at least the small eternity of the redheaded girl's life, and he knew that he didn't have it: he recalled that he had not known her as a virgin.

"I can't bear the idea that someone else is going to touch you and that someone else has already touched you," he said.

"No one's going to touch me."

"But someone's already touched you. And that disgusts me."

She put her arms around him.

He pushed her away.

"How many men have you had before me?"

"Just one."

"Don't lie!"

"I swear there's only been one."

"Did you love him?"

She shook her head.

"How could you go to bed with someone you didn't love?"

"Don't torture me," she said.

"Answer me! How could you do that?"

"Don't torture me. I didn't love him, and it was horrible."

"What was horrible?"

"Don't ask me anything about it."

"Why don't you want me to ask you anything about it?"

She dissolved into tears and, still weeping, confided to him that it had been an old man in her village, that he was revolting, that she was completely in his power ("Don't ask me about it"), that she couldn't even remember him ("If you love me, never remind me of him again!").

She wept for so long that Jaromil forgot his anger; tears are excellent stain removers.

He caressed her: "Don't cry."

"You're my Xavipet," she said. "You came in through the window, and you locked him into a wardrobe, and he'll be a skeleton there and you're going to take me far, far away."

They embraced and kissed. The girl assured him that she couldn't bear anyone else's hands on her body, and he assured her that he loved her. They began to make love again; they made love tenderly, their bodies brimming with soul.

"You're my Xavipet," she said to him afterward, caressing him.

"Yes, I'll take you far away, where you'll be safe," he said, and he knew right away where he would take her: he had a tent for her under the blue sail of peace, a tent above which birds fly on their way to the future, fragrances flow toward the strikers of Marseilles; he had a house for her watched over by the angel of his childhood.

"You know, I'm going to introduce you to my mama," he said, and his eyes were filled with tears.

4

The family that occupied the rooms on the ground floor of the villa could boast of the mother's protuberant belly; a third child was on the way, and the father stopped Jaromil's mama one day to tell her that it was unjust for two people to occupy the same space as five; he suggested she give up one of the three rooms on the second floor. Jaromil's mother replied that this was not possible. The tenant answered that in that case the authorities would have to see to it that the rooms in the villa were equitably redistributed. Mama asserted that her son was about to get married, and that there would soon be three and perhaps four people on the second floor.

Thus, when Jaromil told her a few days later that he wanted to introduce his girlfriend to her, the visit seemed timely to Mama; the tenants would at least see that she hadn't lied when she spoke of her son's forthcoming marriage.

But later, when he admitted to Mama that she already knew the girl from seeing her at the store, she was unable to hide an expression of unpleasant surprise.

"I hope it doesn't embarrass you," he said belligerently, "that she's just a salesgirl. I've already told you that she's a working woman, a simple girl."

It took Mama a few moments to accept the idea that the shallow, unpleasant, and unattractive girl was her son's beloved, but she was able to control herself: "It shouldn't be held against me, but it surprises me," she said, ready to endure whatever her son had in store for her.

So the visit took place; it lasted three painful hours. All three of them had stage fright, but they underwent the ordeal to the end.

When Jaromil was alone again with Mama, he asked her eagerly: "Well, did you like her?"

"I liked her very much, why shouldn't I like her?" she replied, well aware that her tone of voice indicated the opposite.

"So you didn't like her?"

"I just told you I liked her very much."

"No, I can tell from your tone of voice that you didn't like her. You're not saying what you think."

During the visit the redhead had perpetrated numerous awkwardnesses (she was the first to extend her hand to Mama, she was the first to sit down at the table, she was the first to bring her cup of coffee to her lips), numerous impolitenesses (she interrupted Mama), and tactlessnesses (she asked Mama how old she was); while Mama was enumerating these faux pas she suddenly feared that she might seem small-minded to her son (Jaromil regarded excessive attachment to the rules of etiquette as petit-bourgeois), and she quickly added:

"Of course, there's nothing incurable about it. Just keep inviting her here a bit more. In our environment she'll become refined and well mannered."

But the thought that she would have to see this red-headed, ungainly, hostile body with some regularity again gave her an overwhelming feeling of disgust, and she said in a comforting voice: "Of course, you can't blame her for being what she is. You have to imagine the environment in which she grew up and where she works. I wouldn't want to be a salesgirl in a store like that. Everybody takes liberties with you, you have to be at everybody's disposal. If the boss wants to seduce a girl, she can't refuse him. In such an environment, of course, an affair of that kind isn't considered important."

She watched her son's face and saw it flush; a scalding wave of jealousy filled Jaromil's body, and Mama herself seemed to feel that same heat (yes, it was actually the same scalding wave she had felt a few hours ago when she had seen the redhead for the first time, so I might say that they now stood face to face like two communicating vessels through which the same acid flowed). Her son's face was again childlike and submissive; suddenly she was no longer facing a strange, independent man but her suffering beloved child, a child who not long ago would run to her for refuge and whom she would console. She couldn't tear her eyes away from this splendid spectacle.

Jaromil left for his own room, and she surprised herself (after some moments alone) by beating her head with her fists and reprimanding herself in an undertone: "Stop it, stop it, don't be jealous; stop it, don't be jealous."

Nevertheless the deed had been done. The tent stitched up out of airy blue sails, the tent of harmony watched over by the angel of childhood, was in tatters.

For mother and son the era of jealousy was beginning.

Mama's words about affairs that aren't considered important kept resounding in Jaromil's head. He imagined the redhead's fellow workers at the store telling dirty jokes, he imagined the lewd moment of contact established between listener and narrator, and he was horribly tormented. He imagined the store owner rubbing up against her body, surreptitiously touching her breasts or slapping her buttocks, and he was made furious by the thought that such contact wasn't considered important, whereas for him it meant everything. One day when he was at her place, he noticed that she had forgotten to close the toilet door behind her. He made a scene about it, for he immediately imagined her in the toilet at the store and a man inadvertently surprising her sitting on the bowl.

When he revealed his jealousy to the redhead, she managed to calm him with tenderness and pledges of love; but as soon as he found himself alone in his childhood room, the thought recurred that there was no guarantee that the redhead's assurances were true. Besides, wasn't he himself forcing her to lie to him? By reacting so violently to the idea of an insignificant medical consultation, hadn't he prevented her, once and for all, from telling him what she was thinking?

They were over, the happy early days of their love, when the caresses were cheerful and he was full of gratitude to her for having led him with such spontaneous assurance out of the labyrinth of virginity. He was now submitting what he had been so grateful for to a harsh analysis; again and again he evoked the shameless touch of the girl's hand that had so wonderfully aroused him the first time he went to her place; he was now scrutinizing it with suspicion: it wasn't possible, he thought, that he, Jaromil, was the first man she had ever touched that way; if she had dared to employ such a shameless gesture half an hour after meeting him, this gesture must have been totally ordinary and mechanical for her.

What a terrible thought! He had of course already accepted the idea that she'd had another man before him, but only because the girl's words had presented the picture of a liaison that from beginning to end had been bitter and painful, with herself nothing but an exploited victim; that awakened pity in him, and pity diluted his jealousy somewhat. But if the girl had learned that shameful gesture during the liaison, it couldn't have been a total disaster. There was too much joy in that gesture; in that gesture there was an entire little erotic history!

The subject was too painful for him to muster the courage to talk about, for the mere mention of the lover who had preceded him caused him great torment. Nevertheless he tried in a roundabout way to find the origin of the gesture he constantly thought about (and continued to experience, for the redhead delighted in it), and finally he put his mind at ease with the idea that a great love, which abruptly arrives like a lightning bolt, frees a woman at one stroke from all shame and inhibition, and she, just because she is pure and innocent, gives herself to her lover just as quickly as a loose woman; better still: love frees in her such a powerful source of unexpected inspiration that her spontaneous behavior can resemble the expert procedures of a depraved woman. The genius of love instantaneously replaces every experience. This conclusion seemed beautiful and shrewd to him; in its light his girlfriend became a saint of love.

Then one day a fellow student said to him: "Tell me, who was that I saw you with yesterday? She was no beauty!"

He denied her as Peter denied Christ; he claimed she was a casual acquaintance; he spoke of her with disdain. But just as Peter remained faithful to Christ, Jaromil deep down remained faithful to his girlfriend. He did restrict their walks together through the streets, and he was glad when no one he knew saw her with him, but at the same time he actually disagreed with the student and detested him. And he was at once moved by the thought that his girlfriend wore cheap, unattractive dresses, seeing in this not only her charm (the charm of simplicity and poverty) but also and above all the charm of his own love: he reflected that it was not difficult to love someone dazzling, perfect, elegant: such love was a meaningless reflex automatically aroused in us by the accident of beauty; but a great love wishes to create a beloved being precisely out of an imperfect creature, a creature all the more human for her imperfection.

One day as he was once again declaring his love for her (probably after an exhausting quarrel), she said:

"Anyway, I don't know what you see in me. There are so many girls more beautiful than me."

He explained indignantly that beauty had nothing to do with love. He asserted that he loved in her what everyone else found ugly; in a kind of delirium he even began to enumerate: he told her she had meager, sad little breasts with big, wrinkled nipples that aroused pity rather than enthusiasm; he said that she had freckles and red hair and that her body was skinny, and all of that was precisely why he loved her.

The redhead burst into tears because she understood the reality (the meager breasts, the red hair) all too well and the idea not at all.

Jaromil, on the other hand, was carried away by his idea; the tears of the girl, who suffered from not being beautiful, warmed him in his loneliness and inspired him; he thought that he would devote his entire life to making her forget these tears and to convincing her of his love. In this rush of emotion, the redhead's first lover was no more than one of the uglinesses he loved in her. That was a truly remarkable feat of will and of thought; he realized this and began to write a poem:

"Tell me about her I ceaselessly think of, / tell me how she ages [he wanted to possess her completely anew, with all her human eternity], / tell me what she was like as a child [he wanted her not only with her future but also with her past], / give me a drink of the waters she wept [and above all of her sadness, which relieved him of his], / tell me about the lovers who stole her youth; / about all those who pawed her / all those who mocked her / all of that I will love; . . . [and a bit further on]: there is nothing in her soul, in her body / not even the putridity of her old lovers / that I will not drink to intoxication. . . ."

Jaromil was enthusiastic about what he had written, for in place of the great sky blue tent of harmony, in place of the artificial space where all contradictions are abolished, where mother and son and daughter-in-law sit at a common peace table, he had found another dwelling house of the absolute, an absolute more harsh and genuine. For if the absolute of purity and peace does not exist, there does exist an absolute of infinite feeling in which, as in a chemical solution, everything impure and foreign is dissolved.

He was enthusiastic about this poem, even though he knew that no newspaper would publish it, for it had nothing to do with the cheerful era of socialism; but he had written it for himself and the redhead. When he read it to her she was moved to tears, but at the same time she was frightened once again by the allusions to her ugliness, to her being groped, to the coming of old age.

The girl's misgivings didn't bother Jaromil. On the contrary, he liked and savored them; he liked to dwell on them and refute them at length. But the worst was that the girl didn't wish to spend much time discussing the poem, and she changed the subject.

He forgave her her pathetic breasts and the hands of the strangers who had touched them, but there was one thing he couldn't forgive: her endless chatter. Look, he had just read her something that was entirely himself, containing his passion, his sensitivity, his blood, and after a few minutes she began to talk gaily about something else!

Yes, he was ready to make all her faults vanish in the all-forgiving solvent of his love, but only under one condition: that she obediently immerse herself in that solvent, that she never be anywhere else but in that bathtub of love, that she never try, not even in a single thought, to leave that tub, that she be entirely submerged below the surface of Jaromil's words and thoughts, that she be submerged in his world and that the least particle of her body or mind not spend a moment in another world.

Instead she went on talking, and not only talking but talking about her family! Now, her family was what Jaromil disliked most about her, because he didn't know how to object to it (it was a perfectly innocent family, and moreover a proletarian family, a family of the crowd), but he wanted to object to it because when she thought of her family the redhead was constantly escaping from the bathtub he had prepared for her and filled with the solvent of his love.

Thus he had to listen yet again to stories about her father (an old peasant worn out in harness), about her brothers and sisters (it wasn't a family but a rabbit hutch, Jaromil thought: two sisters and four brothers!), and especially about one of her brothers (his name was Jan, and he must have been an oddball—before 1948 he had been the chauffeur for an anti-

Communist cabinet minister): no, it was not just a family, it was primarily an alien milieu he was hostile to, a milieu whose cocoon still stuck to the redhead's skin, a cocoon that estranged her from him and kept her from being totally and absolutely his; and that brother Jan was not so much the redhead's brother but primarily a man who had seen her up close for all of her eighteen years, a man who knew dozens of intimate little details about her, a man with whom she had shared a bathroom (how many times had she forgotten to bolt the door?), a man who recalled the time when she became a woman, a man who had surely seen her naked many times . . .

"You must be mine to die upon the rack if I want you," the ill and jealous Keats wrote to his Fanny, and Jaromil, back home again in his childhood room, was writing a poem to calm himself. He thought about death, that great embrace that soothes everything; he thought about the death of hard men, great revolutionaries, and he thought that he wanted to write the words for a Communist funeral song.

Death; it too, in that time of compulsory jubilation, was among the nearly forbidden subjects, but Jaromil thought that he would be able (he had already written beautiful poetry about death; in his own way he was an expert on the beauty of death) to find a particular viewpoint that would strip death of its customary morbidity; he felt that he would be able to write *socialist* poetry of death;

he thought of the death of a great revolutionary:

"Like the sun setting behind a mountain, the fighter dies. . . ."

and he wrote a poem called "Epitaph": "If I must die, let it be with you, my love, and only by fire turn into heat and light. . . ."

5

Poetry is a domain in which all assertions become true. Yesterday the poet said: "Life is as useless as tears," today he says: "Life is as joyous as laughter," and he is right both times. Today he says: "Everything ends and gives way to silence," and tomorrow he will say: "Nothing ends and everything eternally resounds," and both are true. The poet has no need to prove anything; the only proof lies in the intensity of his emotion.

The genius of lyricism is the genius of inexperience. The poet knows little about the world, but the words that burst forth from him form beautiful patterns that are as definitive as crystal; the poet is immature, yet his verse has the finality of a prophecy by which he himself is dumbfounded.

"Ah, my aquatic love!" When Mama read Jaromil's first poem, she thought (almost with shame) that her son knew more about love than she did; she didn't suspect anything about Magda being seen through the keyhole, for Mama "aquatic love" represented something more general, a mysterious, rather incomprehensible category of love whose meaning could only be guessed at, like those of sibylline pronouncements.

We can laugh at the poet's immaturity, but we must also marvel at it: in his words there is a droplet that has come from the heart and gives his verse the radiance of beauty. But this droplet has no need for a real experience to draw it out of the poet's heart, and it seems to me rather that the poet himself sometimes squeezes his heart like a cook squeezing a lemon over the salad. To tell the truth, Jaromil didn't much care about the striking workers in Marseilles, but when he wrote a poem about the love he bore them, he was truly moved, and he generously sprayed that emotion over his words, which thus became a flesh-and-blood reality.

With his poems the poet paints his self-portrait; but since no portrait is faithful, I can also say that with his poems he touches up his face.

Touches up? Yes, he makes it more expressive, for the imprecision of his own features torments him; he finds himself blurred, insignificant, nondescript; he is looking for a form for himself; he wants the photographic chemical of his poems to firm up the design of his features.

And he makes it more dramatic, for his life is uneventful. The world of his feelings and dreams, materialized in his poems, often looks turbulent and replaces the actions and adventures that are denied him.

But in order to dress himself in his portrait and enter the world behind this mask, the portrait must be exhibited and the poem published. Several of Jaromil's poems had already appeared in *Rude Pravo*, but he was still dissatisfied. In the letters accompanying the poems he addressed the editor, whom he didn't know, familiarly, hoping to induce an answer and to meet with him. But (it was almost humiliating) even after the poems were published, no literary people were interested in meeting him personally and welcoming him among them; the editor never answered.

Among his fellow university students his poems also didn't arouse the reaction he had counted on. If he had belonged to the elite of contemporary poets who gave public readings and whose photographs shone forth in illustrated magazines, he would perhaps have become a curiosity for the students in his class. But some poems buried in the pages of a newspaper barely held anyone's attention for more than a minute or two, and in the eyes of his fellow students, who were heading toward political or diplomatic careers, Jaromil had become a person uninterestingly odd rather than oddly interesting.

And talk about Jaromil's infinite longing for glory! He longed for it like all poets. "O glory! O mighty deity! Ah, may your great name inspire me and my verse gain you," Victor Hugo implored. "I am a poet, I am a great poet, and one day I shall be loved by the whole world, I must tell myself this, it is how I must pray at the foot of my unfinished mausoleum," Jiri Orten consoled himself with the thought of his future glory.

An obsessive desire for admiration is not only a weakness added on to a lyric poet's talent (as it might be regarded in, for example, a mathematician or an architect) but is also part of the very essence of poetic talent, it is the distinctive mark of a lyric poet: for the poet is the one who offers the world his self-portrait in the hope that his face, projected on the screen of his poems, will be loved and worshipped.

"My soul is an exotic flower with a rare and hyper-sensitive fragrance. I have great talent, perhaps also genius," Jiri Wolker wrote in his diary, and Jaromil, disgusted by the editor's silence, selected some poems and sent them to the most prominent literary monthly. What happiness! Two weeks later he received an answer: his poems were considered interesting, and he was asked to visit the magazine's office. He prepared for this meeting as carefully as he used to prepare for his dates with girls. He decided that he was going to present himself, in the deepest sense of the term, to the editors, and he tried to define who exactly he was, who he was as a poet, who he was as a man, what his plans were, where he came from, what he had overcome, what he loved, what he hated. Finally he picked up pencil and paper and wrote down the essentials of his positions, opinions, stages of development. He filled several pages, and then one day he knocked on the door and entered.

A thin little bespectacled man sitting at a desk asked him what he wanted. Jaromil gave his name. The editor once again asked him what he wanted. Jaromil once again (more distinctly and loudly) gave his name. The editor said he was glad to meet Jaromil, but that he would like to know what he wanted. Jaromil said that he had sent some poems to the magazine and that he had received a letter inviting him to come for a visit. The editor said that his colleague who dealt with poetry was out at the moment. Jaromil said that he was very sorry to hear that because he wanted to know when his poems would appear.

The editor lost his patience, got up from his chair, took Jaromil by the arm, and led him toward a big cabinet. He opened it and showed him piles of paper stacked on the shelves: "My dear comrade, in an average day we receive poems from a dozen new contributors. How many is that per year?"

"I can't figure it out in my head," said Jaromil with embarrassment when the editor insisted he guess.

"It comes to 4,380 new poets per year. Would you like to go abroad?"

"Why not?" said Jaromil.

"Then keep on writing," said the editor. "I'm certain that sooner or later we're going to be exporting poets. Other countries export technicians, engineers, wheat, or coal, but our main resource is lyrical poets. Czech lyrical poets are going to establish lyrical poetry in developing countries. In exchange for our lyrical poets we'll get coconuts and bananas."

A few days later Mama told Jaromil that the school janitor's son had come asking for him. "He said that you should go see him at the Police Building. And he asked me to congratulate you on your poems."

Jaromil blushed with pleasure: "He really said that?"

"Yes. As he was leaving he said: 'Tell him that I congratulate him on his poems. Don't forget.'"

"That makes me very happy, yes, very happy," said Jaromil with particular insistence. "It's for people like him that I write my poems. I don't write for editors. A carpenter doesn't make chairs for other carpenters but for people."

And so one day he went into the huge National Police Building, gave his name to an armed guard, waited in the corridor a while, and shook hands with his old classmate, who had come downstairs to greet him warmly. When they arrived at his office, the janitor's son repeated for the fourth time: "Old pal, I didn't know I went to school with a famous man. I kept saying to myself, maybe it's him or maybe it isn't, but finally I told myself that it's not such a common name."

Then he led Jaromil down the corridor to a big bulletin board on which were tacked a number of photographs (policemen training with dogs, with weapons, with a parachute), two circulars, and in the middle of it all a newspaper clipping of a poem by Jaromil; the clipping was nicely outlined in red pencil and seemed to be presiding over the whole board.

"What do you say?" asked the janitor's son, and Jaromil didn't say anything, but he was happy; it was the first time he had ever seen one of his poems live its own life, independent of him.

The janitor's son took him by the arm and led him back to his office. "See, you probably didn't think policemen read poetry," he said, laughing.

"Why not?" said Jaromil, who was very impressed by the idea that his verse was being read not by old maids but by men who wore revolvers on their behinds. "Why not? There's a big difference between policemen nowadays and the hirelings of the bourgeois republic."

"You probably think cops and poetry don't go together, but that's not so," the janitor's son went on, pursuing his idea.

Jaromil, too, pursued his idea: "Besides, poets nowadays aren't the way they used to be. They aren't spoiled little girls anymore."

The janitor's son continued pursuing the thread of his idea: "It's just because our job is so tough—you can't imagine how tough—that we sometimes need something delicate. Without it we wouldn't be able to bear what we have to do here."

Then he suggested (he was just going off duty) that they go across the street for a couple of beers. "Old pal, it's no joke working here every day," he went on, a beer stein in his hand. "Do you remember what I told you last time about that Jew? He's been locked up. He was scum."

Jaromil of course didn't know that the dark-haired fellow who had led the Marxist youth circle had been arrested; he vaguely suspected that there had been arrests, but he didn't know that people had been arrested by the thousands, Communists among them, that they were tortured, and that their crimes were mostly imaginary; he therefore reacted to the news merely with a simple motion of surprise that expressed no opinion but a bit of astonishment and compassion of the kind that caused the janitor's son to assert vigorously: "In these matters there's no room for sentimentality."

Jaromil was frightened by the thought that the janitor's son was again eluding him, was again way ahead of him. "Don't be surprised that I feel sorry for him. It's normal. But you're right, sentimentality could cost us dearly."

"Very dearly," said the janitor's son.

"None of us wants to be cruel," said Jaromil.

"Certainly not," the janitor's son agreed.

"But we'd be committing the greatest cruelty if we didn't have the courage to be cruel toward the cruel," said Jaromil.

"That's right," the janitor's son agreed.

"No freedom for freedom's enemies. It's cruel, I know, but that's how it has to be."

"It has to," the janitor's son agreed. "I could tell you a lot about that, but I can't and I shouldn't tell you anything. It's all secret, my friend. I can't even talk to my wife about what I do here."

"I know," said Jaromil, "I understand," and once again he envied his old classmate's manly job, his secrecy, and his wife, and also that he had to keep secrets from her and that she had to accept this; he envied his *real life*, whose cruel beauty (and beautiful cruelty) always outstripped him (he didn't at all understand why they arrested the dark-haired man, he only knew that it had to be done), he envied his real life, which he himself had not yet entered.

While Jaromil was musing enviously, the janitor's son gazed deep into his eyes (his lips were slightly open and smiling stupidly) and began to recite the poem he had tacked to the bulletin board; he knew the whole poem by heart and didn't make a single mistake. Not knowing how to react (his old friend never took his eyes off him), Jaromil blushed (aware of the ludicrous naïveté of his old friend's performance), but the happy pride he felt was infinitely stronger than his embarrassment: the janitor's son knew and loved his poem! His poems had thus entered the world of men instead of him, ahead of him, as if they were his emissaries, his advance party! His eyes misted over with tears of blissful self-intoxication; ashamed, he lowered his head.

The janitor's son finished his recitation, still looking into Jaromil's eyes; then he told him that a police academy situated at a big, beautiful villa outside Prague, where young policemen took an annual course, occasionally invited interesting people to address the trainees. "We'd like to invite some poets one Sunday. For a big poetry evening."

They had another beer, and Jaromil said: "It's really good that the police in particular is organizing a poetry evening."

"Why not the police? Why not?"

"Of course, why not?" said Jaromil. "The police and poetry maybe go together better than certain people think."

"Why shouldn't they go together?" said the janitor's son.

"Why not?" said Jaromil.

"Yes, why not?" said the janitor's son, and he declared that he would like to see Jaromil among the invited poets.

Jaromil demurred, but in the end he happily accepted. Well, if literature had hesitated to offer to his verse its fragile (puny) hand, life itself now offered to it its (rough and firm) hand.

6

Let's look for a moment longer at Jaromil sitting with his beer stein across the table from the janitor's son; in the distance behind him is the closed world of his childhood, and before him, embodied in his old classmate, is the world of action, an alien world he fears and desperately longs for.

This scene expresses the basic situation of immaturity; lyricism is an attempt to face that situation: the individual expelled from the protected enclosure of childhood wishes to enter the world, but at the same time, because he is frightened of it, he fashions an artificial *replacement* world out of his own verse. He makes his poems revolve around him like the planets around the sun; he becomes the center of a small universe in which nothing is alien, in which he feels as much at home as a child inside its mother, for everything here is fashioned only from the substance of his soul. Here he can accomplish everything that is so difficult "outside"; here he can, like the student Wolker, march with a proletarian crowd to make a revolution and, like the virginal Rimbaud, lash his "little girlfriends" because that crowd and those girlfriends are not fashioned out of the hostile substance of an alien world but out of the substance of his own dreams, and they are thus he himself and do not shatter the unity of the universe he has constructed for himself.

Perhaps you know the beautiful poem by Jiri Orten

about the child who was happy inside its mother's body and experienced his birth as a terrible death, "a death filled with light and frightening faces," and who wanted to go back, back inside its mother, back "into the very sweet fragrance."

In an immature young man, the yearning long persists for the safety and unity of the universe that he alone completely filled inside his mother, and he is anxious about (or angered by) the relativized adult world in which he is now engulfed like a droplet in an ocean of otherness. That is why young people are passionate monists, emissaries of the absolute; that is why the poet weaves the private universe of his poems; that is why the young revolutionary demands a radically new world forged from a single clear idea; that is why he cannot allow compromise, either in love or in politics; the rebellious student proclaims his "all or nothing" throughout history, and twenty-year-old Victor Hugo is enraged when he sees his fiancée Adèle Foucher raise her skirt over a muddy sidewalk, exposing her ankle. "It seems to me that modesty is more precious than a dress," he reproaches her in a harsh letter, and he threatens: "Pay heed to my words, if you don't want me to risk slapping the first insolent fellow who dares to turn toward you!"

The world of adults, on hearing this pathetic threat, bursts out laughing. The poet is wounded by the betrayal of the beloved's ankle and by the laughter of the crowd, and the drama of poetry and the world begins.

The world of adults knows perfectly well that the absolute is an illusion, that nothing human is either great or eternal, and that it is perfectly normal for a sister and brother to sleep in the same room; but Jaromil is in torment! The redhead had announced that her brother Jan was coming to Prague and would be staying with her for a week; she even asked him not to come to her place during that time. That was too much for him, and he complained loudly: he couldn't be expected to give up his girlfriend for a whole week because some character (he called him that with scornful arrogance) was turning up!

"Why are you blaming me?" the readhead retorted. "I'm younger than you, but we're always seeing each other at my place. We can't ever see each other at your place!"

Jaromil knew that the redhead was right, and his bitterness increased; once more he had been made aware of the humiliation of his lack of independence, and, blinded by anger, he announced to Mama that very day (with unprecedented firmness) that he was going to bring his girlfriend to the house because he couldn't be alone with her anywhere else.

How they resemble each other, mother and son! Both are equally bewitched by nostalgia for the monistic paradise of unity and harmony: he wants *to go toward* the "sweet fragrance" of the maternal womb, and she wants *to be* that "sweet fragrance." While her son was growing up, she wanted to enfold him in an ethereal embrace; she espoused all his opinions; she admired modern art, she proclaimed herself a Communist, she had faith in her son's glory, she was indignant about the hypocrisy of professors who said one thing one day and another the next; she wanted always to surround him like the sky, she wanted always to be of the same substance as he.

How could she, an apostle of harmonious unity, accept the alien substance of another woman?

Jaromil saw the opposition in her face, and he became inflexible. Yes, he wanted to return into the "sweet fragrance," he was looking for the old maternal universe, but he had long since stopped looking for it in his mama; in the search for the lost mama it was Mama who hampered him most.

She realized that her son would not give in, and she yielded; Jaromil found himself for the first time alone in his room with the redhead, and it would certainly have been good if both of them hadn't been so nervous; Mama had gone to the movies, but she was really with them the whole time; they felt that she was listening to them; they talked more softly than usual; when Jaromil tried to take the redhead in his arms, he found her body cold, and he realized that he'd better not insist; and so instead of enjoying all the pleasures, they only chatted with embarrassment about this and that, always with an eye on the clock that announced Mama's approaching return; it was actually impossible to leave Jaromil's room without going through hers, and the redhead definitely didn't want to encounter her; so she left half an hour before Mama returned, leaving Jaromil in a very bad mood.

Far from discouraging him, this setback made him still more determined. He realized that his position in the house was intolerable; he wasn't living at his place but at his mother's. This observation aroused stubborn resistance in him: he invited his girlfriend once again, and this time he greeted her with cheerful chattiness, by which he was trying to overcome the anxiety that had paralyzed them the first time. He even had a bottle of wine on the table, and since they weren't used to alcohol they were soon in a state of mind in which they succeeded in forgetting Mama's omnipresent shadow.

For a whole week she came home late in the evening, as Jaromil had hoped, even later than he had hoped. She was away from the house even on days when he hadn't asked her to be. It was neither goodwill nor a sensibly pondered concession on her part; it was a demonstration. By returning late she was trying to expose the brutality of her son by example, she was trying to show that her son behaved as if he were the master of a house in which she was merely tolerated and in which she didn't even have the right to sit in a chair and read in her room when she came home tired from work.

During those long afternoons and evenings when she was out of the house, she unfortunately had not a single person to visit because the colleague who had once courted her had long since tired of his futile insistence, and so she went to the movies and to the theater, she tried (with little success) to take up again with some half-forgotten friends, and with perverse pleasure she entered into the bitter emotions of a woman who, having lost her parents and her husband, was being expelled from her home by her own son. She sat in a dark theater watching two strangers kissing on the distant screen, and tears ran down her cheeks.

One day she came home a bit earlier than usual, ready to show a wounded face and to ignore her son's greeting. She had barely closed the door behind her after entering her room when the blood rushed to her head; from Jaromil's room, barely a few meters away, she heard the panting of her son and, mingling with it, female moans.

She was nailed to the spot and at the same time realized that she could not stay there listening to these love sounds, because she felt she was right beside them looking at them (at that moment she really did see them clearly in her mind's eye), and this was absolutely unbearable. She was seized by a fit of frenzied anger made all the more violent as she immediately realized her powerlessness, for she could neither scream nor stamp her feet nor break furniture nor enter Jaromil's room and hit them; she could do absolutely nothing but stand motionless and listen to them.

At that moment the bit of lucid reason left to her joined with the blind fit of anger into a sudden frenzied inspiration: when the redhead in the next room moaned once more, Mama shouted in a voice filled with anxious concern: "My God, Jaromil, what's wrong with her?"

The moans in the next room ceased instantly, and Mama ran to the medicine chest; she took out a small bottle and came running to Jaromil's door; she pushed down the door handle; the door was locked. "My God, you're scaring me, what's going on? What's wrong with the young lady?"

Holding the redhead, who was trembling like a leaf, in his arms, Jaromil said: "Nothing, nothing at all. . . ."

"Is your girlfriend having cramps?"

"Yes, that's right . . . ," he answered.

"Open the door, I have some drops for her," said Mama, again pushing down the handle of the locked door.

"Wait a minute," said her son, getting up rapidly.

"Those cramps are horrible," said Mama.

"One second," said Jaromil, hastily putting on his trousers and shirt; he threw a blanket over the girl.

"It must be an upset stomach, no?" Mama asked through the door.

"Yes," said Jaromil, and he opened the door and reached for the small bottle of medicine.

"You might let me in," said Mama. An odd frenzy drove her on; she didn't let herself be deterred, and she entered the room; the first thing she caught sight of was a bra and other feminine underclothes thrown over a chair; then she saw the girl; she huddled under the blanket and was as pale as if she were really ill.

Now Mama could no longer retreat; she sat down next to her: "What's wrong with you? I came into the house and I heard those moans, you poor little . . ." She shook out twenty drops on a sugar cube: "But I know all about these cramps, take this and you'll soon be fine . . ." and she brought the sugar cube to the redhead's lips, and the girl obediently opened her mouth and turned it toward the sugar cube as she had opened it moments before and turned it toward Jaromil's lips.

Mama had barged into her son's room in an intoxication of anger, but now only the intoxication remained: she looked at that little mouth tenderly opening and she was suddenly overtaken by a terrible urge to tear the blanket off the redheaded girl's body and to have her naked before her; to shatter the intimacy of the closed little world formed by the redhead and Jaromil; to touch what he touched; to claim it as her own; to occupy it; to enfold both bodies in her ethereal embrace; to slip between their ill-concealed nakedness (it didn't escape her that the gym shorts Jaromil wore under his trousers were lying on the floor); to slip between them insolently and innocently, as if it really were a matter of an upset stomach; to be with them as she had been with Jaromil when she had him drink from her naked breast; to gain access, by way of that bridge of ambiguous innocence, to their games and their caresses; to be like a sky surrounding their naked bodies, to be with them. . . .

Then she became frightened of her own agitation. She advised the girl to breathe deeply, and she quickly withdrew to her room.

7

A minibus, its doors locked, was parked in front of the Police Building, and a group of poets stood waiting beside it for the driver. With them were two police organizers of the poetry evening and of course Jaromil; he knew some of the poets by sight (for example, the poet in his sixties who some time ago had recited a poem about his youth at the meeting at his faculty), but he didn't dare say a word to anyone. His anxieties were allayed a bit by the publication at last, a few days earlier, of five of his poems in the literary review; he saw this as official confirmation of his right to the name of poet; so as to be ready for any eventuality, he had the review in the inside pocket of his jacket, which made one side of his chest flat and male and the other side protuberant and female.

The driver arrived, and the poets (there were eleven in all, including Jaromil) got into the vehicle. After an hour on the road, the minibus stopped in a pleasant countryside, the poets got out, the organizers showed them a river, a garden, a villa, took them into classrooms and the big function room where the evening event would soon begin, obliged them to have a look at the police trainees' three-bed dormitories (caught unawares at whatever they had been doing, the men snapped to attention for the poets with the same discipline they exhibited when an officer inspected the rooms), and at last led them into the director's office. Awaiting them were sandwiches and two bottles of wine, the uniformed director, and as if that weren't enough, an extremely beautiful young woman. When the poets in turn had shaken hands with the director and muttered their names, the director introduced them to the young woman: "This is the supervisor of our film circle," and then he explained to the eleven poets (who one after the other were shaking the young woman's hand) that the people's police had its own social club where cultural activities were pursued intensively; there was an amateur theater and an amateur chorus, and they had just started the film circle, which was supervised by this young woman, who was a student at the film school and at the same time kind enough to help the young policemen; incidentally, they had the best of conditions here: an excellent camera, all kinds of lighting equipment, and, above all, enthusiastic young men, although, the director said, he wasn't sure whether they were more interested in film or in the supervisor.

After shaking all the poets' hands, the young filmmaker motioned to two young men standing at big reflectors; the poets and the director were now munching their sandwiches under the glare of floodlights. Their conversation, which the director tried to make as natural as possible, was interrupted by the young woman's instructions, which were followed by the lights being moved and then by the soft whirring of the camera. After a while the director thanked the poets for having come, looked at his watch, and said that the audience was impatiently awaiting them.

"All right, comrade poets, please take your places," said one of the organizers, and he read their names from a sheet of paper; the poets lined up, and when the organizer motioned to them they mounted the platform; on it was a long table with a chair for each poet marked by a place card. The poets sat down in their chairs, and the room (in which all the seats were occupied) rang with applause.

This was the first time Jaromil had displayed himself before a crowd; he was prey to a feeling of intoxication that never left him until the end of the evening. Besides, everything went wonderfully well; after the poets sat down on their assigned chairs, an organizer went over to the lectern at one end of the table, welcomed the eleven poets, and introduced them. One by one the poets stood up and bowed, and the room applauded. Jaromil, too, stood up and bowed, and he was so stunned by the applause that he didn't immediately notice the janitor's son sitting in the first row and motioning to him; he motioned back, and this gesture from the platform, which could be seen by everyone, made him feel the charm of artificial naturalness, and so during the evening he motioned several times more to his old classmate, like someone who feels at ease and at home on the stage.

The poets were sitting in alphabetical order, and Jaromil found himself next to the poet in his sixties: "My friend, what a surprise, I didn't know it was you! You've had poems recently in a review!" Jaromil smiled politely, and the poet went on: "I remembered your name; they're excellent poems, I enjoyed them very much!" But at that moment the organizer again spoke up, inviting the poets to come to the microphone in alphabetical order and read some of their latest poems.

And so the poets came to the microphone, read poems, were applauded, and returned to their seats. Jaromil anxiously awaited his turn; he was afraid of stammering, he was afraid of using an ineffective tone of voice, he was afraid of everything; but then he got up as if bedazzled; he had no time even to think. He began to read, and from the very first lines he felt sure of himself. And in fact the applause that followed his first poem was longer than anyone's thus far.

The applause emboldened Jaromil, who read his second poem with more assurance than the first, and he felt not at all uncomfortable when two nearby floodlights inundated him with light while a camera began to hum ten meters away. He pretended not to notice any of this, not for a moment hesitating in his recitation and even managing to lift his eyes from his sheet of paper and looking not only at the indistinct space of the room but at the completely distinct spot where (a few steps from the camera) the pretty filmmaker was standing. Again there was applause; Jaromil read two more poems, heard the hum of the camera, looked at the filmmaker's face, bowed, and returned to his seat; at that moment the poet in his sixties rose from his chair, and, solemnly tilting his head back, opened his arms and closed them around Jaromil's shoulders: "My friend, you are a poet, you are a poet!" and since the applause continued, he turned toward the audience, raised his hand, and bowed.

When the eleventh poet had finished his reading, the organizer remounted the platform, thanked all the poets, and announced that after a brief intermission anyone interested was to come back into the room for a discussion with the poets. "That part of the program is not compulsory; only those who are interested are invited to participate."

Jaromil was carried away; people gathered around him to shake his hand; one of the poets introduced himself as also an editor at a publishing house, expressed surprise that Jaromil had not yet published a book, and asked him for a selection of his verse; another invited him to a meeting arranged by the Youth Union; and of course the janitor's son came up to him and stayed, making it clear to everyone that Jaromil and he had known each other since childhood; then the director himself approached him and said: "It seems to me that the laurels of victory this evening belong to the youngest!"

Then, turning to the other poets, he declared that to his great regret he would be unable to participate in the discussion because he had to attend a dance the trainees had organized, which was about to begin in the next room. Many girls from the neighboring villages, he added with a greedy smile, had come for the event because policemen were first-rate Don Juans. "Well, comrades, I thank you for your beautiful poems, and I hope that this isn't the last time we see you here!" He shook the poets' hands and left for the room next door, from which, like an invitation to the dance, a brass band could already be heard.

In the function room, where a few minutes earlier applause had resounded, the small group of excited poets found itself alone at the edge of the platform; one of the organizers mounted the platform and announced: "Dear comrades, the intermission is over, and I return the floor to our guests. I ask those who want to participate in the discussion with the comrade poets to sit down."

The poets returned to their seats on the platform and ten people sat down facing them in the first row of the otherwise empty room: among them were the janitor's son, the two organizers who had accompanied the poets on the minibus, an old gentleman with a wooden leg and a crutch, several less conspicuous men, and two women: one of them (probably a secretary at the academy) seemed to be about fifty; the other was the filmmaker, who had finished shooting and now had her large, calm eyes fixed on the poets; the presence of a pretty woman in the room was all the more remarkable and stimulating to the poets as they heard the increasingly loud and seductive sounds of the band music and growing din of the dance coming from the room next door.

The two rows sitting facing each other were about equal in number, like two soccer teams; Jaromil thought that the silence that had set in was like the silence that precedes a confrontation; and since the silence had already lasted thirty seconds, he figured that the poetic eleven was already losing the game.

But Jaromil had underestimated his teammates; in the course of the year some of them had participated in a hundred various discussions, and so discussion had become their main activity, their specialty, and their art. Let me recall a historical detail: trade union clubs and Party and Youth Union committees organized evenings to which they invited all sorts of painters, poets, astronomers, or economists; the organizers of these evenings were duly noted and rewarded for their initiatives, for the era required revolutionary activity, which, impossible to exert on the barricades, had to blossom in meetings and discussions. Also, all sorts of painters, poets, astronomers, or economists readily participated in such evenings, which enabled them to show that they were not narrow specialists but revolutionary specialists with ties to the people.

Thus the poets were quite familiar with the questions audiences posed, they knew that they were repeated with the stupefying regularity of statistical probability. They knew that someone was certainly going to ask: Comrade, how did you first start to write? They knew that someone else would ask: How old were you when you wrote you first poem? They also knew that someone would ask who their favorite author was, and that you could also expect someone in the audience anxious to display his Marxist learning pose the question: Comrade, how would you define socialist realism? And they also knew that in addition to questions they would be reminded of their duty to write more poetry about (1) the occupations of the people in the audience, (2) youth, (3) the cruelty of life under capitalism, and (4) love.

The initial half minute of silence thus was not caused by any kind of embarrassment; it was rather an oversight on the part of the poets, who knew the routine all too well; or it may have been poor coordination, because the poets had never appeared in this formation before and each one wanted to allow one of the others the privilege of the first shot at the goal. At last the poet in his sixties spoke up. He spoke with ease and forcefully, and after ten minutes of improvisation he invited the facing row not to be afraid to ask questions. These were of a kind that finally enabled the poets to display their eloquence and their aptitude at improvised team play, which from then on was flawless: they knew how to relay, to complement one another, to swiftly alternate a serious answer with an anecdote. Of course, all the basic questions were posed and all the basic answers given (everyone listened with interest to the poet in his sixties, who had been asked how and when he wrote his first poem, explaining that if it hadn't been for his cat, Mimi, he would never have been a poet, for it was she who had inspired him to write his first poem at the age of five; then he recited that poem, and since the facing row didn't know whether he was serious or joking, he hastened to be the first to laugh, and then everyone, poets and audience alike, laughed long and cheerfully).

And naturally the poets were also reminded of their

duty. The janitor's son stood up and spoke at length. Yes, the poetry evening had been remarkable and all the poets were first class, but did anyone notice that of the at least thirty-three poems they had heard (if you figured that each poet read about three poems), there was not a single poem on the subject of the National Police, either directly or indirectly? And yet, can anyone maintain that the National Police occupies less than one thirty-third of a place in our national life?

Then the fiftyish woman got up and said that she agreed completely with what Jaromil's classmate just said, but that she had an entirely different question: Why was so little written these days about love? Stifled laughter could be heard from the audience, but the woman went on: Even under socialism people love each other and like to read something about love.

The poet in his sixties rose, tilted his head back, and said that the comrade was totally correct. Was it necessary in a socialist system to be ashamed of love? Was it something bad? He was an old man, but he was not embarrassed to admit that when he saw women in flimsy summer dresses, which enable one to guess at the young and lovely bodies underneath, he couldn't avoid turning around to look. From the row of eleven questioners came the complicitous laughter of fellow sinners, and the poet, thus encouraged, went on: What should he offer these pretty young women? A hammer with ferns? And when he is invited to visit should he put a sickle in the flower vase? Not at all; he offers them roses; love poetry is like the roses we offer to women.

312

Yes, yes, the fiftyish woman agreed fervently, and so the poet took a sheaf of paper out of his inside pocket and began to read a long love poem.

Yes, yes, that was wonderful, the fiftyish woman gushed, and then one of the organizers stood up and said that these verses were certainly beautiful, but nevertheless even in a love poem it must be obvious that the poem was written by a socialist poet.

But how could it be obvious? asked the fiftyish woman, still fascinated by the old poet's touchingly tilted head and by his poem.

Jaromil had remained silent while all the others spoke up, and he realized that he had to take his turn; he thought that now was the moment; here was a question he had pondered for a long time; yes, since the time when he used to visit the painter and listened obediently to his speeches about modern art and the new world. Alas, once again it was the painter who was expressing himself through Jaromil's mouth, once again it was his voice and his words that were issuing from Jaromil's lips!

What did he say? That in the previous society love had been so deformed by concern for money, by social considerations, by prejudices that it could really not be itself but rather a shadow of itself. Only the new era, by sweeping away the power of money and the influence of prejudice, would make man fully human and love greater than it had ever been in the past. Socialist love poetry is thus the expression of great, liberated emotion.

Jaromil was satisfied with what he had said, and he

noticed the filmmaker's large, dark eyes fixed on him; he thought that the words "love greater" and "liberated emotion" came out of his mouth like a sailboat into the harbor of those large eyes.

But when he finished, one of the poets smiled ironically and said: "Do you really believe that the emotion of love is more powerful in your poems than in the poems of Heinrich Heine? Or that the loves of Victor Hugo are too petty for you? Was love in Macha or in Neruda* crippled by money and prejudice?"

That was a blow. Jaromil didn't know what to say; he blushed and saw a pair of large dark eyes witnessing his debacle.

The fiftyish woman was pleased by the sarcastic questions of Jaromil's colleague, saying: "Why do you want to transform love, comrades? Love will be the same until the end of time."

Once more the organizer intervened: "Oh, no, comrade. Certainly not!"

"No, that's not what I meant to say," the poet quickly said. "But the difference between the love poetry of yesterday and that of today has nothing to do with the intensity of the emotion."

"Then what does it have to do with?" asked the fiftyish woman.

"With the fact that in the past even the greatest love was always a means of escape from social life, which

---

*The nineteenth-century Czech poets Karel Hynek Macha and Jan Neruda.

was loathsome. Today love is bound up with our social duties, our work, our struggle, with which it forms an entirety. That is where its *new* beauty lies."

The facing row expressed its agreement with Jaromil's colleague, but Jaromil gave a scornful laugh: "That kind of beauty, my dear friend, is nothing new. Didn't the great poets of the past lead lives in which love was in perfect harmony with their social struggle? The lovers in Shelley's poem *The Revolt of Islam* are revolutionaries who perish together on a pyre. Is that what you call love cut off from social life?"

Worst of all, just as Jaromil a few moments earlier hadn't known how to answer his colleague's objections, his colleague was stumped in turn, which risked causing the impression (an inadmissible impression) that there was no difference between the past and the present and that the new world did not exist. Besides, the fiftyish woman got up and asked with an interrogator's smile: "So tell me, what is the difference between love today and love in the past?"

At that decisive moment, when everyone was at an impasse, the man with the wooden leg and crutch intervened; he had been following the debate attentively, though with visible impatience; now he got up and leaned firmly against a chair: "Dear comrades, allow me to introduce myself," and the people in his row quickly protested, shouting that it wasn't necessary, that they knew him very well. But he interrupted them: "I'm not introducing myself to you but to the comrades we've invited here," and as he knew that his name would mean nothing to the poets, he gave them a brief account of his life: he had been the caretaker of this villa for thirty years; he was already here in the time of the industrialist Kocvara, whose summer house this was; he was also here during the war, when the industrialist was arrested and the villa became a Gestapo vacation house; after the war the villa was confiscated by the Christian Party, and now the police were installed here. "Well, from what I've seen, I can say that no government takes such good care of working people as the Communist government." Of course, even these days not everything was perfect: "In Kocvara's time, in the Gestapo's time, and in the Christians' time, the bus stop was always right across from the villa." Yes, that was very convenient, it was only ten steps from his basement room in the villa to the bus stop. Then they moved the bus stop two hundred meters away! He had already complained wherever he could. It was absolutely useless. "Tell me," he said, thumping the floor with his crutch, "now that the villa belongs to the workers, why does the bus stop have to be so far away?"

The people in the first row answered (partly with impatience, partly with a certain amusement) that he had already been told a hundred times that the bus now stopped in front of a recently built factory.

The man with the wooden leg replied that he knew this very well, and that he had suggested that the bus should stop at both places.

The people in the first row said that it would be stupid for the bus to stop every two hundred meters.

The word "stupid" offended the man with the wooden leg; he declared that no one had the right to talk to him like that; he thumped the floor with his crutch and turned crimson. Besides, it wasn't true that buses couldn't stop every two hundred meters. He was well aware that on other bus routes the stops were closer together.

One of the organizers stood up and quoted word for word (it was not the first time he had had to do so) the Czechoslovak Transportation Department's decree expressly prohibiting bus stops so close together.

The man with the wooden leg replied that he had suggested a compromise solution: it would be possible to place the stop midway between the villa and the factory.

But it was pointed out to him that then the bus stop would be far away both for the factory workers and the policemen.

The dispute had lasted for twenty minutes, and the poets were vainly trying to join in the debate; the audience was impassioned about a subject it knew in depth and didn't allow the poets to speak. Only when the man with the wooden leg, disheartened by the resistance of his fellow employees, sat down again in exasperation did the room at last lapse into a silence that was immediately broken by the band music coming from the room next door.

Nobody said anything for a while, and then one of the organizers finally got up and thanked the poets for their visit and for the interesting discussion. On behalf of the visitors, the poet in his sixties got up and said that the discussion (as, by the way, was always the case) had certainly been more rewarding for them, the poets, than for their hosts, whom he and his colleagues thanked.

The voice of a male singer came from the next room, the audience gathered around the man with the wooden leg to soothe his anger, and the poets found themselves alone. Then, after a minute or two, the janitor's son along with the two organizers joined them and took them to the minibus.

8

The beautiful filmmaker was in the minibus taking them back to Prague. The poets surrounded her, each one doing his best to attract her attention. Jaromil's seat was unfortunately too far from hers to enable him to participate in the game; he thought of his redhead, and he realized with conclusive certainty that she was irremediably ugly.

The minibus stopped somewhere in the middle of Prague, and some of the poets decided to go into a tavern. Jaromil and the filmmaker went with them; they sat down at a large table, talked, drank, and as they were leaving the tavern the filmmaker suggested they go to her place. Only a handful of poets remained: Jaromil, the poet in his sixties, and the publishing house editor. They settled into armchairs in a handsome room on the second floor of a modern villa the young woman was subletting, and they started drinking again.

The old poet devoted himself to the filmmaker with matchless ardor. He sat beside her praising her beauty, reciting poems to her, improvising odes in honor of her charms, at moments kneeling at her feet and holding her hands. The editor, with almost equal ardor, devoted himself to Jaromil; to be sure, he didn't praise his beauty, but he repeated an incalculable number of times: "You are a poet, you are a poet!" (Let me note in passing that when a poet calls someone a poet, it is not the same thing as an engineer calling someone an engineer or a farmer calling someone a farmer, because a farmer is someone who cultivates the earth while a poet is not merely someone who writes verse but someone— let's recall the word!—who is *elected* to write verse, and only a poet can with certainty recognize in another poet that touch of grace, for—let's recall Rimbaud's letter— all "poets are brothers," and only a brother can recognize the secret family sign.)

The filmmaker, before whom the poet in his sixties was kneeling and whose hands were victims of his assiduous fondling, never stopped looking into Jaromil's eyes. He soon noticed this, was enchanted, and looked into hers. It was a pretty rectangle! The old poet gazed at the filmmaker, the editor gazed at Jaromil, and Jaromil and the filmmaker gazed at each other.

This geometry of gazes was only broken once, when the editor took Jaromil by the arm and led him to the adjacent balcony; he invited Jaromil to urinate with him onto the courtyard below the railing. Jaromil gladly obliged, for he wanted the editor to remember his promise to publish a selection of his poems.

When the two of them returned from the balcony, the old poet got up from his knees and said it was time to go; he was well aware that he was not the one the young woman desired. Then he suggested to the editor (who was much less discerning and considerate) that they leave alone those who wanted and deserved to be, for, as the old poet labeled them, they were the prince and princess of the evening.

The editor finally realized what was going on and was ready to leave, the old poet took him by the arm and led him to the door, and Jaromil saw that he was about to be alone with the young woman, who was sitting in a wide armchair with her legs crossed under her, her dark hair disheveled, and her motionless eyes fixed on him. . . .

The story of two people who are on the verge of becoming lovers is so eternal that we can almost forget the era in which it is taking place. How pleasant it is to recount such love affairs! How delightful it would be to forget what it is that dries up the sap of our brief lives so as to enslave them to its useless work, how beautiful it would be to forget History!

But here is its specter knocking at the door and entering the story. It is not entering in the guise of the secret police or in the guise of a sudden revolution; History does not make its way only on the dramatic peaks of our lives but also soaks into everyday life like dirty water; it enters our story in the guise of underwear.

In Jaromil's country in the era I am speaking of, elegance was a political offense; the clothes worn at the time were very ugly (besides, the war had ended only a few years before, and there were still shortages); and in that austere era elegant underwear was considered a downright reprehensible luxury! Men who were embarrassed by the ugliness of the underwear then being sold (wide shorts that came down to the knees and had the amenity of a comical opening at the crotch) instead wore short pants intended for sports use, that is, for stadiums and gymnasiums. This was strange: everywhere in Bohemia in that era men climbed into their women's beds dressed like soccer players, going to their women as though they were entering the stadium, but from the viewpoint of elegance it was not so bad: the gym shorts had a certain athletic elegance and came in lively colors—blue, green, red, yellow.

Jaromil paid no attention to his clothing, for Mama took care of it; she chose his clothes for him, she chose his underwear, she made sure that he didn't catch cold by seeing to it that he wore warm undershorts. She knew exactly how many pairs of undershorts were stacked in his linen drawer, and she had merely to glance into the linen closet to know which one Jaromil was wearing that day. When she saw that not a single pair of undershorts was missing from the drawer, she immediately became angry; she didn't like Jaromil to wear gym shorts, for she believed that gym shorts were not undershorts and should be worn only for sports. When Jaromil protested that the undershorts were ugly, she answered with concealed irritation that he probably didn't display himself to anyone in his underwear. So whenever Jaromil went to see the redheaded girl, he always took a pair of undershorts out of the linen drawer, hid it in one of his desk drawers, and then put on a pair of gym shorts.

But that day he had not known what the evening would bring, and he wore a pair of hideously ugly, bulky, threadbare, dirty gray undershorts! You might say that this was just a slight complication, that he could, for example, turn off the light so as not to be seen. Alas, there was a bedside lamp with a pink shade in the room, the lamp was on and seemed impatiently waiting to illuminate the caresses of the two lovers, and Jaromil couldn't imagine what he might say to induce the young woman to turn it off.

Or you might perhaps remark that Jaromil could take off his bad-looking undershorts together with his trousers. But Jaromil didn't even think of taking off his undershorts and his trousers at the same time, because he had never undressed in this way; such a sudden leap into nakedness frightened him; he always undressed piecemeal and caressed the redhead for a long time while still in his gym shorts, which he removed only under cover of arousal.

And so he stood terrified before the large dark eyes and announced that he too had to leave.

The old poet was almost in a rage; he told Jaromil that he must not insult a woman, and he lowered his voice to depict the pleasures that awaited him; but his words merely convinced Jaromil all the more of the wretchedness of his undershorts. Looking at the wonderful dark eyes, his heart breaking, he retreated toward the door.

When he reached the street he was overcome by regret; he couldn't get rid of the image of that splendid girl. And the old poet (they had taken leave of the editor at the streetcar stop and were now walking alone through the dark streets) was tormenting him by continuing to reproach him for insulting the young woman and behaving stupidly.

Jaromil told the poet that he hadn't wanted to insult the young woman, but that he loved his girlfriend, who was madly in love with him.

You're naive, said the old poet. You're a poet, you're a lover of life, you wouldn't harm your girlfriend by going to bed with someone else; life is short, and lost opportunities don't recur.

That was painful to hear. Jaromil replied that in his opinion a single great love to which we devote everything we have within us is worth more than a thousand fleeting affairs; that having his girlfriend was having all women; that his girlfriend was so protean, her love so infinite, that he could experience with her more unexpected adventures than a Don Juan with his 1,003 women.

The old poet stopped walking; Jaromil's words had visibly touched him: "You may be right," he said. "But I'm an old man and belong to the old world. I admit that even though I'm married, I'd have loved to stay with that woman."

As Jaromil went on with his reflections on the greatness of monogamous love, the old poet tilted his head back: "Ah, you may be right, my friend, you're certainly right. Didn't I too dream about a great love? About a single, unique love? About a love as boundless as the universe? But I squandered my chance for it, my friend, because in that old world, the world of money and whores, great love was belittled."

Both of them were drunk, the old poet put his arm around the young poet's shoulders, and now they stopped in the middle of the street between the streetcar tracks. The old man raised his arms high and shouted: "Death to the old world! Long live great love!"

Jaromil found this impressive, bohemian, and poetic, and the two of them shouted long and enthusiastically in the dark streets of Prague: "Death to the old world! Long live great love!"

Then the poet knelt before Jaromil on the cobblestones and kissed his hand: "My friend, I pay homage to your youth! My age pays homage to your youth, because only youth will save the world!" He was silent for a moment, and then, his bare head touching Jaromil's knees, he added in a very melancholy voice: "And I pay homage to your great love."

They finally parted, and Jaromil soon found himself back home in his room. Before his eyes he again saw the image of the beautiful woman he had forgone. Driven by an urge for self-punishment, he looked at himself in the mirror. He took off his trousers so as to see himself in his hideous, threadbare undershorts; for a long time he contemplated his comical ugliness with hatred.

Then he realized that it was not he himself he was thinking about with hatred. He was thinking about his mother; his mother, who chose his underwear; his mother, who made him secretly put on gym shorts and hide his undershorts in his desk; he was thinking about his mother, who knew every one of his shirts and socks. He thought with hatred about his mother, who was holding him by the end of a long leash whose collar was embedded in his neck.

9

From that evening on he became still more cruel to the redheaded girl; it was, of course, cruelty ceremoniously cloaked in love: How can she not understand what is preoccupying him just now? How can she not know what mood he is in? Has she become such a stranger that she has no idea what is happening to him deep down? If she really loves him, as he loves her, she should at least be able to guess! How can she be interested in things that don't interest him? How can she always be talking about her brother and still another brother and about a sister and still another sister? Isn't she aware that Jaromil has serious worries, that he needs her involvement and understanding instead of this eternal egocentric chatter?

Of course, the girl defended herself. Why, for example, can't she talk about her family? Doesn't Jaromil talk about his? Is her mother worse than Jaromil's? And she reminded him (for the first time since that day) that his mother had barged into Jaromil's room and shoved a sugar cube with drops on it into her mouth.

Jaromil loved and hated his mother; confronting the redhead, he quickly came to her defense: Had Mama harmed her by wanting to take care of her? That only showed how much she liked her, that she had accepted her as a member of the family!

The redhead laughed: Jaromil's mother wasn't so stupid as to confuse the moans of love with the groans of someone with an upset stomach! Jaromil was offended, fell into silence, and the girl had to ask his forgiveness.

As he and the redhead walked down the street one day, arm in arm and stubbornly silent (when they weren't reproaching each other they were silent, and when they weren't silent they were reproaching each other), Jaromil suddenly noticed two good-looking women coming toward them. One was younger, the other older; the younger one was prettier and more elegant, but (to Jaromil's great surprise) the older one too was very elegant and amazingly pretty. Jaromil knew them both: the younger one was the filmmaker and the older one was his mama.

He blushed and greeted them. Both women returned the greeting (Mama with conspicuous gaiety), and for Jaromil being seen with this unattractive girl was as if the beautiful filmmaker had surprised him in his hideous undershorts.

Back home he asked Mama how she had come to know the filmmaker. Mama answered with whimsical coyness that she had known her for some time. Jaromil continued to question her, but Mama kept evading him; it was as if someone were questioning his lover about an intimate detail and she, to heighten his curiosity, was delaying her answer; at last she told him that this likable woman had visited her about two weeks before. She had said that she admired Jaromil's poetry and wanted to shoot some footage of him; it would be an amateur film produced under the auspices of the National Police film club, and would thus be certain to have a sizable audience.

"Why did she come to see you? Why didn't she come to me directly?" Jaromil wondered.

Apparently the young woman didn't want to disturb him, and she therefore wanted to learn as much as she could from her. Besides, who knows more about a son than his mother? And the young woman was so kind as to ask his mother to collaborate with her on the scenario; yes, together they had devised a scenario about the young poet.

"Why didn't you tell me?" asked Jaromil, who was instinctively displeased by the alliance between his mother and the filmmaker.

"We had the misfortune of running into you. We'd decided to surprise you. One fine day you would come home and find the film crew and a camera."

What could Jaromil do? One day he came home and shook hands with the young woman at whose place he had found himself some weeks before, and he felt as pitiable as he had that evening, even though he was now wearing red gym shorts under his trousers. After the poetry evening with the police, he had never again worn the frightful undershorts, but whenever he faced the filmmaker, there was always someone else playing their role: when he met her in the street with his mother, he thought he had his girlfriend's red hair wrapped around him like a hideous pair of undershorts; and this time the clownish undershorts were represented by Mama's coy remarks and nervous chatter.

The filmmaker announced (no one had asked for Jaromil's opinion) that they were going to shoot documentary material, childhood photographs on which Mama would comment, because, the two women told him in passing, the entire film had been conceived as a mother's account of her poet son. He wanted to ask what Mama was going to say, but he dreaded finding out; he was blushing. Besides Jaromil and the two women, there were three men in the room, along with a camera and two big floodlights; it seemed to him that these fellows were watching him and smiling with hostility; he didn't dare speak.

"You have marvelous childhood photos; I'd love to use them all," said the filmmaker as she leafed through the family album.

"Will they look like anything on the screen?" asked Mama with professional interest, and the filmmaker assured her there was nothing to worry about; then she explained to Jaromil that the first sequence of the film would consist of a montage of photographs of him, with Mama reminiscing off camera. Then Mama would be seen, and only after that the poet; the poet in the house where he had lived all his life, the poet writing, the poet in the garden amid the flowers, and finally the poet out in the country, where he most liked to be; in his favorite spot there, in the middle of a vast landscape, he would recite the poem with which the film will end. ("And where exactly is this favorite spot of mine?" he asked recalcitrantly; he learned that his favorite spot was that romantic landscape on the outskirts of Prague where the rough terrain was strewn with boulders. "What? I detest that spot," he said, but no one took him seriously.)

Jaromil didn't like the scenario and said that he wanted to work on it himself; he pointed out that there were many trite things in it (it was ridiculous to show photos of a one-year-old!); he asserted that there were more interesting problems it would probably be useful to take up; the two women asked him what he had in mind, and he answered that he couldn't say at the moment and that he would prefer that they wait a bit before starting to film.

He wanted at all costs to postpone the shooting, but he didn't win his case. Mama put her arm around his shoulders and said to her dark-haired collaborator: "You see? That's my eternally dissatisfied boy! He's never content. . . ." Then she tenderly leaned close to Jaromil's face: "Isn't that so?" Jaromil didn't answer, and she repeated: "Isn't that so, that you're my dissatisfied little boy? Say it's so!"

The filmmaker said that dissatisfaction is a virtue in a writer, but this time it wasn't Jaromil who was the author but rather the two of them, and they were ready to take all the risks; all he had to do was let them make the film as they understood it, just as they let him write his poems as he pleased.

Mama added that Jaromil shouldn't be afraid that the film would do him harm, for both of them, Mama and the filmmaker, were creating it with the greatest affection for him; she said this so flirtatiously that it was unclear whether she was flirting with him or with her new friend.

In any case she was flirting. Jaromil had never seen her like this; that very morning she had gone to the hairdresser and had her hair done in a youthful fashion; she talked louder than usual, laughed constantly, made use of all the witty turns of phrase she had ever learned, and enjoyed playing her role as mistress of the house, bringing cups of coffee to the men at the floodlights. She addressed the dark-eyed filmmaker with the showy familiarity of a friend (so as to put herself in the same age group) while indulgently putting her arm on Jaromil's shoulder and calling him her dissatisfied little boy (so as to send him back to his virginity, his child-hood, his diapers). (Ah, what a beautiful sight, these two face to face pushing each other: she pushing him into his diapers and he pushing her into her grave, ah, what a beautiful sight these two . . .)

Jaromil gave way; he knew that the two women were building up speed like locomotives and that he wasn't capable of resisting their eloquence; he saw the three men at the camera and floodlights as a sardonic audi-ence ready to jeer at any false step he might take; that's why he spoke in a near whisper while the two women answered him loudly enough for the audience to hear, because the presence of the audience was an advantage to them and a disadvantage to him. And so he told them that he was submitting to them and that he wanted to leave; but they replied (again flirtatiously) that he should stay; it would give them pleasure, they said, if he observed them at work; so he spent a few minutes watching the cameraman shooting various photos from the album before leaving for his room, where he pretended to be reading or working; confused reflections filed through his mind; he tried to find an advantage in this entirely disadvantageous situation, and he thought that the filmmaker might have conceived the idea of this filming to get in touch with him; he reflected that in that case Mama was merely an obstacle to be patiently circumvented; he tried to calm himself and think of a way to utilize this ridiculous filming to his own benefit, that is, to make up for the loss that had tormented him since the night he had stupidly left the filmmaker's room; he tried to overcome his shyness and periodically went out to glance into the next room and see how the filming was going, with the hope of repeating, if only once, their reciprocal gazes, the long motionless look that had so captivated him at the filmmaker's villa apartment; but this time the filmmaker was indifferent to him and absorbed in her work, and their eyes met only rarely and fleetingly; he therefore gave up his attempts and decided to accompany the filmmaker home when she was finished working.

When the three men were going downstairs to stow the camera and lights in their van, he came out of his room. And he heard Mama saying to the filmmaker: "Let's go out somewhere for coffee."

During their afternoon of work together, while he had been shut away in his room, the two women had begun to use the familiar pronoun with each other!

When he realized this, it was as if his lover had just been whisked away from under his nose. He coldly said goodbye to the filmmaker, and as soon as the two women left the house he too left and quickly and angrily headed toward the redhead's building; she wasn't home; he paced up and down in front of the building for nearly half an hour, his mood increasingly gloomy, until he saw her at last; her face expressed delighted surprise, and his expressed harsh reproaches: Why hadn't she been home? Why hadn't she realized that he was probably coming? Where had she gone to be coming home so late?

She had hardly closed the door when he tore off her dress; then he made love to her, imagining that the woman lying under him was the dark-eyed woman; hearing the redhead's sighs but simultaneously seeing dark eyes, he had the impression that the sighs belonged to those eyes, and this so aroused him that he made love several times in a row, but never for more than a few seconds each time. The redheaded young woman found this so peculiar that she began to laugh; but Jaromil was particularly sensitive to irony that day, and the friendly indulgence of the redhead's laughter escaped him; offended, he gave her a pair of slaps; she began to cry; for Jaromil that was like a balm; she cried, and he struck her again; the tears of a woman we have made cry are redemption; they are Jesus Christ dying for us on the cross; for some moments Jaromil enjoyed the sight of the redhead's tears, and then he kissed her face, soothed her, and went home quite serenely.

A few days later the filming resumed; again the van
came and three men (that hostile audience) got out,
along with the beautiful girl whose sighs he had heard
two evenings before at the redhead's; and of course
there was also Mama, getting younger and younger,
resembling a musical instrument that growled, thundered, laughed, and broke out of the orchestra to play a
solo.

This time the camera lens was to be aimed directly at
Jaromil; he had to be shown in his everyday surroundings, at his desk, in the garden (for Jaromil, it seemed,
loved the garden, the flower beds, the lawn, the flowers); he had to be shown with Mama, who, let's remember, had already recorded a lengthy commentary on her
son. The filmmaker sat them down on a bench in the
garden and compelled Jaromil to chat normally with his
mother; this apprenticeship in normality lasted an
hour, and Mama didn't for a moment lose her energy;
she was always saying something or other (in the film
nothing of what they were saying would be heard, their
inaudible conversation would be accompanied by the
prerecorded maternal commentary), and when she
noticed that Jaromil's expression was insufficiently
amiable, she began explaining to him that it wasn't easy
to be the mother of a boy like him, a timid, solitary boy
who always had stage fright.

After that they shoved him into the van and took him
to the romantic spot on the outskirts of Prague where
Jaromil, Mama was convinced, had been conceived. She
was too prudish ever to have dared tell why this land-

scape was so dear to her; even though she had wanted to, she hadn't told anyone, and now she told everyone, with forced ambiguity, that for her this particular landscape had always represented a sensual landscape, a landscape of love. "Look how the soil undulates, it looks like a woman, like her curves, like her maternal shapes! And look at those boulders, those blocks of gigantic boulders rising in the background! Isn't there something virile about those overhanging, steep, vertical boulders? Isn't this a landscape of man and woman? Isn't this an erotic landscape?"

Jaromil wished to rebel; he wanted to tell them that their film was silly; he felt rising in him the pride of a man who knows what good taste means; he might have made a small and useless fuss or at least run away, as he had from the swimming place on the shore of the Vltava, but this time he couldn't; the filmmaker's dark eyes rendered him powerless; he was afraid of losing them a second time; those eyes barred his avenue of escape.

They posed him in front of a huge boulder and told him to recite his favorite poem. Mama was at a height of excitement. It was such a long time since she had been here! Exactly at the spot where she had made love with a young engineer on a Sunday morning so many years ago, exactly here her son was now standing; as if, after so many years, he had sprung up here like a mushroom (ah, yes, as if children came to be like mushrooms exactly at the spot where their parents mingled their seed!); Mama was carried away by the sight of this strange, beautiful, impossible mushroom reciting, in a quavering voice, lines about his wish to die by fire.

Jaromil felt that he was reciting very badly, but he couldn't help it; however much he told himself that he had no stage fright, that in the police villa the other evening he had recited masterfully and splendidly, here it was too much for him; standing in front of this absurd boulder in that absurd landscape, in a panic at the thought that someone might pass by walking his dog or strolling with his girl (you see, he had the same fears as his mother twenty years earlier!), he was unable to concentrate, and he uttered his words unnaturally and with difficulty.

They compelled him to repeat his poem several times in succession, and finally they gave up. "He's always had stage fright!" sighed Mama. "Even in high school he trembled at every exam; often I had to drag him to school by force because of his stage fright!"

The filmmaker said that they would dub an actor reciting the poem and that all Jaromil had to do was stand in front of the boulder and silently move his lips.

That's what he did.

"Dammit!" the filmmaker shouted impatiently. "You have to move your mouth properly, as if you were reciting your poem, not just any old way. The actor will recite the poem by following the movement of your lips!"

And so Jaromil stood in front of the boulder, moved his lips (obediently and properly), and the camera finally hummed.

10

The day before yesterday he had stood outside facing the camera in a light coat, but today he had to wear a heavy winter coat, a scarf, and a hat; it had snowed. He was meeting her in front of her building at six o'clock. But it was already six-fifteen, and the redhead had not yet turned up.

A delay of fifteen minutes was certainly not serious; but Jaromil, after all the humiliations he had undergone the last few days, was unable to bear the merest slight; he had to pace up and down in front of the building in a street full of people who could see that he was waiting for someone in no hurry to join him, thus making his failure public.

He didn't dare look at his watch, fearing that this all-too eloquent gesture would reveal him in the eyes of everyone on the street as a lover waiting in vain; he pulled up the sleeve of his overcoat slightly and slipped its edge under his watchband so as to be able to keep glancing inconspicuously at the time; when he saw that it was six-twenty, he nearly went into a frenzy: Why was he always a few minutes early, and why did she, so stupid and ugly, always turn up late?

She finally turned up and saw Jaromil's stony face. They went into her room, sat down, and the girl apologized: she had been with a young woman friend. She couldn't have found a worse thing to say. Of course nothing could have absolved her, especially not a young woman friend who to Jaromil was the very essence of insignificance. He told the redhead that he was well aware of the importance of her diversions with her friend; that is why he suggested that she turn around and go right back to her friend's place.

The girl realized that things were going badly; she told him that she and her friend had spoken of very serious matters; the friend was about to break up with her boyfriend; the friend seemed to be very sad, she was weeping, the redhead wanted to calm her, and she couldn't leave before she had comforted her.

Jaromil said that it was very generous of her to have dried her friend's tears. But who was going to dry the redheaded girl's tears when Jaromil broke up with her because he refused to continue seeing a girl to whom a friend's stupid tears meant more than he did?

The girl realized that things were going from bad to worse; she apologized again, said she was sorry, and asked his forgiveness.

But this was too little for his humiliation's insatiable appetite; he replied that her excuses made no difference to his conviction: what the redheaded girl called love was not love at all; no, he said, anticipating her objections, it wasn't pettiness that caused him to draw extreme conclusions from an apparently ordinary episode; it was in fact such small details that revealed the basis of the redhead's feelings toward Jaromil; that intolerable flightiness, that typical heedlessness with which she treated Jaromil, just as if he were a woman friend, a customer in the store, a passerby on the street!

She must never again have the gall to tell him that she loved him! Her love was only a paltry imitation of love!

The girl realized that things couldn't possibly get worse. She tried to break into Jaromil's malicious sadness with a kiss; he pushed her away almost brutally; she took advantage of this to fall to her knees and press her head against his stomach; he hesitated for a moment, but then he lifted her up and coldly asked her not to touch him.

The hatred that went to his head like alcohol was beautiful and fascinating; it fascinated him all the more in that it echoed back to him from the young woman and wounded him in turn; it was a self-destructive anger, for he knew very well that by driving the red-headed girl away he was driving away the only woman he had; he sensed that his anger was unjustified and that he was unjust to the girl, but knowing this was probably what made him still more cruel, for what attracted him was the abyss; the abyss of solitude, the abyss of self-condemnation; he knew that he would be unhappy without his girlfriend (he would be alone) and dissatisfied with himself (he was aware that he had been unjust), but this knowledge was powerless against the splendid intoxication of anger. He told her that what he had just said was not only for now but forever: he never wanted to be touched by her hand again.

This was not the first time the girl had encountered Jaromil's anger and jealousy; but this time she perceived an almost frantic obstinacy in his voice; she felt that Jaromil was capable of doing anything to satisfy his incomprehensible fury. Nearly at the last moment, nearly at the edge of the abyss, she said: "I beg you, don't be angry; I lied to you. I wasn't at a friend's."

He was bewildered: "Where were you then?"

"You'll be furious, you don't like him, I can't help it, but I had to go see him."

"Well, who were you with?"

"With my brother. The one who stayed at my place."

He was outraged: "Why do you always need to be with him?"

"Don't get mad; I don't care about him. Compared to you he means nothing at all to me, but you have to understand that he's my brother, after all; we grew up together for fifteen years. He's going away. For a long time. I had to say goodbye to him."

This sentimental farewell to her brother was repellent to him: "Where's your brother going that you have to say such a long goodbye to him and forget everything else? On a job somewhere for a week? Or is he going to the country on Sunday?"

No, he's going neither to work nor to the country; it's something much more serious, and she can't tell Jaromil about it because she knows that he would be furious.

"And that's what you call loving me? Hiding things from me that I don't approve of? Keeping secrets from me?"

Yes, the girl is well aware that to love is to tell each other everything; but Jaromil must understand her: she is afraid, simply afraid. . . .

"What are you afraid of? Where's your brother going that you're afraid to tell me?"

Can it be that Jaromil really has no idea? That he really can't guess?

No, Jaromil can't guess (and at this point his anger is limping far behind his curiosity).

The girl finally confesses: her brother has decided to go across the border, secretly, illegally; by tomorrow he will be out of the country.

What? Her brother wants to abandon our young socialist republic? Her brother wants to betray the revolution? Her brother wants to become an émigré? Doesn't she realize what being an émigré means? Doesn't she realize that every émigré automatically becomes an agent of the foreign espionage services that are trying to destroy our country?

The girl nodded in agreement. Instinct told her that Jaromil would much more readily forgive her brother's treason than her fifteen minutes of tardiness. That's why she kept nodding and said that she agreed with everything Jaromil was saying.

"What do you mean, you agree with me? You should have talked him out of it! You should have stopped him!"

Yes, she had tried to dissuade him; she had done everything she could to dissuade him; now Jaromil would probably understand why she had been late; now Jaromil would probably forgive her.

Curiously Jaromil really did tell her that he forgave her lateness; but he couldn't forgive her brother's leav-

ing the country: "Your brother is on the other side of the
barricades. He's my personal enemy. If war broke out,
your brother would shoot at me and I at him. Do you
understand?"

"Yes, I understand," said the redheaded girl, and she
assured him that she would always be on the same side
as he; at his side and never with anyone else.

"How can you say you're on my side? If you were
really on my side, you'd never let your brother leave!"

"What could I do? Am I strong enough to hold him
back?"

"You should have come to me at once, and I would
have known what to do. But instead of that you lied!
You claimed you were with a friend! You wanted to
mislead me! And you claim to be on my side."

She swore to him that she really was on his side and
that she would stay there whatever happened.

"If what you're saying were true, you'd call the
police!"

What, the police? She couldn't denounce her own
brother to the police! That would be impossible!

Jaromil couldn't bear to be contradicted: "Impossible? If you don't call the police, I'll call them myself!"

The girl again maintained that a brother is a brother,
and that it was unthinkable that she would denounce
him to the police.

"So your brother is more important to you than I am?"

Certainly not! But that's no reason to denounce your
own brother.

"Love means all or nothing. Love is total or it doesn't

exist. I'm on this side and he's on the other side. You have to be with me and not somewhere in the middle. And if you're with me, you have to want what I want, do what I do. To me the fate of the revolution is my own personal fate. If someone takes action against the revolution he is taking action against me. If my enemies are not your enemies then you are my enemy."

No, no, she is not his enemy; she wants to be with him in every way; she is well aware that love means all or nothing.

"Yes, love means all or nothing. Compared to true love everything pales, everything else is nothing."

Yes, she agrees completely, yes, that is exactly how she feels.

"True love is completely deaf to what the rest of the world might say, that's precisely how we recognize it. But you're always ready to listen to what people say, you're always so full of consideration for others that you step all over me."

No, no, certainly not, she doesn't want to step all over him, but she is afraid of doing harm, great harm, to her brother, who would pay dearly.

"And what if he does? It would only be just if he paid dearly. Or are you afraid of him? Are you afraid of breaking with him? Are you afraid of breaking with your family? Do you want to stay stuck to your family all your life? How I hate your terrible pettiness, your abominable incapacity to love!"

No, it isn't true that she is incapable of love; she loves him with all her heart.

"Yes, you love me with all your heart," he replies bitterly, but you don't have the heart to love! You're absolutely incapable of it!"

Again she swears that it isn't true.

"Could you live without me?"

She swears that she couldn't.

"Could you go on living if I died?"

No, no, no.

"Could you go on living if I left you?"

No, no, no. She shakes her head.

What more could he ask? His anger subsided, leaving only a great turmoil; suddenly their death was here with them; the sweet, very sweet death they promised each other if some day one were to be abandoned by the other. In a voice choked with emotion, he said: "I couldn't live without you either." And she said that she couldn't and wouldn't live without him, and they repeated these words again and again until a great, nebulous ecstasy took them into its arms; they tore off their clothes and made love; all of a sudden he felt on his hand the wetness of tears rolling down the redhead's face; that was wonderful; that was something that had never before happened to him, a woman crying for love of him; for him tears were the solution into which a man is dissolved when he is discontented with merely being a man and desires to free himself from the limits of his nature; it seemed to him that, with the aid of a tear, a man escapes the limits of his material nature, merges with the distances, and becomes an immensity. He was terribly moved by the wetness of the tears, and suddenly he realized that he too was crying; they made love and their faces and bodies were drenched, they made love and they actually did dissolve, their fluids mingled and flowed together like the waters of two rivers, they cried and made love, and at that moment they were outside the world, they were like a lake that has got loose from the earth and is rising toward the sky.

Afterward they lay peacefully side by side, caressing each other's faces long and tenderly; the girl's red hair was clumped in comical strands, and her face was red; she was ugly, and Jaromil thought of the poem in which he had written that he wanted to drink down everything she had in her, her former lovers, even her ugliness, even her matted red hair, even the stain of her freckles; he caressed her and gazed at her touching ugliness; he repeated that he loved her, and she repeated the same.

And because he didn't want to let go of this moment of absolute satisfaction, whose promise of mutual death intoxicated him, he once again said: "It's true, I can't live without you; I can't live without you."

"Without you I'd be terribly sad too. Terribly."

He was instantly on his guard: "Are you saying that you can imagine going on living without me?"

The girl didn't perceive the trap behind his words. "I'd be horribly sad."

"But you could go on living."

"What could I do if you left me? But I'd be horribly sad."

Jaromil realized that he had been the victim of a misunderstanding. The redhead had not promised him her death; and when she said that she couldn't live without him, it was only love trickery, a verbal embellishment, a metaphor. The poor fool, she didn't at all grasp what was going on; she promised him her sadness, he who knew only absolute criteria, all or nothing, life or death. Full of bitter irony, he asked her: "How long would you be sad? A day? Or even a week?"

"A week?" she said bitterly. "Let's see, my Xavipet, a week. . . . Much more than that!" She pressed close to him to show with the touch of her body that it was not in weeks that she measured her sadness.

Jaromil reflected on this: What exactly was her love worth? A few weeks of sadness? All right. And what is sadness? A bit of depression, a bit of languishing. And what is a week of sadness? No one is ever sad all the time. She would be sad for a few minutes in the daytime, a few minutes in the evening; how many minutes in all? How many minutes of sadness did her love merit? How many minutes of sadness did he rate?

Jaromil imagined his death, and he imagined the redhead's subsequent life, a life unconcerned and unchanged, coldly and cheerfully rising up above his nonbeing.

He had no desire to resume the exacerbated jealousy dialogue; he heard her voice asking why he was sad, and he didn't answer; the tenderness of that voice was an ineffectual balm.

He got up and dressed; he was no longer angry; she kept asking him why he was sad, and by way of an answer, he melancholically caressed her face. Then, looking closely into her eyes, he said: "Are you going to the police yourself?"

She thought that their wonderful lovemaking had definitively allayed Jaromil's wrath against her brother; so Jaromil's question caught her off guard, and she didn't know what to say.

Once again he (sadly and calmly) asked her: "Are you going to the police yourself?"

She mumbled something; she wanted to persuade him to change his mind, but she was afraid to say so clearly. The evasive meaning of her mumbling was obvious, however, so Jaromil said: "I understand your not wanting to go there. All right! I'll take care of it myself." And again (in a compassionate, sad, disappointed gesture) he caressed her face.

She was confused and didn't know what to say. They kissed and he left.

When he woke up the next morning, Mama had already gone out. While he was still sleeping she had laid out on his chair a shirt, tie, trousers, jacket, and, of course, a pair of undershorts. It was impossible to break this twenty-year habit, and Jaromil had always passively accepted it. But that day, when he saw folded on the chair the light-beige undershorts with their long legs and that big opening at the crotch that was a glaring invitation to urinate, he was overcome by a towering rage.

Yes, he had gotten up that morning as one gets up on a great, decisive day. He held the undershorts in his extended hands and examined them; he examined them with an almost loving hatred; then he put the end of one leg into his mouth and bit down on it; he gripped the leg with his right hand and pulled it violently; he heard the sound of ripping cloth; then he threw the torn undershorts on the floor. He hoped that Mama would see them there.

Then he put on a pair of yellow gym shorts and the shirt, tie, trousers, and jacket that had been prepared for him and left the villa.

11

He surrendered his identity card in the lobby (as anyone who wished to enter the National Police Building
had to do) and climbed up the stairs. Look at the way
he climbs, how he gauges every step! He climbs as if he
were carrying his entire destiny on his shoulders; he is
not climbing to reach a higher level of a building but to
a higher level of his own life, from which he is going to
see something he has never seen before.

Everything favored him; when he entered the office,
he saw that his old classmate's face was the face of a
friend; it greeted him with a happy smile; it was pleasantly surprised; it was cheerful.

The janitor's son said he was delighted by Jaromil's
visit, and Jaromil's soul was blissful. He sat down on the
chair that was offered him, and for the first time felt he
was facing his friend as man to man; as an equal facing
an equal; as one tough man facing another.

They chatted for a few minutes about this and that, as
friends do, but for Jaromil this was merely a piquant
overture, during which he waited impatiently for the
curtain to rise. "I want to tell you something extremely
important," he said very seriously. "I know about a fellow who is getting ready to leave secretly for the West in
the next few hours. Something should be done about it."

The janitor's son was instantly on the alert and asked
Jaromil a number of questions. Jaromil answered them
quickly and precisely.

"This is a very serious matter," the janitor's son said at last. "I can't decide what to do on my own."

He then led Jaromil down a long corridor and into another office, where he introduced him to an older man in civilian clothes; he introduced him as a friend, which caused the man in civilian clothes to smile amicably at Jaromil; they called for a secretary to take down a statement; Jaromil had to be precise about everything: his girlfriend's name; where she worked; her age; how he had come to know her; her family background; where her father, brothers, and sisters worked; when she had told him of her brother's intention to leave for the West; what kind of man her brother was; what Jaromil knew about him.

Jaromil told them that he knew quite a bit about her brother from his girlfriend; that's precisely why he regarded this matter as extremely grave and had lost no time in informing his comrades, his comrades in arms, his friends before it was too late. Because his girl's brother hated our system of government; how sad that was! His girl's brother came from a very poor, very modest family, but because he had worked for some time as a chauffeur for a bourgeois politician he was now body and soul on the side of people who are plotting against our system; yes, he could affirm this with utter certainty, for his girl had very exactly described her brother's opinions to him; this fellow was ready to shoot at Communists; Jaromil could easily imagine what he would do if he joined the ranks of the émigrés; Jaromil knew that his sole passion was to destroy socialism.

With manly conciseness the three men finished dictating the statement to the secretary, and the older man told the janitor's son to go quickly and make the necessary arrangements. When they were alone in the office, the man thanked Jaromil for his help. He told him that if the entire populace were as vigilant as he, our socialist country would be invincible. He also said that he hoped this meeting would not be their last. Jaromil was probably aware that our system had enemies everywhere; Jaromil was part of the university environment and perhaps also knew people in the literary milieu. Yes, we know that most of them are decent people, but perhaps there are also quite a few subversive elements among them.

Jaromil gazed enthusiastically at the policeman's face; it seemed beautiful to him; it was furrowed with deep wrinkles testifying to a hard, manly life. Yes, Jaromil, too, hoped this meeting would not be their last. He wished for nothing else; he knew where he stood.

They shook hands and exchanged smiles.

With this smile in his soul (the splendid wrinkled smile of a man), Jaromil left the Police Building. Descending the broad front steps, he looked at the frosty morning sun rising over the city rooftops. He breathed the cold air, felt exuberant with the virility that flowed from his every pore, and felt like singing.

At first he thought he would go straight home, sit down at his desk, and write poems. But after a few paces he turned around; he didn't want to be alone. It seemed to him that during the past hour his features had hardened, his step become firmer, his voice grown lower, and he wanted to be seen in this transformation. He went over to the university and engaged in conversation with everyone. Of course, no one told him that he was any different, but the sun was still shining, and up above the chimneys an unwritten poem was still floating. He went back home and shut himself into his room. He filled several sheets of paper, but he was not very satisfied.

So he put down his pen and reflected for a while; he mused about the mysterious threshold an adolescent must cross so as to become a man; he believed he knew the name of that threshold; its name was not love, the threshold was called "duty." It is difficult to write poems about duty. How can this harsh word kindle the imagination? But Jaromil knew that it was precisely the imagination stimulated by this word that would be new, unheard of, surprising; for he wasn't thinking of duty in the former sense of the word, duty assigned and imposed from outside, but duty man himself creates and freely chooses, duty that is voluntary and bold and the glory of man.

This meditation filled Jaromil with pride, for he was thus sketching an entirely new self-portrait. He once again wanted to be seen in this surprising transformation, and he rushed to his redheaded girl. It was about six in the evening by now, and she should long since have returned from the store. But the landlady told him that she had not yet come home. She said that two gentlemen had been looking for her about half an hour before, and she had had to tell them that her tenant wasn't back yet.

Jaromil had time to spare, and he walked up and down the redheaded girl's street. After a while he noticed two gentlemen also walking up and down; Jaromil thought they were probably the same ones who had spoken to the landlady; then he saw the redheaded girl coming from the other side of the street. He didn't want her to see him, so he hid in the carriage entrance of a building and saw his girl walking rapidly toward her building and vanishing inside. Then he saw the two gentlemen follow her. He felt uncertain and didn't dare move from his observation post. After about a minute, the three of them left the building; it was only then that he noticed a car parked a short distance from the building. The two gentlemen and the girl got into the car and drove away.

Jaromil realized that the two men were probably policemen; but the fright that chilled him soon mingled with a feeling of elated amazement at the idea that what he had done that morning was a real act that had set things in motion.

The next day he hurried over to his girl's place, to surprise her when she came home from work. But the landlady told him that the redhead had not returned since the two gentlemen had taken her away.

He was very shaken by this. The following morning he went at once to the police. As before, the janitor's son was very friendly, shook his hand, gave him a jovial smile, and when Jaromil asked him what had happened to his girl, who had not yet come home, he told him not to worry. "You put us on a very important trail. We're going to give them a good grilling." His smile was eloquent.

Once again Jaromil came out of the Police Building and into a frosty, sunny morning; once again he breathed the cold air and felt big and filled with his destiny. But it wasn't the same as it was two days before. Because now he reflected for the first time that his act had *caused him to enter tragedy*.

Yes, that is what he told himself, word for word, as he descended the broad steps: I am entering tragedy. He kept hearing the jovial and threatening "We're going to give them a good grilling," and these words stirred his imagination; he realized that his girl was now in the hands of strange men, that she was at their mercy, that she was in danger, and that interrogation lasting several days was no small matter; he recalled what his old classmate had told him about the dark-haired Jew and about the grimness of police work. All these ideas and images filled him with a kind of sweet, fragrant, and noble substance, so that it seemed to him that he was growing bigger, that he was walking through the streets like an itinerant monument of sadness.

Then he thought that he now knew why the lines he had written two days earlier were worthless. Because at the time he didn't know yet what he had just done. Only now did he understand his own act, understand himself and his destiny. Two days ago he wanted to write poems about duty; but now he knew more about it: the glory of duty flowers from the hacked-open head of love.

Jaromil walked though the streets, fascinated by his own destiny. When he returned home he found a letter for him: I'd be very glad if you could come next week to a small party, on such and such a day and hour, to meet some people who will interest you. The letter was signed by the filmmaker.

Even though the invitation didn't promise anything definite, Jaromil was immensely pleased, for he saw in it proof that the filmmaker was not a lost opportunity, that their story was not yet over, that the game was continuing. And the vague, strange idea crept into his mind that there was a profound meaning in the fact that this letter had reached him exactly on the day when he had realized the tragedy of his situation; he had the confused and exhilarating feeling that everything he had experienced during the last two days finally qualified him to face the radiant beauty of the dark-haired filmmaker and to attend the sophisticated party with self-confidence, without fear, and like a man.

He felt happier than ever before. He felt full of poems, and he sat down at his desk. No, it wasn't right to put love and duty into opposition, he reflected; that was just the old conception of the problem. Love or duty, the beloved woman or the revolution—no, no, that's not it at all. He had exposed the redhead to danger not because love didn't matter to him; what Jaromil wanted was precisely a world in which man and woman would love each other more than ever. Yes, that's how it was: Jaromil had exposed his girl to danger precisely because he loved her more than other men loved their women; precisely because he knew what love and the future world of love were. Of course, it was terrible to sacrifice an actual woman (redheaded, nice, delicate, talkative) for the sake of the future world, but it was probably the only tragedy of our time that was worthy of beautiful verse, worthy of a great poem!

So he sat down at his desk and wrote and then got up and paced the room, saying to himself that what he was writing was greater than anything he had ever written before.

It was an exhilarating evening, more exhilarating than all the amorous evenings he could imagine, it was an exhilarating evening even though he was spending it alone in his childhood room; Mama was in the next room, and Jaromil had completely forgotten that he had detested her a few days earlier; when she knocked on the door to ask him what he was doing, he tenderly called her "Mama" and asked her to help him find the calm and concentration he needed because, he said, "Today I'm writing the greatest poem of my life." Mama smiled (a maternal, considerate, understanding smile) and left him in peace.

When he went to bed later he realized that at that very moment his girl was surrounded by men; that they could do with her whatever they wanted; that they watched her change into prison clothes; that the guard watched her through the peephole while she was sitting on a bucket, urinating.

He didn't much believe in these extreme possibilities (they were probably interrogating her and would soon let her go), but the imagination doesn't allow itself to be bridled: tirelessly he imagined her in her cell, sitting on a bucket as a strange man watched, imagined interrogators tearing off her clothes; one thing astounded him: despite these images, he felt no jealousy!

"You must be mine to die upon the rack if I want you!" John Keats's cry resounds through the centuries. Why should Jaromil be jealous? The redhead is his now, she belongs to him more than ever: her destiny is his creation; it is his eye that watches her urinate into the bucket; it is his palms in the hands of the guards that are touching her; she is his victim, she is his creation, she is his, his, his.

Jaromil is not jealous; he is sleeping the manly sleep of men.

PART SIX

The Man in His Forties

1

The first part of this novel encompasses fifteen years of Jaromil's life, but the fifth part, which is longer, covers barely a year. In this book, therefore, time flows in a tempo opposite to the tempo of real life; it slows down.

The reason for this is that we're looking at Jaromil from an observatory I've erected at the point of his death. For us his childhood is in the distances where months merge into years; he has come with his mama from these misty distances right up to the observatory, where everything is as visible as the foreground of an old painting in which the eye can distinguish every leaf on a tree and every leaf's delicate tracing of veins.

Just as your life is determined by the profession and marriage you have chosen, so this novel is limited by the view from the observatory, from which one always sees only Jaromil and his mother while other characters are caught sight of only when they appear in the presence of the two protagonists. I've chosen this way as you have chosen your destiny, and my choice is equally irreparable.

But everyone regrets being unable to live lives other than his own; you too would like to live all your unrealized potentialities, all your possible lives (ah! inaccessible Xavier!). This novel is like you. It too would like to be other novels, those it might have been.

That is why I am constantly dreaming of other possible unbuilt observatories. What if I were to put one, for example, in the painter's life, in the janitor's son's life, or in the redheaded girl's life? We don't know much about them. Hardly more than did foolish Jaromil, who never knew anything about anyone! What kind of novel would it be if it followed the career of that downtrodden janitor's son, and his former classmate the poet appeared in it only once or twice as a minor character? Or if I followed the painter's story and finally found out what exactly he thought of his mistress, whose belly he decorated with drawings in India ink?

A man cannot simply walk out of his life, but a novel has much more freedom. What if I swiftly and secretly dismantled my observatory and transported it elsewhere, if only temporarily? For example, well beyond Jaromil's death! For example, all the way to the present, where there is no longer anyone, absolutely no one (his mother, too, died a few years ago) who still remembers Jaromil. . . .

2

My God, transport the observatory right here! And pay a visit to the ten poets who sat on the platform with Jaromil at that evening with the cops! Where are the poems they recited then? No one, no one remembers them, and the poets would deny having written them.

What actually remains of that distant time? Nowadays everyone regards it as an era of political trials, persecution, forbidden books, and judicial murder. But we who remember must bear witness: that was not only a time of horror but also a time of lyricism! The poet reigned along with the hangman.

The wall behind which people were imprisoned was made entirely of verse, and in front of the wall there was dancing. No, not a *danse macabre*. Here innocence danced! Innocence with its bloody smile.

Was it a time of bad poetry? Not quite! Novelists, who wrote about that time with the blind eyes of conformism, created mendacious, stillborn works. But lyrical poets, who exalted the time in an equally blind manner, often left behind beautiful verse. Because, I repeat, in the magical territory of verse all assertions become true as long as they are backed by the power of experienced emotion. And the poets experienced their emotions with such fervor that from their souls a vapor mounted and a rainbow extended in the sky, a miraculous rainbow above the prisons. . . .

No, I'm not going to transport the observatory into

the present, because it is not important to me to portray that time and once again offer it new and newer mirrors. I did not choose those years because I wanted to draw their portrait, but only because they seemed to me to be a matchless trap to set for Rimbaud and Lermontov, a matchless trap to set for poetry and youth. And is a novel anything but a trap set for a hero? To hell with portraying an era! What interests me is a young man who writes poems!

That's why this young man, whom I've named Jaromil, must never go completely out of our sight. Yes, let's leave this novel for a while, let's transport the observatory beyond Jaromil's life, and let's place it in the mind of an entirely different character made of completely different stuff. But let's move it no more than two or three years beyond his death, so that it remains in a time when Jaromil has not yet been forgotten by everyone. Let's construct a part of the novel that will be related to all its other parts as the cottage on an estate is related to the mansion:

The cottage to which I compare this sixth part of the novel is several dozen meters away from the mansion; it is an independent structure, which the mansion can do without; besides, the former owner long ago sublet it. But through the open cottage windows voices from the mansion can be faintly heard.

3

This sixth part of the novel, which I've compared to a cottage, takes place in a studio apartment: a foyer with a clothes closet that has been casually left wide open; a bathroom with a spotlessly clean tub; a small, untidy kitchen, a room containing a wide daybed with a large mirror facing it, bookshelves all around, some engravings behind glass (reproductions of paintings and sculpture from classical antiquity), a coffee table with two armchairs, and a window over the courtyard looking out on rooftops and chimneys.

It is late afternoon, and the owner of the apartment has just come home; he opens his briefcase and takes out a rumpled pair of overalls that he hangs up in the closet; he enters the room and opens the window wide; it is a sunny spring day, a cool breeze wafts into the room, and he goes into the bathroom, turns on the hot water, and undresses; he examines his body with satisfaction; he is a man in his forties, but from the time he began working with his hands he has been feeling in excellent shape; he has a lighter brain and heavier arms.

He is stretched out in the bathtub, across which he has put a board to serve as a desk; books are spread out in front of him (that odd predilection for the authors of antiquity!), and as he warms himself in the hot water, he reads.

Then he hears the doorbell. One short ring, two long, and after a pause, another short ring.

He doesn't like to be disturbed by unexpected visits, and so he has arranged signals with each of his friends and mistresses. But whose signal is this one?

It seems to him that he is getting old and losing his memory.

"Just a minute!" he shouts. He gets out of the tub, unhurriedly dries himself, puts on his bathrobe, and goes to open the door.

4

A girl in a winter coat stood before him.

He recognized her immediately and was speechless with surprise.

"They let me go," she said.

"When?"

"This morning. I was waiting for you to come home from work."

He helped her out of her coat; it was heavy, brown, and shabby; he put it on a hanger and hung it up. The girl was wearing a dress the man in his forties knew well; he recalled that she had been wearing that dress the last time she had come to see him, yes, that dress and that coat, and it seemed that a winter day of three years ago was entering this spring afternoon.

The girl was astonished, too, that the room was still the same while so much had changed in her life since that day. "Everything here is just the way it was," she said.

"Yes, everything is just the way it was," the man in his forties agreed, and he motioned her to sit down in the chair she had always sat in; then he hastened to question her: Are you hungry? Have you really eaten? When did you eat? Where are you going from here? Are you going to your parents' house?

She told him that she had to go to her parents' house, that she had gone to the railroad station but then had hesitated and decided to come here first.

"Wait, I'm going to get dressed," he said. He had just noticed that he was still in his bathrobe; he went into the foyer and closed the door behind him; before starting to dress he picked up the phone; he dialed a number, and when a woman's voice answered, he apologized, saying that he would be unable to see her today.

He was under no obligation to the girl waiting in the room; nevertheless he didn't want her to overhear his conversation, and he spoke in a low voice. While he was talking, he kept looking at the heavy brown coat hanging on the peg and filling the foyer with poignant music.

5

It had been about three years since he had last seen her, and about five years since he had come to know her. He had had prettier girlfriends, but this one possessed fine qualities: she was barely seventeen when they had met; she had an amusing spontaneity and was erotically gifted and malleable: she did exactly what she read in his eyes; she understood within fifteen minutes not to talk about feelings with him, and without his having to explain anything, obediently came to visit only (it was hardly once a month) when he invited her over.

The man in his forties didn't hide his penchant for lesbian women; one day, amid the intoxication of physical love, the girl had whispered in his ear that she had once surprised a strange woman in a swimming-pool cubicle and made love with her; the story greatly pleased the man in his forties, and later, after realizing its improbability, was still more touched by the effort the girl had made to please him. Furthermore the girl didn't confine herself to fabrications; she readily introduced the man in his forties to some of her girlfriends, and she inspired and organized a good many erotic entertainments.

She understood that the man in his forties not only didn't require her faithfulness but also felt safer when his girlfriends had serious affairs with other men. She therefore talked to him with innocent indiscretion about her boyfriends past and present, which interested and entertained him.

Now she is sitting before him in an armchair (the man in his forties had put on a pair of slacks and a sweater), and she says: "As I was leaving the prison, I saw horses coming toward me."

6

"Horses? What horses?"

As she was going through the prison gate early that morning she came across a group of horseback riders. They sat straight in the saddle, upright and firm, as if they were attached to the animals to form huge inhuman bodies. The girl felt herself level with the ground, tiny and insignificant. Far above her she heard laughter and the snorting of the horses; she crouched against the wall.

"Where did you go after that?"

She had gone to the last stop of the streetcar line. It was morning, but the sun was already hot; she was wearing the heavy coat, and the stares of passersby intimidated her. She was afraid that there would be a crowd at the stop and that people would be eyeing her. Fortunately, there was no one but an old woman on the traffic island. That was good; it was like a balm to find only an old woman there.

"And you decided right away that you were going to see me first?"

Her duty was to go home, to her parents. She had gone to the railroad station, she was standing in line at the ticket window, but when her turn came she ran away. She shivered at the idea of her family. She was hungry, and she bought a piece of salami. She sat in a square and waited until four o'clock, when she knew the man in his forties would be coming home from work.

"I'm glad you came to me first, it was nice of you," he said.

"Do you remember," he said a moment later, "do you still remember what you said? That you would never come here again?"

"That's not true," said the girl.

He smiled. "Yes, it is," he said.

"No, it isn't."

7

Of course it was true. When she had come to see him that day, the man in his forties had opened the liquor cabinet; when he was about to pour two glasses of cognac, the girl shook her head: "No, I don't want anything. I'm never drinking with you again."

The man in his forties was surprised, and the girl went on: "I'm not coming here anymore, I only came today to tell you that."

As the man in his forties continued to show surprise, she told him that she really loved the young man she had told him about, and that she didn't want to deceive him any longer; she had come to ask the man in his forties to understand her and to hold no grudge against her.

Even though he enjoyed a colorful erotic life, the man in his forties was basically an idyllist and saw to it that his adventures were calm and orderly. To be sure, the girl gravitated as a humble intermittent star in his erotic constellation, but even a single small star suddenly torn out of its place can unpleasantly rupture the harmony of a universe.

He was also hurt by her lack of understanding: he had always been happy that the girl had a boyfriend who loved her; he had urged her to talk about him, and he gave her advice about how she should behave with him. The young man so amused him that he kept in a drawer the poems the fellow had written for her; he disliked these poems, but at the same time they interested him, just as he was interested in and disliked the world that was taking form around him, which he observed from his bathtub.

He was willing to watch over the lovers with all his cynical benevolence, and the girl's sudden decision struck him as ungrateful. He was unable to control himself enough to let nothing show, and the girl, seeing his sullen look, kept on talking to justify her decision; she swore that she loved her young man and that she wanted to be honest with him.

And now she sat (in the same armchair, wearing the same dress) facing the man in his forties and claiming that she had never said anything of the kind.

8

She was not lying. She was one of those rare souls who don't distinguish between what is and what should be, and who regard their moral wishes as reality. Of course she recalled what she had said to the man in his forties; and yet she also knew that she should not have said it, and therefore she now denied her recollection the right to a real existence.

But she recalled it perfectly! That day she had stayed with the man in his forties longer than she had intended, and had been late for her date. Her boyfriend had been mortally insulted, and she had felt that she would only be able to placate him with an excuse of equally mortal gravity. And so she had invented the story that she had stayed for a long time with her brother, who was about to leave secretly for the West. She had not suspected that her boyfriend would urge her to denounce her brother to the police.

So after work the very next day, she ran to the man in his forties to ask for advice; he was understanding and friendly; he advised her to stick to her lie and to convince her boyfriend that after a dramatic scene her brother had sworn to give up the idea of leaving for the West. He had instructed her exactly how to describe the scene in which she dissuaded her brother from secretly crossing the border, and told her to suggest to her boyfriend that he was indirectly her family's savior, for without his influence and intervention her brother

375

would perhaps already have been arrested at the border or—who knows?—already be dead, shot by a border guard.

"How did your conversation that day with your boyfriend end up?" he asked her now.

"I never talked to him. They arrested me just as I was coming home from seeing you. They were waiting in front of my house."

"So you never talked to him again?"

"No."

"But surely you know what happened to him."

"No."

"You really don't know?" asked the man in his forties, amazed.

"I don't know anything."

The girl shrugged her shoulders apathetically, as if she didn't want to know anything.

"He's dead," said the man in his forties. "He died soon after you were arrested."

9

She had not known that; from far away came the words of the young man who had readily weighed love and death on the same scales.

"Did he kill himself?" she asked in a soft voice that was suddenly ready to forgive.

The man in his forties smiled. "No. He just got sick and died. His mother moved away. You wouldn't find a trace of them now in the villa. There's nothing but a big black monument in the cemetery. Like the tombstone of a great writer. His mother had it inscribed: 'Here lies the poet. . .' and underneath his name there's the poem 'Epitaph' you once brought me: the one in which he says he wants to die by fire."

They fell silent; the girl was thinking that her boyfriend had not committed suicide but had died an entirely ordinary death; that even his death turned its back on her. When she left the prison she had firmly resolved never to see him again, but she had not imagined that he was no longer alive. If he didn't exist, the reason for her three years in prison no longer existed, and all of it was merely a bad dream, nonsense, something unreal.

"Listen," he said, "we're going to make dinner. Come and give me a hand."

10

They went into the kitchen and sliced bread; they made ham and salami sandwiches; they opened a can of sardines; they found a bottle of wine; they took two glasses out of the cabinet.

That had been their habit when she used to visit him. It was comforting to her to notice that this stereotypical bit of life always awaited her, unchanged, immutable, and she was able today to reenter it without difficulty; she thought that it was the most beautiful part of life she had ever known.

The most beautiful? Why?

It was a part of life in which she was safe. This man was good to her and required nothing from her; in his eyes she was neither guilty of nor responsible for anything; she was always safe with him, as one is safe when one finds oneself for the moment beyond the reach of one's own destiny; she was safe as a character in a play is safe when the curtain falls after the first act and the interlude begins; the other characters, too, remove their masks and chat casually.

For a long time the man in his forties had felt that he was living outside the drama of his own life; at the beginning of the war he had slipped out of the country to England with his wife, fought against the Germans with the British air force, and lost his wife in an air raid on London; when he returned to Prague, he remained in the military, and at just about the time that Jaromil decided to study political science, the authorities determined that he had been too closely tied to capitalist England during the war and that he was therefore not reliable enough for a socialist army. And so he found himself working in a factory, his back turned on History and its dramatic performances, his back turned on his own destiny, he himself entirely preoccupied with himself, with his private, responsibility-free amusements and his books.

Three years earlier the girl had come to say goodbye, because he had merely offered her an interlude whereas her young boyfriend had promised her a life. And now she is chewing a ham sandwich, drinking wine, boundlessly happy that the man in his forties is bestowing on her an interlude during which she feels a delightful silence slowly blossom within her.

Suddenly she feels more at ease, and she begins to talk.

11

Only crumbs on the empty plates and a half-empty bottle of wine were still on the table, and she talked (freely and simply) about the prison, about her fellow prisoners and the guards, and she lingered, as she always did, over details that interested her, combining them in an illogical but charming stream of chatter.

And yet there was something new in her talk today; in the past her sentences had naively headed toward the essentials, but today they seemed to be merely a pretext to avoid the heart of the matter.

But what matter? Then the man in his forties thought he could guess, and he asked: "What happened to your brother?"

"I don't know . . . ," said the girl.

"Did they let him go?"

"No."

The man in his forties finally understood why the girl had run away from the ticket window and why she was so afraid to go home; for she was not only an innocent victim but also the guilty one who had brought calamity to her brother and to her whole family; he could easily imagine how the interrogators had made her confess, how her attempts to evade them had enmeshed her in ever more suspect lies. How can she now explain that it was not she who had denounced her brother by accusing him of an imaginary crime but some unknown young man who, moreover, was no longer alive?

The girl was silent, and a wave of compassion overwhelmed the man in his forties: "Don't go to your parents' today. There's plenty of time. You've got to think about it first. If you like you can stay here."

Then he leaned over her and put his hand on her face; he didn't caress her, he merely kept his hand tenderly and for a long while pressed against her skin.

The gesture expressed such kindness that tears began to flow down the girl's cheeks.

12

Since the death of his wife, whom he had loved, he had hated female tears; they frightened him just as he was frightened by the idea that women could make him an actor in the dramas of their lives; he saw tears as tentacles that tried to drag him away from the idyll of his nondestiny; tears repelled him.

So he was surprised to feel their unpleasant wetness on his hand. But he was even more surprised to find that this time he was unable to resist their melancholy power; he knew that these were not actually tears of love, that they were not directed at him, that they were neither a ruse nor a means of coercion nor a scene; he knew that they were content, simply and for themselves, to be, and that they streamed from the girl's eyes the way sadness and joy invisibly slip out of one's body. He had no shield against their innocence and was touched by them to the inmost depths of his soul.

He reflected that throughout the time of their acquaintance he and the girl had never done each other harm; they had always been considerate of each other; they had always given each other the gift of a brief moment of well-being and had wanted no more than that; they had nothing to reproach themselves for. And he felt particular satisfaction that after the girl's arrest he had done everything he could to free her.

He raised her from the armchair. He wiped the tears from her face with his fingers and tenderly took her into his arms.

13

Beyond the windows of this moment, somewhere distant, three years back, death stamps its feet impatiently in the story we have abandoned; its skeletal figure has already come onto the illuminated stage and projects its shadow so far that the studio apartment in which the girl and the man in his forties are now standing face-to-face is invaded by twilight.

He tenderly embraces the girl's body, and she is nestled motionless in his arms.

What does this nestling mean?

It means that she is abandoning herself to him; she is settled in his arms and she wants to stay there.

But this abandonment is not an overture! She is settled in his arms, closed, locked up; her hunched shoulders guard her breasts, her head is turned away from his face and leans on his chest; she is staring into the darkness of his sweater. She is settled in his arms, sealed up so that he hides her in his embrace as in a steel safe.

14

He lifted her wet face to his own and began to kiss her. He was driven by compassionate warmth and not by sensual desire, but situations have their own automatism, which one cannot escape: while he was kissing her he tried to pry her lips open with his tongue; in vain; the girl's lips remained shut and refused to respond.

Strangely enough the less his kisses succeeded, the more he felt the wave of compassion in him increase, for he realized that the girl he was holding in his arms was under a spell, that her soul had been torn out of her and that all that was left after this amputation was a bloody wound.

He felt a bloodless, bony, pitiable body in his arms, but the damp wave of sympathy, sustained by the twilight that had begun to fall, obliterated contour and size, depriving them both of their distinctness and their materiality. And just at that moment he felt himself desiring her physically!

It was entirely unexpected: he was sensual without sensuality, he was aroused without arousal! Pure kindness had, perhaps by some mysterious transubstantiation, turned into arousal of the body!

But perhaps just because it was unexpected and incomprehensible, this arousal carried him away. He caressed her body eagerly and began to unbutton her dress.

"No, no! Please don't! No!" she defended herself.

15

Since words were unable to stop him, she ran for refuge into a corner of the room.

"What's the matter with you? What's happened?" he asked.

She pressed herself against the wall and remained silent.

He approached her and caressed her face: "Don't be afraid of me, you needn't be afraid of me. Tell me what's the matter. What's happened to you?"

She was motionless, silent, unable to find words. She saw looming up above her the horses passing the prison gate, great robust beasts that with their riders formed arrogant creatures with double bodies. She was so far beneath them and so incommensurable with their animal perfection that she wished to merge with something within her reach, with a tree trunk perhaps, or with a wall, to hide in their lifelessness.

He persevered: "What's the matter with you?"

"What a pity you're not an old woman or an old man," she said at last.

Then she added: "I shouldn't have come here, because you're neither an old woman nor an old man."

16

He silently caressed her face for a long time, and then (the room was already dark) he asked her to help him make the wide daybed; they lay side by side on it, and he talked to her in a soft, comforting voice, in a way he had not talked to anyone in years.

The physical desire had vanished, but his great and steady warmth for her was still there, and he felt a need for light; the man in his forties turned on the small bedside lamp and gazed at the girl.

She was stretched out tensely, staring at the ceiling. What had happened to her? What had they done to her? Beaten her? Threatened her? Tortured her?

He didn't know. The girl was silent, and he caressed her hair, her brow, her face.

He caressed her until he felt the terror vanishing from her eyes.

He caressed her until her eyes closed.

17

The studio apartment window was open, allowing the breeze of a spring night to enter; the bedside lamp had been turned off, and the man in his forties, lying motionless beside the girl, was listening to her agitated breathing and watching her drowsiness, and when he was sure she was asleep, he once more caressed her hand very gently, happy to have been able to provide her the first sleep in the new era of her sad freedom.

The window of the cottage to which I have compared this sixth part is also always open, allowing entrance to the fragrances and sounds of the novel that we left a bit before its climax. Do you hear death stamping its feet impatiently in the distance? Let it wait, we are still here in that stranger's studio apartment, secluded in another novel, in another story.

In another story? No. In the lives of the man in his forties and the girl, their encounter is an interlude in the middle of their stories rather than a story itself. This encounter will hardly engender a series of events. It is only a brief moment of respite the man in his forties bestows on the girl before she embarks on the long scramble her life will be.

In this novel, too, this sixth part has been only a quiet interlude in which a stranger suddenly lights the lamp of kindness. Let us keep looking at it a few moments more, that gentle lamp, that kindly light, before the novel's cottage vanishes from our sight.

PART SEVEN

The Poet Dies

1

Only a real poet knows how sad it is inside the poetry house of mirrors. The crackle of distant gunfire is heard through the window, and the heart longs for departure. Lermontov is buttoning his military uniform; Byron is putting a pistol into the drawer of his night table; Wolker, in his poems, is marching with the crowd; Halas is rhyming his insults; Mayakovsky is stomping on the throat of his own song. A splendid battle is raging in the mirrors.

But beware! The moment a poet mistakenly steps outside the house of mirrors he will perish, for he is a poor shot, and when he fires he will hit his own head.

Alas, do you hear them? A horse is proceeding on a winding Caucasian road; the horseman is Lermontov, armed with a pistol. And here are other hoofbeats and a creaking carriage proceeding! This time it is Pushkin, also with a pistol and also heading for a duel!

And what do we hear now? A streetcar; a Prague streetcar, clanking and decrepit; Jaromil is inside it, on his way from one suburb to another; it's cold: he's wearing a dark suit, a necktie, an overcoat, and a hat.

2

What poet never dreamed of his death? What poet never imagined it? "If I must die, let it be with you, my love, and only by fire turn into heat and light. . . ." Do you think that it was merely an accidental play of the imagination that induced Jaromil to visualize his by fire? Not at all; for death is a message; death speaks; the act of dying has its own semantics, and it matters how a man dies, and in what element.

Jan Masaryk's life ended in 1948 with a fall into the courtyard of a Prague palace, after he had seen his destiny shattered by the hard shell of History. Three years later the poet Konstantin Biebl, frightened by the face of the world he had helped to bring about, threw himself from a sixth floor onto the pavement of the same city (the city of defenestrations), perishing on the element earth and with his death offering an image of the tragic discord between the air and weight, between dream and awakening.

Jan Hus and Giordano Bruno could not have died by the rope or by the sword; they could have died only at the stake. Their lives thus became the incandescence of a signal light, the beam of a lighthouse, a torch shining far into the space of time. For the body is ephemeral and thought is eternal and the flicker of fire is the image of thought. Jan Palach, who twenty years after Jaromil's death drenched himself with gasoline in a Prague square and set his body afire, would have been less likely to succeed in making his cry ring out to the nation's consciousness as a man who had drowned.

On the other hand Ophelia is inconceivable afire and had to die by water, for the depth of water converges with the depths of the human soul; water is the exterminating element of those who have been led astray in their own selves, in their love, in their feelings, in their madness, in their mirrors and their whirlwinds; in old folk songs girls whose fiancés fail to return from war drown themselves; Harriet Shelley threw herself into the water; Paul Celan drowned in the Seine.

3

He got off the streetcar and headed toward the snow-covered villa he had so precipitously run away from the other night, leaving the beautiful dark-haired young woman alone.

He thought of Xavier:

In the beginning there was only Jaromil.

Then Jaromil created Xavier, his double, and with him his other life, dreamlike and adventurous.

And now the moment has come to end the contradiction between dream and waking, between poetry and life, between action and thought. At the same time the contradiction between Xavier and Jaromil has also vanished. Both have merged into a single creature. The man of daydreams has become the man of action, the adventure of dreams has become the adventure of life.

He approached the villa and felt the return of his old timidity, heightened by a sore throat (Mama had not wanted to let him go to the party; he would have been better off listening to her and staying in bed).

He hesitated at the door, and to give himself courage he had to summon up all the big days he had recently experienced. He thought of the redhead, he thought of the interrogation she had undergone, he thought of the police and of the train of events he had set in motion by his own strength and his own will. . . .

"I am Xavier, I am Xavier . . . ," he told himself, and he rang the bell.

4

The people at the party were young actors and actresses, painters, and art students; the owner of the villa was present, and he had made all the rooms available for the evening. The filmmaker introduced Jaromil to a few people, put a glass in his hand, asked him to serve himself from any of the many bottles of wine, and left him.

Jaromil felt ridiculously stiff in his dark suit, white shirt, and tie; everyone around him was dressed casually, and a number of the guests were in sweaters. He squirmed in his chair and finally came to a decision; he took off his jacket and put it over the back of his chair, loosened his tie, and unbuttoned his shirt collar; after that he felt a bit more at ease.

The guests were surpassing one another in calling attention to themselves. The young actors were behaving as if they were on stage, speaking loudly and unnaturally, and all were trying to impress with their wit or the originality of their opinions. Jaromil, too, after having emptied several glasses of wine, tried to raise his head above the surface of the conversation; he managed a number of times to utter remarks that he considered audaciously witty and that attracted the attention of the others for a few seconds.

5

She hears noisy dance music coming from a radio on the other side of the wall; not long ago the authorities had assigned the third room on the floor to the tenant family; the two rooms left to the widow and her son are a shell of silence besieged on all sides by noise.

Mama hears the music, she is alone, and she is thinking about the filmmaker. From the very first time she saw her, she had sensed the far-off danger of love between her and Jaromil. She tried to become friends with her solely in order to occupy a favorable position in the impending battle to keep her son. And now she realizes with humiliation that her efforts had been in vain. The filmmaker had not even thought of inviting her to her party. They had shoved her aside.

One day the filmmaker had confided to her that she worked at the National Police film club because she came from a wealthy family and needed political protection to enable her to pursue her studies. And now it occurs to Mama that this unscrupulous girl knows how to exploit everything in her own interest; to her, Mama had merely been a stepping stone to get to Jaromil.

6

The competition continued: everyone tried to be the center of attention. Someone played the piano, couples danced, adjacent groups loudly laughed and talked; people tried to outdo each other in wit, everyone tried to surpass the others and be seen.

Martynov was there, too; tall, handsome, almost operetta elegant in his uniform and with a large dagger, surrounded by women. Oh, how much he irritated Lermontov! God was unjust to give such a handsome face to that idiot and short legs to Lermontov. But if the poet lacked long legs, he had a sarcastic wit that had lifted him high.

He approached Martynov's group and awaited his opportunity. Then he made an insolent remark and watched the stunned faces near him.

7

At last (after a long absence) the filmmaker reappeared in the room. She came over toward him and gazed at him with her large dark eyes. "Are you having a good time?"

It seemed to Jaromil that he was going to relive the beautiful moment they had experienced together in her room, when they had sat gazing at each other.

"No," he answered, looking into her eyes.

"Are you bored?"

"I came here because of you, and you're always off somewhere. Why did you invite me if I can't be with you?"

"But there are a lot of interesting people here."

"But for me they're only a pretext to be near you. For me they're only steps I'd climb to get to you."

He felt bold and pleased with his eloquence.

She laughed: "This evening there are many of those steps here!"

"Instead of steps, perhaps you could show me a secret staircase that would bring me to you more quickly."

The filmmaker smiled: "We're going to try," she said. She took him by the hand and led him away. She took him upstairs to the door of her room, and Jaromil's heart began to pound.

In vain. The room he was familiar with was filled with still more guests.

8

The radio in the adjoining room has long since been turned off; it's dark, and Mama waits for her son and thinks about her defeat. But then she tells herself that although she has lost this battle, she will go on fighting. Yes, that is exactly how she feels: she will fight, she will not permit anyone to take him away, she will not allow herself to be separated from him, she will be with him always, she will follow him always. She is sitting in an armchair, but she has the feeling of being on the move; she is on the move through a long night, to rejoin him, to regain him.

9

The filmmaker's room is filled with talk and smoke, through which one of the guests (a man of thirty or so) has for a while been watching Jaromil attentively. "I believe I've heard about you," he says at last.

"About me?" says Jaromil, pleased.

The man asks Jaromil if he wasn't the boy who used to visit the painter.

Jaromil was glad that a mutual acquaintance tied him more firmly to this gathering of strangers, and he hastened to nod his head.

"But you haven't been to see him for a long time," the man said.

"Yes, not for a long time."

"And why is that?"

Jaromil didn't know how to answer, and he shrugged his shoulders.

"I know why. It would jeopardize your career."

Jaromil tried to laugh: "My career?"

"You publish poetry, you recite your work in public, our hostess has made a film about you for the good of her political reputation. Whereas the painter doesn't have the right to show his work. Don't you know that he's been called an enemy of the people in the press?"

Jaromil was silent.

"Do you know it—yes or no?"

"Yes, I've heard about it."

"Apparently his paintings are contemptibly bourgeois."

Jaromil was silent.

"Do you know what the painter is doing now?"

Jaromil shrugged his shoulders.

"They fired him from his teaching job, and he's working as a construction laborer. Because he doesn't want to give up his ideas. He can only paint evenings, by artificial light. But he's painting beautiful canvases, while you're writing beautiful shit!"

10

And still another insolent remark, and then another, so that the handsome Martynov is insulted at last. He reprimands Lermontov before the entire company.

What? Should Lermontov take back his witty remarks? Should he apologize? Never!

His friends warn him. It's insane to risk a duel over foolishness. It's best to calm things down. Your life, Lermontov, is more precious than that laughable will-o'-the-wisp, honor!

What? Is there something more precious than honor?

Yes, Lermontov, your life, your work.

No, there is nothing more precious than honor!

Honor is merely the hunger of your vanity, Lermontov. Honor is a mirror illusion, honor is merely a spectacle for this insignificant audience, which will no longer be here tomorrow!

But Lermontov and the moments in which he is living are as immense as eternity, and the ladies and gentlemen watching him are the world's amphitheater! Either he will cross this amphitheater with a firm and virile step, or he will not deserve to live!

11

He felt the mud of humiliation running down his cheek, and he knew that with such a dirtied face he could not stay there a minute longer. They tried in vain to calm him, to soothe him.

"It's no use trying to make peace between us," he said. "Sometimes reconciliation is impossible." Then he stood up and turned tensely toward the man he had been speaking with: "Personally I regret that the painter is a laborer and has to paint by artificial light. But looking at things objectively, it makes absolutely no difference if he paints by candlelight or doesn't paint at all. The whole world of his paintings has been dead for a long time. Real life is elsewhere! Entirely elsewhere! And that's why I stopped seeing the painter. I'm not interested in discussing nonexistent problems with him. I wish him well! I've got nothing against the dead! May the earth cover them gently. And I say that to you, too," he added, pointing at the man. "May the earth cover you gently. You're dead and don't even know it."

The man stood up, too, and said: "It might be interesting to see a fight between a poet and a corpse."

Jaromil felt the blood rise to his head: "Let's try it," he said, and he raised his fist at the man, who caught Jaromil's arm, violently twisted him around, then seized him by the collar with one hand and by the seat of the pants with the other and lifted him off the ground.

"Where shall I take Mister Poet?" he asked.

The young men and women who a few moments earlier had tried to reconcile the two opponents could not resist laughing. The man went across the room carrying Jaromil, who struggled high in the air like a tender, desperate fish. The man brought him to the balcony doors. He opened them, set the poet down on the balcony, and gave him a kick.

12

A shot rings out, Lermontov clutches his chest, and Jaromil falls to the icy concrete floor of the balcony.

O my Bohemia, how easily you transform the glory of a pistol shot into the buffoonery of a kick in the pants!

And yet, should we laugh at Jaromil because he is merely a parody of Lermontov? Should we laugh at the painter because he imitated André Breton with his leather coat and his German shepherd? Was André Breton not himself an imitation of something noble he wished to resemble? Is not parody the eternal destiny of man?

Besides, nothing is easier than to reverse the situation:

13

A shot rings out, Jaromil clutches his chest, and Lermontov falls to the icy concrete floor of the balcony.

He is strapped up tight in the dress uniform of a czarist officer, and he rises to his feet. He is terribly alone. There is no literary history with its balms that could give a dignified meaning to his fall. There is no pistol whose firing would obliterate his childish humiliation. There is only the laughter that reaches him through the balcony doors and dishonors him forever.

He goes over to the railing and looks down. Alas, the balcony is not high enough for him to be certain of killing himself if he jumped. It's cold, his ears are frozen, his feet are frozen, he hops from one foot to another and doesn't know what to do. He is afraid that the balcony doors will open, afraid that mocking faces will appear. He is trapped. He is trapped in a farce.

Lermontov isn't afraid of death, but he's afraid of ridicule. He would like to jump, but he doesn't jump, for he knows that while suicide is tragic, failed suicide is laughable.

(But how's that? How's that? What an odd sentence! Whether a suicide succeeds or fails, it is always still the same act, to which we are led by the same reasons and by the same courage! What, then, distinguishes the tragic here from the ridiculous? Merely the accident of success? What distinguishes pettiness from greatness?

Tell us, Lermontov! Merely the stage props? A pistol or a kick in the pants? Merely the scenery History imposes on a human adventure?)

Enough! It is Jaromil who is on the balcony, in a white shirt and loosened necktie, shivering with cold.

14

All revolutionaries love fire. Percy Shelley, too, dreamed of a death by fire. The lovers in his famous poem perish together on a pyre.

Shelley cast them in his own and his wife's image, and yet he died by water. But his friends, as if trying to correct death's semantic error, erected a large funeral pyre on the seashore and incinerated his fish-nibbled body.

Is death, too, trying to mock Jaromil, by assaulting him with ice instead of fire?

For Jaromil wants to die; the idea of suicide attracts him like a nightingale's song. He knows he has the flu, he knows he is falling ill, but he does not go back into the room, he cannot bear the humiliation. He knows that only the embrace of death can soothe him, an embrace that would entirely fill his body and soul and in which he would at last achieve greatness; he knows that only death could revenge him and indict for murder those who had snickered at him.

He decides to lie down in front of the balcony doors and let the cold roast him from below so as to make death's work easier. He sits down on the floor; the concrete is so frozen that in a few minutes he can no longer feel his bottom; he wants to lie down, but he lacks the courage to press his back against the icy floor, and he stands up again.

Frost completely gripped him: it was inside his thin

socks, it was under his trousers and gym shorts, it slid its hand under his shirt. Jaromil's teeth chattered, his throat hurt, he couldn't swallow, he sneezed, and he had to piss. He unbuttoned his fly with numb fingers; then he urinated on the ground below, and he saw that the hand holding his member was trembling with cold.

15

He was doubled up with pain on the concrete floor, but nothing in the world could induce him to open the balcony doors and rejoin those who had snickered at him. But what were they doing? Why weren't they coming out to get him? Were they so malevolent? Or so drunk? And how long had he been out here shivering in the icy cold?

The overhead light in the room suddenly went out, leaving only a subdued glow.

Jaromil approached the balcony doors and saw a small lamp with a pink lampshade shedding a dim light onto the couch; after a while he was able to discern two naked bodies embracing.

His teeth chattering, his body shivering, he went on looking; the half-drawn curtain prevented him from being certain whether the woman's body covered by the man's was that of the filmmaker, but everything indicated that it was she: the woman's hair was long and dark.

But who is the man? My God! Jaromil knows him well! For he has already observed this scene! Cold, snow, a mountain chalet, and at an illuminated window, Xavier with a woman! Starting today, however, Xavier and Jaromil were to become one and the same person! How can Xavier betray him like this? My God, how can Xavier make love to Jaromil's beloved under his very eyes?

16

Now the room was dark. Nothing could be seen or heard. And in his mind, too, there was no longer anything: neither anger, nor regret, nor humiliation; in his mind there was no longer anything but terrible cold.

And then he couldn't bear to stay here any longer; he opened the balcony doors and went inside; not wanting to see anything, he looked neither left nor right, and he quickly crossed the room.

A light was on in the hall. He went down the stairs and opened the door to the room where he had left his jacket; it was dark, except for the glow from the hall faintly illuminating some heavily breathing sleepers. He kept shivering with cold. He felt around on the chairs for his jacket, but he couldn't find it. He sneezed; one of the sleepers awoke and mumbled a complaint.

He went into the vestibule. His overcoat was hanging on the coat rack. He put it on over his shirt, picked up his hat, and rushed out of the villa.

17

The procession has already started. At the head of it, a horse is pulling the hearse. Walking behind the hearse is Mrs. Wolker, who notices that a corner of white pillow is sticking out of the coffin's black lid; this pinched tip of fabric is like a reproach, the last bed of her little boy (he is only twenty-four years old!) has been badly made; she feels an overwhelming desire to rearrange the pillow under his head.

Then the coffin, surrounded by wreaths, is set down in the church. Grandmother has had a stroke and must raise her eyelid with her finger in order to see. She examines the coffin, she examines the wreaths; one of them has a ribbon with the name Martynov. "Throw that away," she orders. Her aged eye, its paralyzed lid held up by her finger, faithfully watches over the last journey of Lermontov, who is only twenty-six years old.

18

Jaromil (he is not yet twenty years old) is lying in his room with a high fever. The doctor has diagnosed pneumonia.

On the other side of the wall the tenants are noisily quarreling, and the two rooms occupied by the widow and her son are a small island of silence, an island under siege. But Mama doesn't hear the racket from the adjoining apartment. She is only thinking about medicines, hot herbal teas, and cold compresses. When he was small, she had spent day after day by his side to bring him back, red and hot, from the realm of the dead. Now she is watching over him again, just as passionately, just as faithfully.

Jaromil sleeps, is delirious, wakes up, goes on being delirious; fever's fire licks at his body.

Really fire, then? Will he, after all, be transformed into heat and light?

19

A man unknown to her is standing before Mama, asking to talk to Jaromil. She refuses. The man mentions the name of the redheaded girl. "Your son informed on her brother. Now they're both under arrest. I need to talk to him."

They are face to face in Mama's room, for her now merely the entrance hall to her son's room; she mounts guard here like an armed angel barring the gate of paradise. The visitor's tone is insolent and arouses her anger. She opens the door to her son's room: "All right then, talk to him!"

The man sees the flushed face of a young man in a fevered delirium, and in a low, firm voice Mama says: "I don't know what you want to talk about, but I assure you that my son knew what he was doing. Everything he does is in the interests of the working class."

As she utters these words, often spoken by her son but up to now alien to her, she feels a sense of boundless power; now she is linked to her son more strongly than ever; she and he form a single soul, a single mind; she and he form a single universe carved from the same matter.

20

Xavier was holding his schoolbag, which contained a Czech notebook and a science textbook.

"Where are you going?"

Xavier smiled and pointed at the window. The window was open, the sun was shining, and from afar came the voice of the city filled with adventures.

"You promised to take me with you. . . ."

"That was a long time ago," said Xavier.

"Do you want to betray me?"

"Yes, I'm going to betray you."

It took Jaromil's breath away. All he felt was boundless hatred for Xavier. Until recently he had thought that he and Xavier were a single being with two appearances, but now he realized that Xavier was someone else entirely and Jaromil's sworn enemy.

Xavier leaned over him and caressed his face: "You are beautiful, you are so beautiful. . . ."

"Why are you talking to me the way you talk to a woman? Are you crazy?" Jaromil shouted.

But Xavier went on: "You are very beautiful, but I must betray you."

Then he turned on his heels and headed toward the open window.

"I am not a woman! You know very well I am not a woman!" Jaromil shouted after him.

21

The fever has temporarily subsided, and Jaromil is looking around; the walls are bare; the framed photograph of the man in the officer's uniform has vanished.

"Where's Papa?"

"Papa isn't here anymore," Mama says tenderly.

"Why? Who took him down?"

"I did, my darling. I don't want you to look at him. I don't want anyone to come between us. It's pointless now to lie to you. There's something you should know. Your father didn't want you to be born. He didn't want you to live. He tried to prevent me from bringing you into the world."

Jaromil is exhausted from fever and no longer has the strength to have a conversation or even to ask questions.

"My beautiful little boy," says Mama, her voice breaking.

Jaromil realizes that the woman speaking to him has always loved him, never evaded him, never made him afraid of losing her, and never made him jealous.

"I'm not beautiful, Mama. You're beautiful. You look so young."

Mama hears her son's words and feels an urge to weep with happiness. "Do you think I'm beautiful? And you look like me. You've never wanted to admit that you look like me. But you do look like me, and that makes me happy." She caressed his downy yellow hair and covered it with kisses: "You have the hair of an angel, my darling."

Jaromil feels great fatigue. He no longer has the strength to look for another woman, they are all so far away, and the road to them is so endlessly long. "Actually, I never really liked any woman," he says. "Only you, Mama. You're the most beautiful of all."

Mama weeps and kisses him: "Do you remember our vacation in the spa town?"

"Yes, Mama, I loved you most of all."

Mama is seeing the world through a huge tear of happiness; everything around her is blurred by moisture; freed from the shackles of form, things dance and rejoice: "Is that really so, my darling?"

"Yes," says Jaromil, taking Mama's hand into his burning palm and feeling tired, immensely tired.

22

Earth is already piling up on Wolker's coffin. Mrs. Wolker is already back from the cemetery. The stone is already in place above Rimbaud's coffin, but his mother, it is said, has had them open the family vault in Charleville. Do you see her, that austere lady in the black dress? She is examining the dark, damp hole to make sure that the coffin is in place and that it is closed. Yes, everything is in order. Arthur is at rest and is not going to run away. Arthur will never again run away. Everything is in order.

23

So it's to be water after all, just water? Not fire?

He opened his eyes and saw leaning over him a face with a gently receding chin and fine yellow hair. That face was so close to him that he thought he was stretched out over a well and seeing the reflection of his own image.

No, no sign of fire. He was going to die by water.

He looked at his face on the surface of the water. Suddenly he saw great fear on that face. And that was the last thing he saw.

COMPLETED IN BOHEMIA IN 1969

AUTHOR'S NOTE

Life Is Elsewhere was written in Czech. In 1985 I revised its French translation so completely that I was able to include, in the subsequent new edition, a note affirming that it was "equal in authenticity to the Czech text." My intervention did not result in a variant of my original; I was led to it only by a wish for fidelity to my thought and style.

Like his earlier translations of *The Book of Laughter and Forgetting* and *Farewell Waltz* (also from my revised French versions), Aaron Asher's present translation results from a uniquely close and fruitful collaboration between author and translator. And so yet again I thank him with all my heart for the fulfillment of my wish.

Paris, April 2000

OOKS BY MILAN KUNDERA

FICTION

IGNORANCE *A Novel*

ISBN 0-06-000210-7 (paperback)

Set in contemporary Prague, *Ignorance* takes up the complex and emotionally charged theme of exile and creates from it a literary masterpiece.

IDENTITY *A Novel*

ISBN 0-06-093031-4 (paperback)

"A beguiling meditation on the illusions of self-image and desire." —*Time Out New York*

"A fervent and compelling romance, a moving fable about the anxieties of love and separateness." —*Baltimore Sun*

SLOWNESS *A Novel*

ISBN 0-06-092841-7 (paperback)

"Irresistible. . . . An ode to sensuous leisure." —*Mirabella*

"Audacity, wit, and sheer brilliance." —*New York Times Book Review*

IMMORTALITY *A Novel*

ISBN 0-06-093238-4 (paperback)

From a woman's casual gesture to her swimming instructor springs a novel of the imagination that both embodies and articulates the great themes of existence.

"Ingenious, witty, provocative, and formidably intelligent, both a pleasure and a challenge to the reader." —*Washington Post Book World*

THE UNBEARABLE LIGHTNESS OF BEING *A Novel*

ISBN 0-06-093213-9 (paperback)

"Mr. Kundera's novel composed in the spirit of the late quartets of Beethoven is concerned with the opposing elements of freedom and necessity among a quartet of entangled lovers." —*The New Yorker*

THE BOOK OF LAUGHTER AND FORGETTING *A Novel*

ISBN 0-06-093214-7 (paperback)

"*The Book of Laughter and Forgetting* calls itself a novel, although it is part fairy tale, part literary criticism, part political tract, part musicology, and part autobiography. It can call itself whatever it wants to, because the whole is genius." —*New York Times*

FAREWELL WALTZ *A Novel*

ISBN 0-06-099700-1 (paperback)

Farewell Waltz poses the most serious questions with a blasphemous lightness that makes us see that the modern world has deprived us even of the right to tragedy.

"*Farewell Waltz* shocks. Black humor. Farcical ferocity." —*Le Point* (Paris)

LIFE IS ELSEWHERE

ISBN 0-06-099702-8 (paperback)

"A remarkable portrait of an artist as a young man." —*Newsweek*

"A sly and merciless lampoon of revolutionary romanticism." —*Time*

LAUGHABLE LOVES

ISBN 0-06-099703-6 (paperback)

"Kundera takes some of Freud's most cherished complexes and irreverently whirls them about in acts of legerdemain that capture our darkest, deepest human passions. . . . Complex, full of mockeries and paradoxes." —*Cleveland Plain Dealer*

THE JOKE

ISBN 0-06-099505-X (paperback)

A student's innocent joke incurs hard punishment in Stalinist Czechoslovakia.

"A thoughtful, intricate, ambivalent novel." —John Updike

NONFICTION

THE CURTAIN

ISBN 0-06-084186-9 (hardcover)

Available Winter 2007

A brilliant, delightful exploration of the novel— its history and its art—from one of the genre's most distinguished practitioners.

TESTAMENTS BETRAYED *An Essay in Nine Parts*

ISBN 0-06-092751-8 (paperback)

"A fascinating idiosyncratic meditation on the moral necessity of preserving the artist's work from destructive appraisal. . . . One reads this book to come in contact with one of the most stimulating minds of our era." —*Boston Globe*

THE ART OF THE NOVEL

ISBN 0-06-009374-9 (paperback)

"Every novelist's work contains an implicit vision of the history of the novel, an idea of what the novel is. I have tried to express the idea of the novel that is inherent in my own novels." —Milan Kundera

PLAYS

JACQUES AND HIS MASTER

ISBN 0-06-091222-7 (paperback)

Kundera's three-act stage adaptation of Diderot's eighteenth-century philosophical novel *Jacques le Fataliste*.

For more information about upcoming titles, visit www.harperperennial.com.

Visit www.AuthorTracker.com for exclusive information on your favorite HarperCollins authors.

Available wherever books are sold, or call 1-800-331-3761 to order.

HARPER PERENNIAL   HarperCollins*Publishers*